A

D0481101

A SMALL DECEIT

Margaret Yorke

ARROW BOOKS

This edition published by Arrow Books in 1992

3 5 7 9 10 8 6 4 2

© 1991 by Margaret Yorke

The right of Margaret Yorke to be identified as the
author of this work has been asserted by her in accordance
with the Copyright, Designs and Patents Act, 1988

First published in Great Britain by Hutchinson in 1991

Random House, 20 Vauxhall Bridge Road, London SW1V 2SA

Random House Australia (Pty) Limited
20 Alfred Street, Milsons Point, Sydney,
New South Wales 2061, Australia

Random House New Zealand Limited
18 Poland Road, Glenfield
Auckland 10, New Zealand

Random House South Africa (Pty) Limited
PO Box 337, Bergvlei, South Africa

Random House UK Limited Reg. No. 954009

A CIP catalogue record for this book
is available from the British Library

ISBN 0 09 987740 6

Printed and bound in Great Britain by
Cox & Wyman Ltd, Reading, Berkshire

All the characters and events, and most of the places in this story, are fictional. Resemblance to real people is coincidental.

PART ONE

1

The boy heard the front door open. He sat at his desk, his body tense, listening for the heavy tread in the hall below. Next came the boom of the deep voice and the high, anxious response from his mother. He waited for the footsteps to approach on the stairs, crouching over his homework, unable to concentrate until the steps had passed his door. Even then he was not safe: there would be thumps and bangs from the bedroom as cupboards and drawers were opened and closed, sounds from the bathroom; afterwards, the return.

Sometimes, before going downstairs, the footsteps would stop, the door handle would turn, and he would receive a visit.

He had already had his supper. His mother gave him his meal as soon as she could when she returned from work. By then he had been back from school for over an hour. To help her, he would do the ironing, or peel potatoes, or vacuum the floors. Usually, she was grateful, but once he had broken a dish in the kitchen, and another time scorched a new shirt when the telephone rang and he set the iron down flat on the board instead of resting it upright. The call had been a wrong number. When he made these mistakes his mother would be angry and then she would be clumsy, too. She would get in a fluster, fearing things would still be in a muddle when the front door key was turned. Now the boy had almost given up trying to help her, and he spent most of his time at home alone in his room. When his homework was done, he would lie on his bed and dream. Sometimes, in fantasy, he saved his mother from a burning building or pulled her out of the path of an oncoming train. There was no need, in these escapes from reality, to explain why she had got into danger; all that mattered was that he was in time to save her. Dreaming was safe: you could overcome anything in a dream.

In dreams you could kill.

PART TWO

1

You met all sorts in prison: murderers, rapists, fraudsters, and minor offenders who had failed to pay bills or fines, drunks, petty thieves, confidence tricksters, and the mentally ill who should be in hospital, not gaol.

But he was a killer.

He sat in his cell, looking at his long thin hands which had ended a life, though he had not been convicted for that crime. He had never confessed, even when charged with rape and criminal assault, for which he had received a sentence of eight years; nor had he admitted to other, lesser attacks upon women. Sometimes, in dreams, he saw his victims' faces, their anguished eyes, but he felt no remorse. He was punishing them for the offence of being women.

Now he was nearing the time of release. He had not qualified for parole, but would soon be freed at the end of his term, though he had lost remission for bad conduct. Tomorrow he would go to an open prison to prepare for his return to society.

During his time in prison, no one had helped him find out why he had these violent impulses, or how to prevent them recurring. There were very few places where you received such help; all that happened was that you were taken out of circulation to punish you and protect the public; then, after what was considered an appropriate time, you were returned to the world with a pittance and, if you were lucky, a place in a hostel and maybe even a job.

He was not interested in a job, but he had funds in a building society where interest would have been added during his incarceration. In prison he had learned various ways of making money which could be quite diverting, and he had made some useful contacts. Though he longed, in part, to be free, he was afraid of the future. One day, when the opportunity arose, he knew he would commit another terrible crime, and he might be caught and locked up again. He didn't want that. Or so he thought.

2

The sign loomed up through the fog: *Bed and Breakfast*, he read, scripted in black on a white board which hung from a post by the gate.

He had hoped to find a hotel, but the only one he had passed since leaving the scene of the accident had been full. Fog had swirled down over the main road, and cars which were travelling too fast had hurtled into an obstruction where someone had overtaken without being able to see the road ahead. He had missed being involved more by luck than skill, but he was a naturally cautious and careful driver; a man in his position could not afford to take risks. He had seen the red rear lights of the car in front in time to pump his own brakes gently in warning to the driver behind him. A line of vehicles, either stationary or crawling along, stretched before him, and he could not see where the trouble was, but as he slowed down he saw a road leading off to the left and had just time enough to turn down it.

He was in a narrow lane, unmarked by white lines or cat's-eyes, with untrimmed hedges on either side, so that for a short distance the fog seemed thinner, but when the high hedges gave way to neatly shorn ones, the fog again became dense.

He edged along carefully, not sure, now, of the wisdom of shedding the pathfinders. The lane seemed interminable and wound along in a circuitous way. In the end, he reasoned, it must join some other more major road, and he would reach a signpost which would point him in the right direction so that eventually, after making a loop, he could pick up his original route.

His meeting had ended much later than was normal. Usually he was nearly home by now but today, when he left, it was already dark and the air was heavy as the fog began to form. The first twelve miles of the journey had been slow because of the mass of rush hour traffic travelling out of the city, and he had resigned himself to a tedious drive, but he had expected to reach home in not much more than the two hours which ordinarily it took. He had never before deviated from the main road, part of which was notoriously dangerous as it was too narrow and twisty for the amount of traffic which used it.

His speed had dropped to not much more than walking pace as he peered through the windscreen, the wipers sweeping mist from the glass but their action blurring what visibility there was. He tried to pick out the grass at the side of the road by which to steer. Suddenly, out of the fog, loomed the lights of an oncoming car. He braked hard and pulled over, nearside wheels mounting the verge and his heart thudding as he braced himself for collision, but the car was further away than it had seemed and its driver, too, was proceeding cautiously. It slid past without harm and he engaged gear and went forward, a little more confident now for unless other traffic were hurtling towards him, the headlights would give good warning of approach. At last he met some crossroads, and turned right on to what appeared to be a better road. Here and there it carried a broken white line, and this was an aid. He passed through a village, lights on in houses, people warm and safe within. He must be travelling parallel to the road on which he had met the tailback. Should he try to work round towards it? Perhaps he had passed the accident. He drove on, looking for signposts, but by now he was disoriented and was travelling in an easterly, not a southwards direction. The fog seemed to be getting worse. He had at least another sixty miles to go, even if he managed to find his way back to his original route before long. Unless the fog suddenly lifted, it would be most unwise to proceed. He must surely reach another village soon; there would be an inn; he would put up for the night.

He passed a small country hotel ten minutes later, but it had very few rooms and they were all let; the fog had brought them extra custom. Reluctantly, he started the car and set off once more, and he had driven another fifteen anxious miles before he saw the sign. He had taken a wrong turning at a junction and had found himself back in a lane he had been down before; he recognised, or thought he did, a strip of white fencing marking off a pond, and a huddle of houses, some with cars parked outside, without lights, creating a further hazard. At that point he had begun to consider pulling into a gateway and spending the night in the car. Then he saw the painted board.

He turned in at the guesthouse gate. Unless it proved to be an unsavoury sort of place, he would make do with whatever it offered.

The house, when he could see it through the murk, was reassuring: it was large, made of stone, with a plant of some kind creeping up the wall between the front porch and a window. An outside light shone over the door, and when he rang, a woman appeared. She was small, with short grey hair cut in a cap round her head, and she wore black trousers and a long scarlet tunic. Her striking appearance surprised him; he had expected some sort of cosy body.

'Good evening,' he said, in his measured tones. 'I wonder if you have a room free? I don't think it would be wise if I continued my journey tonight because of the fog.'

'It's dreadful isn't it?' she said, while she studied him. She had already had a quick glance at him through a peephole in the door. He wore a navy overcoat which was undone to reveal a dark suit, and, behind his wire-rimmed spectacles, he looked strained. Beyond him was parked his Volvo. He was older than most of the businessmen she put up, some of them regulars, representatives covering the area or accountants on audits.

'I've got one room free,' she decided. She never displayed a vacancy sign; that gave her leeway to refuse anyone whose appearance she did not like.

'I'll get my case,' he said. He had only his briefcase, but he carried a spare shirt and toilet things because his beard grew fast and he always liked to be spruce; this was a habit begun in youth and maintained even when unnecessary.

She watched him cross to the car, extract the case, then lock the door, testing it afterwards; a cautious man, she deduced.

'Is the car all right there?' he asked. 'Not in anyone else's way?'

'No. It's quite all right. There's room for my other guests,' she said. There was plenty of space on the sweep in front of the house, which had a large garage to one side. Perhaps he could have put the Volvo away.

He was too tired to ask.

'I planned to get home tonight,' he told her. 'But there was an accident on the main road and I made a detour. The lanes are rather confusing.'

'Yes,' she agreed. 'You didn't come through Witherstone, then?'

'No,' he said. 'Unless it's so small that I missed it.'

'It's not. It's to the left – I'm just on the edge of the town,' she said. 'I imagine you came the other way.'

She led the way upstairs, her legs thin in the slacks.

'I hate the fog,' she said. 'It makes me think of Magwitch. That wonderful scene in the film.'

'Indeed,' he agreed, though he could not remember seeing the film of *Great Expectations* and was not sure if fog played a part in the book. 'Do you do meals?' he asked.

'No. I'm sorry – only breakfast,' she said. 'That's included. It's fifteen pounds for a night, for a single.'

She opened the door of a small room, comfortably furnished with a single bed, a table bearing tea-making equipment and a portable television, and a button-back armchair upholstered in deep gold velvet. The curtains were flowered, yellow, blue and green on a deeper gold background. He seldom noticed such details, but he absorbed these; after the gloom outside, the whole impression was of warmth and light.

'There's a hotel and several restaurants in Witherstone,' she said. 'My guests usually go there, if they haven't had dinner before they arrive.'

If he had driven on just a short way, he would have found this hotel and been able to stay there. Even now it was not too late; he could tell her he had changed his mind and drive on. But the effort was just too much, and besides, the hotel might be full.

'I won't bother about eating,' he said.

She could see that he had almost reached his limit.

'I'll make you some sandwiches,' she said. 'Ham and cheese, and some soup. You must have something. You settle in and I'll bring them up.'

She showed him the bathroom across the landing. It was large, with a shower and a bidet. While she was downstairs, he relieved himself quickly and washed his hands. He was embarrassed by bodily functions and hoped the cistern, which was noisy, would have finished refilling before she came back.

He had no pyjamas or hairbrush to unpack, though he had a comb as well as his toothbrush and razor. He combed his grey hair and thick eyebrows, and put his things away. When she returned he was studying the spines of books arranged on some shelves under the window. There were Kilvert, and Strachey's *Eminent Victorians*, some modern novels and detective stories and several volumes of short stories.

'An eclectic collection,' he said, as she entered after knocking on the door.

'Yes. I think visitors like something to dip into,' she replied. 'And short stories are good at bedtime. They don't keep you from sleep for hours, like a thriller can. I brought you a whisky, too,' she added

11

as she set down his tray. 'You look as if you could do with one after your drive.'

'How thoughtful of you,' he said. 'Thank you.'

'Just put the tray outside when you've done,' she said. 'My other guests won't be late. They've been here before and they're not noisy. Breakfast's at eight, unless you want to be away earlier.'

'No. That will do very well,' he said.

'Is there anyone you want to telephone, to say you're held up?' she asked.

'No. No, there isn't anyone waiting for me,' he said.

'I'll get you to sign the book in the morning,' she said.

'My name's Desmond Baxter,' he told her.

'And mine's Judith Kent,' she answered. 'Goodnight, Mr Baxter.'

'Goodnight,' he said. 'And thank you.'

The soup was tinned tomato. He enjoyed it, and his sandwiches which were made with crusty brown bread, and he finished his whisky – a strong one. After a while he felt drowsy, so he had a bath and washed his shirt, hanging it up by the radiator in his room with his towel below to catch the drips. He slept in his other shirt for he was not of a generation to take easily to sleeping in the nude.

Since that night he had often stayed at Willow House, dining first at The White Hart in Witherstone. On those nights, no one in the world knew where he was, except Mrs Kent, and she did not know his real name, for it was not, as he had led her to believe, Desmond Baxter.

3

He had been sent to work in an old woman's garden, and had pruned the overgrown roses and pulled withered flowers from the beds.

She had come out of the house to see what he had done and was grateful, noticing that he had cut the rose stems to an outside bud in a professional way.

'I like gardening,' he told her. 'I used to help my mother.'

'Where is she now?' asked the old woman. 'Waiting for you?' She was not afraid of him, confident that dangerous men were not sent on gardening duty.

'That's right,' he said. 'Counting the days, I expect.'

It wasn't true. No one outside waited for his release.

'Well, it's nice that you've somewhere to go,' she said. 'So many haven't.'

She went off to make him some tea. She would have liked to give him money, but it wasn't allowed.

Later, he was sent to work at a factory and stayed in a hostel with other pre-release men. All knew that if they broke any of the rules by which their lives were bounded they would lose remission and might be returned to a closed prison instead of enjoying their present limited freedom.

The men talked. Some boasted about what they would do to their women when they got out, or what had happened on their weekends away, for before being freed they were allowed leave to see about jobs and start the adjustment to normal life. Some talked about their children, often sentimentally, reluctant to accept that they would all come together as strangers. Some had nowhere to go and would be looking for digs, dependent on NACRO or probation officers to help them. Some would be back inside within weeks, if not days. A few would go straight. Some had jobs; a few had done training of various kinds which depended on where they had spent their time. Until they came here, to the open prison, most of them had passed their days banged up in small cells, two or three together, with nothing to do.

No one had shown much interest in him. He had been on Rule

43, isolated among other sex offenders, for a considerable period. Once, he had broken up his cell from frustration and had been kept in the hospital for a week, with sedatives administered to calm him down. Since coming here, he had been late back from work three times; on each occasion he had followed a woman but he did not admit it, merely said he had lost all sense of time. In a way it was true.

Now his sentence was over, finished. He would not be on parole so no one would be checking up on him; he would not have to report to anyone outside. He could disappear.

He would use the money in the building society to buy clothes and set himself up in an office. He'd do all right, make a quick profit, buy a good life for himself. He had a plan for that, based on what he had learned from other cons who had done well until they got caught.

He didn't want more trouble. Perhaps if he found someone regular, he wouldn't feel the temptation. But he liked the submission, the terror he caused, the sense of power.

The main thing was not to let anyone pin it on him, if he did it again.

PART THREE

1

The judge's wife liked her house, which was tranquil within, although sometimes out in the street there was noise and bustle, especially on market days. Even an occasional Saturday night drunken punch-up was not unknown. Waite House, so named after the man who had built it in the eighteenth century, was made of brick which had mellowed to a soft rose. The tall sash windows, now double-glazed, overlooked Rambleton's market square, separated from it only by the pavement, and through them Felicity could watch the life of the town passing by. She knew many of the inhabitants by sight and wondered about their lives, while any who looked in might, in their turn, wonder at hers, if they could see past the fine net curtains which her husband insisted they hang. At the side of the house, long double gates, heavy to move, opened to admit the car when the judge returned from court. Behind the house there was a long garden, walled from its neighbours on either side, and in it grew apple trees, carpeted beneath with snowdrops. There were rose beds, and a curving border where Felicity grew flowers which provided splashes of colour through most of the summer and which could be cut for the house. There were peonies and lupins, delphinium, scabious; later, Michaelmas daisies and dahlias came into bloom. Felicity enjoyed gardening; the flowers were her responsibility, while the judge grew vegetables in an area behind a tall hedge. Here he planted beans, peas, marrows, new potatoes, onions and various other things, aided by Joe, a retired postman, who also cut the lawn if the judge had no time. The judge would not allow Felicity to use the mower; he said she would not understand its ways and might wreck the engine, but she was expected to trim the edges and apply lawn-sand at the appropriate times.

They had lived here for seven years, since Colin was appointed to the Bench. He was a circuit judge and sat in Titchford, twenty miles away. Because Felicity did not drive – in the judge's opinion it had never been necessary for her to learn – they had to live well placed for public transport, and a house in a country town, served by buses and trains, seemed the wisest choice. Waite House should suit, until either of them died and the other found life alone in so large a place untenable.

The most likely one to be left was Felicity, who was twelve years younger than her husband. She sometimes thought about the future, and wondered if Stephen, their son, would move in with his wife when that time came. He loved the house, and could easily commute to London, where he was an accountant. Felicity sighed when she thought about Stephen, who had changed so much from the solemn but affectionate little boy he once was; he had become pompous; indeed, she thought now, he had been born middle-aged. His wife was still, to Felicity, an enigma. Emily was nine years older than Stephen, only five feet tall, and extremely thin, and she wore little pleated skirts which Felicity felt must come from the girl's department of Harrods or some such store. She had a King Charles spaniel called Ferdy, which she cuddled to her flat Fair Isle chest and crooned over, expecting everyone else to do the same. Stephen often did, but a rare bond, implicit but never discussed, between Felicity and her husband was their antipathy to this cossetted animal which, on the couple's fortnightly visits, shed silken hairs on the furniture and was allowed to sleep on Emily's bed.

When she looked at the years ahead, quiet despair was Felicity's main emotion. She could see no prospect of change. Every other weekend, Stephen and Emily would continue to visit, with Ferdy or his successor, but never a child for, as Stephen had confided when they became engaged, Emily could not have children. Eventually the judge would retire, and might be persuaded to write a book, but what if he decided to supervise Felicity's shopping trips in the town? She had seen retired couples shopping together: glum, elderly men with brisk wives consulting lists in the supermarket; livelier men and cheerier wives choosing cereals or biscuits; solemn men selecting wine while their wives pawed over the vegetables. Women who had ruled supreme in home and kitchen for upwards of forty years were suddenly challenged as new schemes for doing the housework were proposed by frustrated men who were no longer heads, if not of companies, at least of departments or sub-sections. She feared the judge would become one of them, since he had always tried to dictate how she spent her time.

When she was young – they met when she was nineteen – she had found what she saw as his worldly poise reassuring. At the time, she was sharing a flat in London with three other girls and working in an estate agency. Her father was employed by an oil company and her parents were often abroad. The advent of Colin into her life, and his instant, dignified courtship – for it had to be described like that, consisting as it did of invitations to art exhibitions or the theatre, and the sending of flowers – was flattering to the shy, insecure girl. Her flatmates were impressed because she was pursued by someone 'so grown up', as one of them described him. No other visitor to the flat, except their parents, was over twenty-three.

The girls wondered why he was still unmarried. In those days, bachelors of thirty or more were suspected of being many things, not least philanderers, but it seemed clear that Colin was no playboy.

'They have to wait, at the Bar,' Felicity told them, looking wise. 'It takes them so long to earn, you see, when they first go into chambers.'

Her use of the jargon made the oldest girl in the flat smile; however, as the years passed, Colin rarely discussed his work with his wife, keeping it a thing apart, as he did everything in his life. Sometimes Felicity thought she knew as little about him now as she had done then.

They had met at a dinner party given by one of the men in his chambers. For some time his colleagues had jokingly been trying to find him a wife and introducing him to likely girls produced by their own wives. Though he made light of their teasing, Colin had agreed with them that the time had come to settle down. He had established himself as sound and industrious, though not brilliant. The days of devilling and too few briefs were past; he could look forward to a modestly prosperous career, and should acquire its proper concomitants, namely a wife and family. In fact, if you looked at it one way, said the hostess who introduced the pair, he was quite a catch, but he hadn't much soul.

'Soul doesn't pay the bills,' said her husband. They had just finished washing up while they discussed the party, almost the best part of the evening.

'He'll go for Felicity, just you see,' said the wife, who had not had this in mind when inviting her guests. Another girl had dropped out, and Felicity, who worked in the same office and whom the hostess had met when she called one day to see her friend, was suggested as a late stopgap.

She was not in the least offended by a last-minute invitation. She seemed timid, having met, of those present, only the hostess and that on a single occasion, but she was pretty in an unassuming way,

19

quite tall, with curly dark brown hair, and blue eyes which reflected the colour of the simple dress she wore.

Three months later, she and Colin were married.

The judge prided himself on his impassive demeanour on the Bench. In wig and gown, clothed in the majesty of justice, he was meticulous in drawing novice barristers' attention to any neglect of clients' rights, and in steering those who diverged back on course. His summings-up were masterpieces of impartiality and juries were sometimes left wishing he would direct them one way or the other. When it came to sentencing those found guilty, however, he could be extremely stern.

He rarely sat in judgement on a major crime. Theft, embezzlement, false pretences, failure to pay fines, assaults of varying degrees and drug offences were the usual traffic of his day; just occasionally he would have a case of arson, or a rape, or a death by careless driving.

Early in his career, he had accepted the knowledge that he would not reach the status of a High Court judge; indeed, he had done well to become a judge at all, lacking as he did a network of useful friends who would help to waft him upwards. He had won success on his ability alone and his achievement was a demonstration of what could be attained by sheer application. This was a lesson he had passed on to his son, hoping that Stephen would follow and surpass him, but it was not to be. Stephen had no wish to study law. He liked figures. The neatness of equations, abstract calculations, fascinated him, and he enjoyed chasing sums that had gone astray, columns that did not balance as they should; here he was painstaking like his father, but much slower. At primary school, aged five, he had won the egg and spoon race, lumbering stoutly but slowly along, tongue clenched between his teeth, hand steady, eyes fixed upon the potato which masqueraded as an egg. Never one for speed, he had subsequently become a long-distance runner at his minor public school. The judge had not sent him to a more illustrious establishment, partly because he feared the boy might not perform too well among strong competition, and partly because, never having benefited from influence himself, he ostracised the network into which it might admit his son. Besides, Stephen could have been outclassed in more ways than the strictly academic. As it was, he had never caused his parents a day's serious anxiety, but nor had either of them ever glowed with real pride in him since Felicity felt weepy when he appeared as Joseph in a Nativity play at the age of six.

The judge was sorry that he had no daughter. In idle fancies, rarely indulged, he imagined spoiling one, a pretty little girl with blonde hair – unlikely, since he and Felicity, and Stephen, were all dark – who would idolise her father, but he was disciplined in his fantasies. Life was not make-believe, and whimsy must be recognised for what it was.

His marriage had proved satisfactory. Felicity had been, as he recognised when first they met, a malleable, biddable girl, and he had managed to ensnare her before she was spoiled by sophistication or by sexual licence. He had sent her to cookery classes after they were married, explaining that as he rose in his profession it was important that she should be able to entertain appropriately, and those months were the happiest of her marriage. She had a sense of purpose, setting forth for the school each morning, and there was pleasant company and laughter, which compensated for the bleakness already present in her emotional life with Colin.

As a young man, the judge had been afraid of women. Their bodies were mysterious, ruled by complicated rhythms like the moon, and in pregnancy and other matters not subject, as he liked to think his own was, to their owners' control. He was in court when she gave birth to Stephen. When he saw her afterwards, she was pale and tired, but clean and tidy; he had no concept of the process she had just endured. The baby, three hours old by now, was plain but healthy, and, said a nurse, very like his father.

Felicity was very quiet when she came home. For a long time she seemed to cry a lot, though seldom in front of Colin. She took to going off alone into any room in the house except where Colin was, and would push the pram for lengthy walks across the common at weekends. At this time they lived in Wimbledon, but later they moved out to the Chilterns. Felicity lost a lot of weight after Stephen's birth and soon had to put him on to bottles, advised to do so by an older mother at the clinic where she took him to be checked at intervals. In those days, post-natal depression was seldom looked for or suspected in such cases, and hers was never recognised. Nowadays the judge knew about it, and on occasion had to take it into account when assessing punishments for shoplifters, but it never occurred to him, with hindsight, that his wife had suffered from it all those years ago.

On the Bench, he slid easily into his sagacious role; now experienced and confident, if he had doubts about a point of law there was always a volume to consult and a lesser person who would look it up. Once they had been found guilty by a jury, he would reprove offenders and tell them they were worthless men or women, for by then the judgement was the verdict of the common man. He would often hope, aloud, that the criminal before him would see the error of his ways and emerge reformed from prison.

Lunching with his fellow judges, wig and gown removed, he would enjoy legal discourse and, because he was considered sound but unadventurous, his opinion was quite often asked. He never sought publicity, but he did not shirk what seemed to him his duty: crimes against the person were severely punished, to the maximum prescribed; minor peccadilloes were more leniently treated.

As he never asked her for it, Felicity rarely gave her opinion on any of his judgements, though recently he had begun to tell her about some of his cases. It helped with conversation during dinner, and he could be amusing when he described any quaint event that had happened in his day.

When another judge sent a girl to prison for stealing a tin of baked beans worth less than a pound, Colin was disgusted. The sentencing judge had said that theft was theft, and the offender must be taught a lesson. It seemed that she was living in a squat with some undesirable young people and in prison would be fed and housed.

'But when she comes out, what then?' demanded Colin, waving his fork across the table at Felicity. 'Where will she live? What will she live on? Social security, of course. She should be put into some sort of hostel and a job should be found for her.'

Felicity agreed. She liked these rare conversations, and wished that they could have more of them. All the same, she wanted to escape, and she had begun to make a plan. She had had the idea of leaving Colin for a long time, but where could she go, and what about his humiliation? After all, he had never really treated her badly. Latterly, recognising the long dolour of the years ahead, she had begun to think about it more, and to concoct schemes, even to build up a nest egg which might make it possible.

After they had been living at Waite House for a year, when everything was working smoothly – the safe Sanderson fabrics hanging at the windows and covering the chairs and big four-seater sofa, the kitchen newly fitted out, the heating checked, the wiring done – she had lost what impetus the move had given her and had looked about for chances to rebel. Wandering round the market, so conveniently held weekly just outside her house, she saw the stalls of bric-a-brac, of small antique goods and old jewellery, some of which appealed to her and often seemed extremely cheap. Finding cash to buy them was her problem, for though Colin did not query her expenses for their food and other household items, he required a breakdown of them, and she could not abstract odd sums for herself. This had been the pattern through the years; he denied her nothing that she needed but the liberty to budget for herself; Felicity had no spending money and could not buy herself a coffee in a café when she went to Titchford or to London, without accounting for it at the next time of reckoning. However, there were ways and means: she sold a brooch she never wore, one given to her as a child, and with that to start her off, began to buy and sell. There were several shops in Titchford where she found an outlet for her purchases and her journeys there were regarded by Colin as legitimate necessities; he took her in when he went to court, and she returned by bus. She would be on her way to an excellent delicatessen which sold cheese he particularly liked, or to buy some shoes, or to see an exhibition at the gallery – he approved of trips like that. It amused her to sit in the car with a large handbag containing a china figure or a locket, or a snuffbox, carefully wrapped, balanced on her lap, and return that evening with some money in its place. She made mistakes; she suffered losses now and then, but on the whole she made a modest profit and she was not greedy, content if she gained a mere two per cent on what she had paid for any item. At first she worked by instinct, having one day seen a small bronze cat priced at two pounds which seemed to her ridiculously cheap for an object so delicately moulded. She sold it for five pounds, and then saw it in the window of the shop which bought it from her priced at twelve pounds fifty. Later, she borrowed books from the library which increased her knowledge and she went to Fine Arts lectures which were approved of by her husband. She'd make nice friends there, he declared, and it would give her a new interest. The nice friends all had ready money in their purses; when she went on trips to museums, Felicity needed cash for teas and coffees, even wine; she asked for it and got it, but she had to explain where it had gone.

She lied a little; not a lot. Deception did not come easily to her.

Where should she go and what would she do, when she had made a thousand pounds? She thought she could not flee with less, and at this patient rate of operation it would take her a long time to amass as much. She made exciting plans. She could go to Australia and visit her parents, who had retired there because they liked the climate and her sister lived in Adelaide with her doctor husband, two sons and a daughter. But she'd have to come back. No, she must invest it somehow, put it in a business. Would it be enough? With every year that passed, the ceiling rose; it had to be another two hundred, then another five hundred, finally a second thousand. She laid out more on buying and had periods when her capital was in goods, not money. Her cash was kept in a biscuit tin beneath the floor boards in her bedroom; if she put it in Savings Certificates or a building society account, Colin might find out about it through the tax office, so she had to forego the interest it might have earned.

You came out of prison with – what was it – forty-four pounds? Surely it was more? And you had nowhere to go. You could sign on at once, however, for social security.

So could she, if destitute, presumably, though no individual card had been stamped for her since marriage. Think of the headlines if she made her claim: JUDGE'S WIFE ON BREADLINE.

Her small intrigue, with her sales and profits, fuelled her; if caught – and why should Colin ever find out? – it was an innocent deception; it was not as if she had a lover. Often, she wished she had: wished some man had come along to sweep her off her feet, ride off with her into the sunset yonder, but what she had seen of such episodes among people whom they knew seemed anguished affairs, full of pain, the joy so often transitory. Anyway, the temptation had never come her way; she sometimes wondered how she would respond, if ever it should happen: but it wouldn't now. It was too late. She was not the sort of woman to attract in quite that way, or so she felt, having acquired, by osmosis, some attitudes more typical of Colin than of her own nature.

The world must think her fortunate. She lived in an attractive house, comfortably furnished. Some of their nicer pieces Colin had acquired during his bachelor days, knowing they were 'good'; others had been bought at Heal's. She went to dinners and receptions with her husband, had a dull but unworrying son, dressed well, and entertained, when it was her duty, with competence. What more could be expected in this life? In his turn, Colin had equipped himself with a good-looking, docile wife who, on social occasions, could be trusted to bat back the conversational ball in a steady, uncontroversial manner and who would listen with attention to the words of others better informed than she. She ran his house efficiently, saw

24

that he had fresh shirts and socks and that his suits were cleaned and pressed. She polished his shoes and cooked his food and at appropriate intervals had acceded to his intimate embraces. These interludes were infrequent and were swiftly concluded, undignified as they were, even embarrassing, to both participants. The judge, fearful of possible failure, had ceasing making overtures of this kind years ago.

Sometimes, reading novels, Felicity was sure that there was more to all that side of life than she suspected, though the consequences often seemed to be disastrous.

Colin, though he had once read Dickens and the other classics, read no fiction now, and saw no films either in the cinema or on television. It did not cross his mind that both might be instructive: to him, lust was a sin; it led to wantonness and vice, aspects of human weakness often revealed to him in court. He had always felt shamed by the physical manifestations his body had exhibited despite his mind's instructions. Lawfully indulged, such episodes were uncomfortably pleasant, but control must not be lost.

He was tough with sex offenders, but he preached homilies to young women who took risks by walking home alone along dark streets at night, or who accepted lifts from men at pubs or discos. Felicity, reading of his comments in the local press, sometimes challenged him.

'They've got to get home,' she said. 'They can't afford taxis and the buses stop before the parties.' When he rebuked one young woman for wearing revealing clothes, she wanted to know why the girl shouldn't dress as she chose.

'Because it may inflame these ill-controlled men,' he answered. 'It's dangerous.'

'You mean it gives them come-on signals?'

'Felicity, where do you pick up these vulgar expressions?' he asked wearily.

'That one's common knowledge,' she replied.

'You've led a sheltered life, my dear,' he said. 'Please don't give opinions on things you know nothing about.'

Like rape, you mean, she thought. But I do know about it, for it was what you did to me, though with my consent, by default. Once it was called having conjugal rights, and men could sue for them, if they were withdrawn.

All that was over now, at least, and she could sleep in peace.

*

Felicity had one true friend in Rambleton, and that was Mrs Turner, her cleaning lady, who came with the house. She found Felicity a most congenial employer, and willingly spared her three hours twice a week. On other days she helped in a pub and she sometimes sat with an elderly invalid man to enable his daughter, who looked after him, to go out.

Mrs Turner thought Felicity was rather tense and nervy, especially when her son and his wife were due for a weekend, though over the years this seemed to improve somewhat and she appeared more eager for their visits now. Emily was not a cosy sort of girl, Mrs Turner realised; perhaps she frightened her mother-in-law, with her pert round face, hair cut in an old-fashioned fringe and bob, and her way of saying exactly what she thought. But Stephen was an agreeable young man, though he could not compare with Mrs Turner's idol, the Prince of Wales, but then, who could?

Mrs Turner shared her birth date with the Queen, April 21st, 1926, and because of this bond had followed the monarch's fortunes with devotion all her life. She kept scrapbooks about the major events in the royal calendar and could easily have answered *Mastermind* questions on her subject. Alas, there were few similarities in the lives of herself and her twin, if Mrs Turner might, without disrespect, so regard Her Majesty, though she had also been a Guide and had joined the ATS, but as a clerk. It was then that she met Alfred Turner, a corporal who was trained as a mechanic; he later became a garage foreman, dying of a heart attack at the age of fifty-five. Fortunately, the Duke of Edinburgh had been spared thus far to partner the Queen into her evening years, not yet reached by any means. Mrs Turner had no time for those who thought that she should abdicate: she was wise and vigorous, and it wouldn't be fair to load Charles with all that responsibility while the little boys were young. Besides, he might have to stop saying what he thought about things if he became King. Mrs Turner approved unquestioningly of his every utterance, and even the judge, in the privacy of Waite House, had commended his remarks about the decline in English usage.

In place of the Queen's numerous family, Mrs Turner had just one daughter, Betty, and so far no grandchildren. Betty had trained as a hairdresser and now had her own salon in a suburb of Birmingham, in partnership with her friend Zoe, whom she had met on a training course years before. They lived in a flat above the shop, and Mrs Turner was proud of Betty's success. She sometimes worried, however, because neither Betty nor Zoe had boyfriends, or none that they mentioned. Mrs Turner was not sure what to think about the possible significance of this, and, telling Felicity about Betty, skated quickly past the peril. After all, everyone had family problems of one sort or another, even the Queen.

Mrs Turner soon learned about Felicity, as much from what she deduced as what she was told. You discovered a lot when working in a person's house, and she could tell, from the way Felicity stopped whatever she was doing promptly at a quarter to eleven to make coffee for them both, which they drank together at the kitchen table, that she was lonely. It was not surprising. The judge was a lot older, and he was a busy man. When not in court, he had papers to read, opinions to give, and from time to time he had to sit on various committees concerned with matters of importance. He had to remain aloof from the hurly-burly; Mrs Turner understood that; but it was hard on Mrs Drew who was prevented, because of his position, from undertaking various things others in her income group, with children off their hands, might do. Mrs Turner was vague about the nature of these exclusions; surely other judges' wives had jobs?

Yes, they did, but certain things were frowned on, Mrs Drew had said. She could not enter politics, for instance, not that she wanted to; and she was not trained to be a teacher or a lawyer, which would have been approved. She felt no urge to be a magistrate, and thought she was not suitable.

Mrs Turner knew about the sales. Felicity was not aware of this, but once, in Titchford, Mrs Turner noticed her in an antique shop and later, in its window, saw a little figure which she had watched the judge's wife buy in the market the week before and had expected to see displayed in the house. Observation told her more, but she never mentioned it and would not have told the judge, no, not if you were to stick red-hot needles in her. She wondered why Mrs Drew did not open her own shop; surely one selling antiques would not be controversial? It never occurred to her that her employer could not raise the necessary capital from her husband.

It was a shame Mrs Drew had never been to Australia to see her parents. Once, she had suggested they fly out for a holiday but the judge was not enthusiastic; he preferred his few weeks touring in the car in France. Mrs Turner, on the other hand, went on package tours with her friend Mrs Jones.

Recently a firm of contract cleaners had started in the town and had approached Mrs Turner to see if she would join their team.

They travelled round in a small green van, whisking from house to house with a powerful vacuum cleaner and a range of scented sprays. Mrs Turner did not hold with aerosols and was glad to use Antiquax from a tin. She was not tempted by their blandishments and remarks about valuing her experience. She liked following her own methodical routine and being friendly with her employer, but would never have dreamed of addressing her informally, and, in her turn, Felicity always called her Mrs Turner.

In Mrs Turner's opinion, some of today's bad behaviour by youngsters could be put down to all these instant Christian names across the generations, showing no respect for older people. She had said as much to Felicity, who agreed and said that in France you always addressed those you met as *Monsieur* or *Madame* and shook hands on arrival and departure. She would tell Mrs Turner about her holidays with the judge in France, the small hotels in Provence or the Dordogne; Mrs Turner imagined them fraternising with the locals, although little of this happened, for Felicity spoke better French than Colin, who did not like being placed in any sort of inferior position and discouraged conversations in which he could take no part. Felicity, meanwhile, attended classes in the town and every year her French improved; on holiday she slipped off when she could and engaged in long talks with shopkeepers or chambermaids. Colin had decided they they would go to Italy next year, and Felicity, determined to keep one jump ahead, had enrolled for Italian lessons.

Mrs Turner seldom saw the judge, unless there were people to dinner at Waite House and she came to help. She enjoyed that; they had the local Member of Parliament and his wife once, and various legal men who must be important, one of them a retired judge who was sometimes to be seen on television giving his opinion on controversial matters. Mrs Turner soon saw that Felicity was glad of her moral support on these occasions. She was a good hostess and always looked nice, with her curly hair well cut – she went to Anton's in Titchford every month and did it herself between times – and she always wore a becoming dress, though in unadventurous colours like black or navy blue; once, in dark red velvet, she looked stunning, Mrs Turner thought. Round the house she wore jeans and her husband's cast-off shirts. Mrs Turner looked forward to Monday and Thursday mornings and would tell Felicity what had been happening at Sandringham or Windsor, or discuss the Queen's clothes if she had been on one of her tours, and say how nice it must be when she could stay aboard *Britannia* among all her own things instead of in some Governor's house or foreign palace, eating alien food.

The judge and his wife had been to a garden party at Buckingham Palace, and Felicity gave Mrs Turner a detailed account of this experience from the minute they arrived by taxi at a point from which they could walk, so avoiding the queue of arriving cars, until their departure the same way. If only the judge could get a medal, or be knighted: then they would go to an investiture, right inside the palace! That would be the day!

Felicity said that it might happen in the end; not a knighthood, but perhaps a modest decoration.

'When he retires,' she said.

It wouldn't be for ages; judges could work on until they were seventy-two years old, and they needed to, for they were well paid compared with being successful at the Bar, and they were not entitled to a full pension until they had served for fifteen years.

The judge never grudged her money for new clothes or for the hairdresser; to do so would reflect on him, if she were clad in rags or were to be unkempt; but as she grew older, she saw that this was one of the ways in which he controlled her. When they moved to Waite House, though, he surprised her by opening an account for her at a bank in the town and said she could use this to pay the household bills. He would still want full details of her expenditure, her statement analysed, cheques explained, and she must obtain receipts from every shop. Formerly, he had given her a weekly sum in cash but she had had to account for every penny, even down to chemist's items. He never queried anything; he merely wanted to know where the money had gone. It had made supermarket shopping difficult; she had had to check things off against the till slips. Now, however, things were easier; she could buy herself an illicit bar of chocolate or a packet of ginger nuts, not because she craved them but as a gesture of defiance.

As time went on, she developed more.

2

He sat in the train. Round him were representatives of the law-abiding populace, or so he supposed, surveying them, but then he looked ordinary, too. In prison he had grown a moustache, a long, soft one which hid his upper lip. It made him look quite mild.

He flexed his hands, cracking his knuckles, and a woman facing him looked up from her *Daily Mail* and frowned, then returned her gaze to the paper. She was middle-aged, dressed in a mock suede jacket and black skirt, with patterned tights. Silly cow, he thought, tarted up like that at her age. He began wondering about her, lasciviously; what if he followed her when she left the train, waited for his chance? That would wipe the smug look off her face. But she wasn't the sort he went for; she was too old, too heavy. There would be other opportunities, safer ones, and what he really needed was an acquiescent woman with a flat or house who would take him in while he readjusted to the world.

He was going to the hostel where he had spent his pre-release leaves. After a night or two there, he would take off. He'd made his plans already and had found a place to rent.

He hadn't got a long-term strategy: that had always been a problem for him; he preferred to improvise.

When her husband died, Judith Kent did not want to leave her house or the district where she had lived for the past twenty-five years.

It was a modern house, and they were its first owners, buying it when Dick, until then a physician in a London hospital, had decided to go into general practice. Neither had regretted the change; Dick had enjoyed the continuity with his patients which had been missing in his hospital appointment, and she had been glad to move into the country. The children's lives had opened up, with freedom to ride their bicycles about the countryside, and Veronica had a pony which was kept in the field beyond the garden. Now she was a nurse, working her way around the world and at present in California. David was a physicist, with a university appointment in Toronto, and Tim had joined the Army. At present he was stationed in Germany.

During the last weeks of their father's final illness, they had all managed to come home, and Veronica, when he died, had wanted to cut short her tour to keep her mother company, but Judith had been firm.

'You must carry on with what you've planned,' she said. 'It's wonderful to travel while you're young. I won't sell the house for at least a year or two. Later, maybe, when we see how things work out.'

There was enough money for the moment. Dick had been well insured.

The idea of taking paying guests had come about by chance. When the daughter of one of Dick's partners got married in some style in Witherstone church, her parents sought among their friends for people who would put up those who had to travel from a distance to attend the service. Judith at once agreed to take in two couples. She was going to the wedding, and she was able to sit with them, which made the occasion easier for her in her new, raw, single state. It was good to talk it over with them later, have the house full again. Tim was the only one of her children able to come home often, and though she had many friends, and took part in local activities, the centre of her life had gone and she lacked purpose.

The day after the wedding, while eating a large breakfast, one of the guests was talking about a holiday spent touring the Cotswolds, visiting different bed and breakfast places which they had discovered from a book. Most of them were very comfortable, a happy blend of the private and the personal.

'Almost as perfect as here, Judith,' said the husband. 'You should take it up professionally. You're good at it.'

He had been embarrassed at accepting hospitality from a widow. Judith had prepared a buffet luncheon for her visitors, who arrived in time to change into their wedding finery before the ceremony; in the evening, both couples took her out to dinner at The White Hart in Witherstone.

'Have you ever thought of being a landlady?' One of the wives took up the idea.

Judith hadn't.

'It's a good area. You aren't completely in the country, but it's quiet with fields around, and you're not far from interesting places for sightseers,' said the woman. 'Oxford's what – thirty miles? And

31

Stratford-on-Avon much the same. There's Blenheim, and Warwick Castle – plenty of attractions.'

Judith found the idea intriguing, and after they had gone, found her mind returning to the subject. She had enjoyed having the house full, humming once again with life. She had asked the touring couple about the places they had stayed in, whether dinner was provided, what duties devolved upon the landlady. She resolved to find out more: there must be books one could consult, or established land-ladies, or the tourist board.

So the scheme was born, and rapidly began to flourish. Her regular visitors soon became undemanding friends who enjoyed the familiarity of the comfort she provided.

Desmond Baxter was among their number. He would book in by telephone and, because she knew him, she never asked for written confirmation. He would arrive at nine o'clock or so, exchange some small talk with her, then retire to his room – a larger one, on subsequent visits, than where he had slept on that first foggy night.

She made a note of his car number; she always did that with guests. He gave his address as care of a branch of Barclays Bank, and paid in cash. No more was necessary.

The room was adequate. There was a large window, equipped with a Venetian blind, overlooking the street; the floor was sound, wood laid on concrete, and would need no covering during his short tenure.

He bought a chipped desk, two chairs and a filing cabinet from a place selling second-hand furniture, paying cash. He had drawn all his money out of the building society, closing the account, and opened a bank account in the name of Ray Evans. As proof of identity, he showed an envelope addressed to Ray Evans, and a driving licence in that name. While he was on pre-release leave he had made arrangements to buy several stolen licences from inmates released earlier. That was something he could not have done before his sentence.

It took him a few days to prepare the place. He painted the walls pale yellow to look bright and warm. In the room behind the office there was a sink with a small geyser, and, at the back, a lavatory. He slept in a sleeping bag on an inflatable mattress on the office floor: no hardship after years in prison.

He put posters advertising the service he offered in the window, but he had no big sign outside. This was a short-term venture and he would have to move on swiftly before his customers grew suspicious.

The first couple arrived the day his advertisement appeared in the local paper. They had been trying in vain to sell their house for several months and were becoming desperate. They had to move because the husband's firm had appointed him to another of its branches.

'I've got plenty of people on my books,' he told them. 'Some I can send round at once, even before I take the particulars of your residence. First there's this agreement. I charge only half a per cent commission on the sale, but I need a small deposit for expenses while negotiating. Only a hundred pounds, and it's deducted at completion of the sale.'

It was amazing how they fell for it. That weekend, he attracted ten vendors and his takings were therefore a thousand pounds, to be offset against the month's rent already paid. He hoped he could keep going for as long as that before someone grew impatient at achieving no result. All his new customers swallowed his story of waiting impatiently for the telephone to be installed; it was a matter of days, he said. He never called at any house; all his clients had details from other agents which he took to a copy shop and recopied under his own bogus heading.

'Just until I can get round to list the special features your property is sure to have,' he said, smiling guilelessly at a thin young man and his pregnant girlfriend who sat before his desk. The man was unemployed and they could not meet their mortgage payments so they were selling their small terraced house and moving in with his parents until something turned up. They found the hundred pounds which he requested; pawned something, he supposed, but that was not his problem.

He made appointments for people to view, who of course never arrived since they were fictitious buyers. In his room at the back, he cooked beans on toast and fried eggs, brewed tea and coffee. He seldom drank alcohol; it soon wound him up, out of control. He bought sandwiches and sometimes he went to McDonald's or to a takeaway. He melted into the background, a nondescript-looking man, not tall, with large, thin hands.

Sometimes, walking back at night, he would follow a woman; then, when he sensed that she noticed his presence, he would turn down a side street. If he kept off drink, he might be able to restrain the impulse which had driven him to violence. And finding a legitimate partner, even marrying, might be the best way to keep out of that sort of trouble. Soon he had the money, and in his business suit he looked respectable.

He met Sandra Dean at a sandwich bar one lunch time; she was buying egg and cress sandwiches for herself and another girl in the office where she was a filing clerk. Tomato and cheese was his own choice. Standing behind her, he knocked into her, apparently by accident, and apologised effusively. When he met her there a second time, it was natural to pass the time of day, and he walked with her back to her door, thus discovering where she worked.

The third time they met, he invited her out for a Chinese meal.

Much later, she said he had been ever so nice and quite the gentleman.

3

The boy learned to evade some of his difficulties. He found ways of shutting home from his mind as he set off for school, but there were problems: when his bike was damaged by an older boy, he had to make the excuse that he had ridden it into a wall to avoid a passing car as the truth would not have been accepted. Even so, he received a beating.

His crime was carelessness: shut in his room for a whole weekend, his meals – only bread and water were allowed – were pushed into his room each morning, the ration for the day. He was let out to wash and go to the lavatory each morning, then again at night.

'That will be quite sufficient,' the angry voice had said.

His mother had slipped up later and had unlocked his door, intending to pass in a pail he could use in between, but she was caught and forbidden to do it; after that, she had no key, and the boy knew that she, too, would be punished.

When he needed to urinate, he opened the window. He did not try climbing out to escape because, if he did, his mother would be made to suffer.

Gradually, he taught himself to blot his misery from the surface of his mind, but it lay dormant, haunting him in dreams where sometimes he was shut in a narrow vault, like an upright coffin, in total darkness and unable to breathe. He would wake with a warm rush of relief, gasping for air, heart thudding.

He told no one about the nightmares: no one could cure them, only time, or himself, or, maybe, revenge.

He flitted from the office four days before the month he had paid for was over. He'd done quite well to last so long, he thought; several clients, discouraged by his lack of progress in their interests, had expressed concern but he had reassured them; in each case, because he had the keys and, allegedly, had shown intended buyers round while the vendors were out, he said that offers were expected.

He cleaned the place up before leaving, wiping every piece of furniture to remove his prints, which were, of course, on file with the police, and polishing light switches and doorknobs.

He felt happy, charged with success, and he had made nearly three thousand pounds profit, taking into account what he had paid for rent. For a month's work, that was pretty good. He closed his Ray Evans bank account, removing all the money, mentioning that he was leaving the country. Then he took the train westwards, for a new area and another identity, where he ran the same scheme again.

He soon found a girl to take out, replacing Sandra Dean, one who worked in a fast food restaurant making beefburgers and frying chips. When you got her away from the stove, and she'd had time to wash away the smell of fat, she was quite attractive. He felt no hostility towards her, but he might have, if she had irritated him. He didn't see enough of her for that.

He needed a new line to exploit. The housing market had become so uncertain that sellers were not coming forward in the numbers he had hoped for; perhaps, in this area, they were less gullible. Certainly their houses were superior to those he had had on his files before.

He was Frank Brown here, and he rented an office in a block destined for renovation in a grandiose scheme which had misfired when the developer went bankrupt. Another firm had bought it and would carry out the transformation in a few months' time. Here, he stayed in a cheap lodging house, basic in the extreme.

Poppy, the fast food girl, was upset when Frank Brown went away without saying he was leaving, and with no goodbye. He had said he was a civil servant, and she believed him, for he looked so smart in his grey suit and his white shirt and sober tie: very clean, he was, and polite. She remembered him very well, later. They had exchanged kisses and some minor groping when he walked her home after a cinema visit, but no more.

He left the place by car, which he had hired in the name of Frank Brown, after closing the bank account which he had used during his three-week stay. He had thought of inviting Poppy to go away with him for the weekend, but he felt too restless to trust himself. It was all boiling up again, he knew, and he would have to be careful for when it happened he must be able to cover his tracks, choose a stranger, not someone with whom he had been seen. The police were devils now, and could get on to you if you left so much as a hair on the whore, for that was what he saw them as, those buttoned-up women who wouldn't give you the time of day.

People were so easy to string along. He had supplied himself with credentials on notepaper obtained as samples from firms advertising personalised stationery. He had practised several different scripts, writing as though from satisfied vendors, and he had displayed them on a cork board in each office. His next venture would be different; something new; another challenge.

He left on Friday, not wanting to face irate clients on the Saturday; he had cleaned up a nice little profit, not spectacular, but enough to last him for a while and let him buy some comfort, which he had not had since coming out of gaol. He'd go north, to Birmingham, or Wolverhampton: some large city big enough to offer anonymity.

As he cruised along in his hired Sierra, a police car came up behind him and he dropped his speed, at once uneasy. But his car was legitimately hired, and he had arranged to keep it for a week, which he did not plan to do as he knew where he could dispose of it for quite a lot of cash to someone who would soon equip it with new plates and sell it on before it was missed.

The police car overtook him and hastened on its way, its passage having caused dozens of law-abiding motorists to check their speeds and examine their consciences. Perhaps there was trouble ahead, he thought: an accident: a road block. Like another man, in fog, several years before, he turned off, forking right into a minor road, and, in fifteen minutes, arrived at Witherstone, where he stopped and went into the public library to look at old newspapers. He wanted to study advertisements, to help with his next money-extracting ruse. He spent the afternoon there, and made some useful notes. By the time he left it was getting dark, which made him uneasy. In prison you were safely locked up during the hours of darkness, and in strange territory he felt unsafe. It was too late to drive all the way to Birmingham and find somewhere to stay – or so, in his uncertain condition, he felt. The weather was blowing up; rain gusted down as he crossed the street to where he had left the car. He saw the sign for The White Hart Hotel but decided against staying there; though he wanted comfort, this might be too grand for him at the moment. He drove slowly on through the town into the outskirts, and at last, as he approached open countryside and the sign denoting the end of the speed restriction, he saw Judith Kent's board, hanging outside Willow House.

That would be just right: an up-market guest-house where the bed would be soft, the sheets clean and pressed, and someone else would cook his breakfast. He rang the bell and smiled his best smile at Judith when she opened the door. He told her his name was Frank Brown and invented an address in Shropshire. To her eyes, he looked respectable; he was well-spoken and polite, and his car was new. She told him she had a room vacant, and gave him the name of an Italian restaurant in Witherstone where he could dine, mentioning that it was popular with some of her regular guests. Or, she added, there was The White Hart Hotel, and a newly opened Indian restaurant about which, as yet, she had no reports.

While he was consuming pasta and veal in Marsala in the Trattoria Vicenza, the man Judith Kent knew as Desmond Baxter was in The White Hart, having a drink before dinner, at which he ordered grilled steak with half a bottle of good claret, and cheese and biscuits afterwards.

They met in the morning.

A couple had also been staying overnight, an elderly husband and wife who had come for a weekend break before winter closed in. When the pair came down to breakfast, they found two other places set at the large dining table. Judith had thought about getting small tables where people could sit individually, but as breakfast was all she provided, and she owned a big mahogany table which could seat ten with ease, and which she would need when the family were at home, she decided to keep things as they were. She laid the guests' places well apart, so that strangers need not talk if they felt unsociable.

She brought in tea, which the couple had said they preferred; cereal and fruit juice were on the sideboard, and she asked them what they would like to follow. Since it was paid for, most visitors ate a large cooked breakfast; well fed, they would need little for lunch. The couple chose scrambled egg, bacon and tomato, and while she was away in the kitchen, preparing it on the Aga, a man appeared, rather thin, with thick dark hair and a large, soft moustache. He was pale, and greeted them uncertainly.

'Morning,' he said.

'Good morning,' said the elderly man, echoed by his wife.

Mrs Kent came in then, with their plates.

'Oh, good morning, Mr Brown,' she said. 'Do help yourself to fruit juice and cereal.' She set down the plates, then smiled at him. 'Tea or coffee?' she asked.

'Coffee, please,' he said. It would be good here, real, not instant.

'Eggs and bacon? Sausage? Tomato? Fried bread?' she recited, smiling pleasantly, impersonal but friendly. Many of her business visitors wore sharp grey suits like this man, and brightly patterned ties – he had exchanged his everyday sober one for a gaudier one – and many were anxious, competitive salesmen, short on time and confidence. To her, he was another such. Seeing him hesitate about what to order, she suggested, 'The works?'

'Yes, please,' he said.

He did not smile. The husband and wife noticed this.

He helped himself to cornflakes, sprinkled them with sugar, poured on milk, and sat down at one of the vacant places.

'Going far today?' asked the woman. 'Or home for the weekend?'

'Oh – to Leeds,' he invented. 'I've got a new job.'

'Ah – that's nice,' said the woman, who was kind. 'What's that?'

'Selling cars,' said the man. 'What's your line?' He knew that the way to divert attention from himself was to give it to another.

'We're retired,' said the husband. 'We're having a little holiday, staying here till Sunday. There's lots to see round about. Have you stayed here before?'

'No.'

'We'd heard about it. Friends came in the summer. Said you couldn't go anywhere better, not for double the money,' said the woman.

'I'm sure of that,' said the man. He had drunk Valpolicella wine with his meal and had slept like a baby.

He was tucking into the heaped plate of food which Mrs Kent had brought him when the fourth guest came downstairs. Mrs Kent greeted him by name.

Desmond Baxter said a general good morning, then helped himself to fruit juice and a small bowlful of muesli. Mrs Kent would boil him an egg, four and a half minutes, just as he liked, and would bring him some toast. He sat down in one of the vacant places, opposite the couple, alongside the lone man. He never liked conversation in the morning. Mrs Kent knew that; male guests, business-men, were often quiet: they would say 'good morning' and leave it there, but couples were sometimes verbose; some thought they must be friendly. This elderly woman now asked Mr Baxter if he had been here before and he said that he had. She volunteered that the house was just like home, so comfortable, and there were pleasant spots to visit, and some lovely countryside. Today, if it kept fine, they meant to go to Chipping Campden.

'How nice,' he said, discouragingly, and no, he had never been there himself.

'Oh, you should. It's a delightful place. So unspoiled,' said the wife.

The younger man, seated beside him, was eating fast. He had cast one startled glance across the room at Desmond Baxter as he poured orange juice into a glass, then kept his head bent over his plate.

It happened that Mrs Kent came in with Mr Baxter's egg just as the man rose to leave the table. For the first time, Mr Baxter looked at him. He frowned.

The man had gone in seconds.

'He was in a hurry,' said the elderly woman.

'We must get off, too, dear, if we're to have a good day,' her husband urged her. He wanted to go to Snowshill and look at the view, if it stayed fine.

'He ate well,' said the woman. 'But he's left his coffee.'

'He's got a fair way to go,' said her husband.

From their room, as they collected maps and guide books, they heard the man drive off with a flurry of gravel from the wheels of his blue Sierra.

The man calling himself Desmond Baxter finished his egg and toast, and drank his coffee. He folded his napkin neatly. Mrs Kent always supplied fabric napkins, though of a kind you did not have to iron, slightly crinkled, in a pleasing pattern of checks. He knew that she wanted to get the washing into the machine as soon as her guests had gone. Unless any were returning for a second night, she had to put clean sheets on all the beds, clean towels on the rails, and do the bedrooms. Mr Baxter wondered if she had help in the house; perhaps a woman to do some of the rough work, he thought vaguely, though nowadays most houses had little of that. Floors were no longer scrubbed, though some were polished.

He went upstairs and cleaned his teeth. His bag was already packed, his bedroom window on the latch to air the room. At first, he had felt quite awkward, thinking of Mrs Kent cleaning up after him, for she seemed such a lady, so superior. He knew now that she was a doctor's widow. In summer, he had walked round her garden and admired the roses. At the end of the large plot there was a willow, which gave the house its name, and a small stream gurgled past; the doctor had been a keen gardener and had created a water garden governed by gravity from a spring in the lawn. It seemed the area was full of natural springs.

'*There is a willow grows aslant a brook*,' had kept ringing in Mr Baxter's head, and he had to look it up. Ophelia's suicide: '*There with fantastic garments did she come.*' It had made him shiver with unease, a feeling rare for him; now he felt that apprehensive *frisson* again.

He delayed until the couple had driven off on their excursion. Then he went to bid Mrs Kent farewell.

'I'll telephone when I'm next this way,' he told her, as he always did, then added, 'That other man – with the moustache. Has he been here before?'

'Frank Brown? No,' she answered. 'Why?'

So that was what he was calling himself. Well, he would hardly give his real name here, thought Mr Baxter, who had committed the same deceit himself.

'Did he book ahead, or just drop in?'

'He dropped in, just as you did,' she replied, smiling.

But Mr Baxter was not smiling back, though that was not unusual; he was a real old sobersides, she thought, and rather sad. She had started a competition with herself to see if she could make him laugh; so far, she had not succeeded.

'If he calls again, or telephones, I advise you not to let him have a room,' he told her.

'Why? You've met him before, have you?'

'I think so, though he had no moustache then. I don't know if he recognised me,' said Mr Baxter, though he felt sure, by the way the man had scuttled off, that he had done so.

'What's wrong with him?' she asked. 'You'll tell me next that he's been to gaol.'

'Yes. That's exactly what I would say,' Mr Baxter acknowledged.

'For all I know, so have you,' Mrs Kent declared. 'Some things have to be taken on trust.'

'Yes,' he agreed. 'And this time, please trust me.'

4

What was there to fear?

The man known as Frank Brown drove fast down the road, remembering where he had last seen the older man. But it didn't matter now; he'd done his time and he had not offended again. He ignored the matter of defrauding house vendors; he had not been sentenced for that sort of crime.

All the same, there was something alarming in the fact that both of them had spent the night in the same guest-house, and, now that he came to think about it, hadn't he heard the landlady address the other man as Mr Baxter?

That wasn't his name. What was he playing at? Brown was certain that he had made no mistake in recognition; that was a face which he would never forget. He couldn't be having it off with the landlady, could he? Surely they were much too old? But you read strange things in the papers. There had been all sorts in prison; however mighty you were, you could still be caught out doing wrong, and how great was the fall when you crashed so far. There was an opportunity here.

He abandoned his immediate plans, slowing down when he was two or three hundred yards away from Willow House, then taking the first side road he met, where he turned the car in a gateway and parked it facing the main road along which he had just travelled. Mr Baxter, as he called himself, might come this way; he would wait a while and watch. Then, if he appeared, he would trail him, see what happened.

He might not come this way, of course; he could turn in the other direction when he left Willow House. Brown decided to give it half an hour.

His luck was in. Twenty minutes later, the blue Volvo he had seen parked outside the guest-house went past the end of his road. Brown started the engine and set off in pursuit, without a plan, except to follow 'Mr Baxter'. He would have to be careful; the man was no fool and might recognise the Sierra. He must allow other cars to separate them, hope that he could keep his quarry in view.

He liked tracking people. He had tracked a lot of women in the past.

Soon a fine rain began to fall. That was a help; there was a need to pay more attention to the road ahead, less, perhaps, to looking in the mirror.

Even if 'Mr Baxter' realised that he was being followed, what could he do about it? The roads were not his alone; anyone could take the same route. The man calling himself Frank Brown felt bold now, his first anxiety erased by the knowledge that there was a puzzle here which might, when solved, yield dividends.

Even if he lost sight of the Volvo, there were other ways of tracking down the man. He might force the landlady to reveal his address, he thought, tightening his grip on the steering wheel; people talked if you hurt them: everyone knew that.

Felicity had certain selected friends and activities. When they first moved to Waite House, she and Colin received invitations to dinner and drinks parties, and soon Felicity was asked to sit on committees concerned with raising funds for various good causes and to attend charity luncheons. Colin approved of her involvement in these things, which were appropriate interests for a judge's wife. Because she had no car and did not drive, she usually ended up doing much of the catering for events, preparing Coronation chicken or making elaborate puddings in her own kitchen.

Most of the women she met on her committees were pleasant and friendly, but they knew each other already and formed little groups or cliques. Some were in their late thirties, married to prosperous men in the city; they lived in expensive houses beautifully renovated. Others were older, the wives of professional men or politicians. Each organisation managed a title or two. Felicity felt herself to be an outsider, lacking the confidence the others displayed; she was not aware that much of what she perceived as this was superficial.

She was considered, by these new acquaintances, something of a mouse, because of her timidity. She had a settled, almost elderly way with her, the result, they decided, of long years of marriage to an older man with little humour in him. The fact that she did not drive was a nuisance; she had to be collected and returned, and could not transport her contributions to repasts. She was also over-meticulous in submitting accounts for repayment and acquired a reputation for being mean. Most of the other women gave at least

43

some of the ingredients they used, or certainly never worried about the odd pound here or there, but Felicity was accurate to the final penny.

The trouble was largely her own fault, she knew; she did not fit in because she did not really want to, yet what the women did was entirely admirable and produced excellent results. She felt that part of their satisfaction came, in a few instances, from complacency at hobnobbing with Lady Hearn or the Honourable Mrs Powell, two ladies who were both unassuming for they had no need to assert themselves; neither of them could ever remember Felicity's name. 'The dull woman with the curly hair,' they said.

Golf featured largely in the lives of the heartier ladies Felicity met; and bridge with others. Some played both. Felicity had never learned either, though at first Colin had hoped she would take up bridge because it was so useful as a way of passing time after dinner. He tried to teach her, but the lessons lapsed when she became pregnant with Stephen and suffered severe sickness.

From time to time they were invited out to dinner, and in return, gave dinner parties at Waite House. Felicity felt constrained, on these occasions, about giving her true opinion on topics that arose in conversation round the table, for if it did not tally with Colin's views, he would chide her as though she were a child or a delinquent in court, and he sometimes did this in company.

Once, she turned on him after they returned home following such an incident.

'Just because we're married doesn't mean I have to agree with you about everything,' she said angrily. 'You spoke to me as if I was ten.'

'Naturally, because you sounded as if you were no older,' Colin replied.

The discussion had touched on putting children into care whence sometimes they were adopted without the parents having knowledge of their fate, thus losing all rights to regain them. Colin thought that such children were better in a safe background than at hazard in the wider world; Felicity considered that the child would think it had been rejected by its own parents when that was not in fact the case, and its whole future would be marred.

'You don't know what you're talking about, my dear,' he had reproved her, and went on to relate a harrowing tale of a child battered when returned home, which was not, in fact, the point at issue.

The man next to her had turned to her, during the judge's discourse, and asked where she and the judge had been for their holiday – all he could think of as a distraction in the circumstances. He managed to offer her a lifebelt on which to float back into the talk around the table, and, by creating a second conversation, to puncture the judge's self-importance. Colin was not popular; he easily grew pompous, and his stiff good manners sprang from contrived, not natural courtesy.

'The man's a bully,' Felicity's dinner companion told his wife, driving home. 'Poor woman, how does she stand him?' He found Felicity attractive, in a baffled, faun-like way, but did not mention this.

They continued their journey speculating about the home life of the judge and his wife, developing ever wilder theories which made them laugh a great deal and reflect that they were a luckier couple.

'He's years older than she is,' said the wife. 'And because he's a judge, I suppose she daren't break out and become liberated. He might clap her into prison.'

'She is in prison,' said her husband. 'Though it may be a gilded cage.'

'All marriages are prisons,' said the wife. 'Even ours.'

'But in some the doors are unlocked, and the key's been thrown away,' said her husband, patting her knee.

They decided not to invite the judge and his wife to a dinner party they were planning; public discord between couples was embarrassing; better to include them in a large drinks party in the summer.

'It would have been fun if she'd fought back,' said the wife.

'She's much too insecure,' said the husband, a management consultant.

'It's never too late to rebel,' said his wife. 'He'd have to provide for her, if she walked out. She'd surprise herself by what she'd find that she could do. It happens.'

'Perhaps a bolt from the blue will strike him down,' said her husband cheerfully.

'What a thing to say,' rebuked his wife, and added, 'No such luck.'

5

It was a long time before the boy had learned that the man was not his father. By then he was seven years old and had been sent to stay with his grandmother during a summer holiday. She had returned to England after the death of his grandfather, who had farmed somewhere in Africa. Now she lived in a cottage in Somerset and, to the boy, it was paradise. There were hens in an orchard, the sea nearby, and a local woman called Hilda who came in daily to cook and clean.

His grandmother told him about his father, her son, who had died as quite a young man. He had not known that before.

During her years abroad, he had received presents and postcards from his grandmother, and it seemed they had met while he was a baby, but he did not remember that. He had written back to her, solemn letters, neat and well spelled, supervised by his mother who had, he learned, met his stepfather when he was only two.

Why had he not known about this? Why had he, all this time, been led to believe that the man was his father? It was too puzzling; he did not enquire aloud.

His grandmother said she was pleased when she heard his mother was going to marry again. It meant she and the boy would be cared for, and perhaps there would be brothers and sisters later for her grandson, who by now was using the surname of his stepfather. He wondered why this had to be: still, it was better not to ask such a difficult question, and best, too, not to tell his grandmother how hard things were at home, for what could an old lady do, and it might make life worse for his mother. So he talked cheerfully about his friend Tony, who had a pet rabbit, and about the things he was learning at school.

There followed a time during which he spent part of every holiday in Somerset. In the summer his grandmother drove them both to the sea in her small car, and he played on the sand and attempted to swim. She was shocked that he could not really manage it, but she was too old to teach him, she said, and the water was too cold. He had never seen the sea until he stayed with her, and soon, by *sheer persistence, he managed to stay afloat for five or six strokes before sinking.*

'All you need now is practice,' his grandmother said. 'It's true of most things in life, once you master the elementary skill.'

When she asked about his mother, he would reply that she had a cold, or was well, and would find some diversionary remark to make, perhaps that the people next door had a new dog which barked a lot, annoying the neighbours, but that he had offered to take it for walks after school. His grandmother rarely asked a direct question, and if she did, he learned to parry and make a reply which hid the true state of things. The boy knew that his mother was unhappy; she often looked as if she had been crying, and once he saw a big bruise on her arm which she said had been caused by knocking into the kitchen door. Another time there was a purple mark on her forehead, which she tried to hide by wearing her hair in a fringe. He had bruises too, but his stepfather had few excuses to beat him because the boy was so docile; he preferred shutting him up in his room for hours at a time, until the boy learned to do it himself and isolate himself from trouble.

Then came the last visit to Somerset. He had longed for it with such impatience that he had scarcely slept the night before, and sat in the train in a turmoil of excitement, only to feel, on arriving at the station, a shock of disappointment as though a bucket of cold water had been thrown over him, for his grandmother was not there to meet him. Instead, there was a taxi with an unknown driver, who was kind and gave him a bull's-eye to suck.

At the house, his grandmother did not seem very pleased to see him. Before, she had always hugged him, but this time she simply said in a new, gruff voice that he was getting too old for kisses now and must learn to shake hands in a manly way. She wasn't interested when he told her how nice the taxi driver had been, and he soon developed a horrible sick feeling inside.

She didn't like him any more.

What had he done to upset her? He worried throughout his visit, which was suddenly cut short after less than a week.

His grandmother said, 'I think an old lady's company is boring for you now, and you'd better go home. I shall telephone your mother tonight.'

He cried himself to sleep, though he knew he was too old to cry. He must have behaved badly in some way, talked with his mouth full or forgotten to open a door for her. In his mind he rehearsed his every action since his arrival, but could not detect his offence.

Until now, his grandmother, since she entered his life in a real sense, had offered him escape. He would imagine that he and his mother had run away from his stepfather and had moved in with her. There was room in the cottage; his mother would soon be happy again in such a lovely place. Now that fantasy was ended.

Hilda, who still came every day, had not changed. She made him a gingerbread man and his special pudding, treacle tart, and taught him some card games after tea when she said his grandmother was resting. His grandmother had always rested in the afternoons, unless they were out somewhere; it was the custom in warm countries during the heat of the day, she had said, but now she lay on the sofa most of the time and they did not go out in the car once.

After that visit he never saw her again, but he went on writing to her, though she did not reply. Christmas came and went with no present, and finally he asked his mother what he had done to make his grandmother angry with him.

His mother did not look at him.

'Nothing,' she said. 'She's dead, that's all.'

The boy stared at her, shocked, and two tears spilled from his eyes but he blinked to hold back more. He would never see his grandmother again, never have the chance to find out what was wrong; she was gone, gone, gone; she had left him alone for ever.

At the time, he thought she had only just died but he found out that it had happened weeks before. He never understood why his mother had kept the knowledge from him, not comprehending that she lacked the strength of will to confront such a painful duty.

6

Felicity was back, that weekend, from her regular Saturday morning shopping trip before Colin's return, though she made no special effort about this on the occasions, several times a year, when he spent Friday night away after attending meetings of a charitable organisation of which he was a trustee. So she never saw the man outside the house.

Stephen and Emily were coming down. Sometimes, especially in the summer, they arrived on Friday evening, but most weekends they came in time for lunch on Saturday. The dog would run yapping round the garden, pleased at his release from the car, and would raise his leg against any handy plant. Though Colin found her pet difficult to tolerate, he approved of his daughter-in-law who worked appropriately in an art gallery, and was not a tiresome modern girl given to demonstrations at nuclear bases or other extremes of behaviour which could lead to trouble with the law and cause her to become an embarrassment; nor was she over-assertive; he was rarely at ease with women solicitors or barristers. Clever women were a threat.

He was always surprised that Felicity found it necessary to go out shopping on a Saturday; surely she could get what she needed ahead of time and devote herself, over the weekend, to her duties in the house? But in this, as in other ways, she had been a disappointment to him. She had never acquired the poise and elegance he had expected her to develop. Still, they existed peaceably enough; there were no raised, angry voices within Waite House, and he lived comfortably, as he deserved after his years of hard work and self-discipline.

Felicity knew her Saturday excursions irritated Colin; she made them as a gesture more than anything. It would not do to run out of something to read over the weekend, so she always went to the library; she bought cream and fresh bread, and wandered round the town enjoying all the weekend bustle before she had to settle down inside.

The man calling himself Frank Brown parked outside the Primrose Café and waited in the car, watching while people went in and out of shops and gossiped on the pavement. Gradually, the town grew very busy. At one point, a space in the market square near Waite House became vacant, and he moved the Sierra into it, remaining there behind the wheel. He observed the shoppers, especially the women, but not the old or ugly ones, or the large or fat; it was the thin, young ones that attracted his attention.

Eventually a small white Peugeot pulled in front of Waite House. This was not the car which he had followed all the way from Witherstone; that one, a Volvo, had arrived much earlier and the driver had stepped out to open the large double gates before taking it inside. Such a household, though, would run to two cars. As he watched, a young man in a tweed hat got out of the car and opened the gates. The car moved forward: the gates were closed: the little traffic flutter ended.

There was a woman in the car. Brown saw her small pointed face and the white blob of the dog she held on her knee.

Colin, after his rare Friday nights in Witherstone, was always secretly pleased if Felicity was out when he returned, though he never failed to comment on her absence when they met. If the house were empty, he had time to unpack, put his soiled linen in the clothes basket, and shed his role as Mr Baxter. He would change into tweed jacket and flannels, his weekend garments, worn with a checked shirt and a tie that was less austere than his daily grey or navy.

Felicity could be relied on to return in plenty of time to greet Stephen and Emily; looking after them was her business, and after he had welcomed them with a peck on the cheek for Emily and a handshake for Stephen, his custom was to retreat once more into his study, where he always had plenty of work on hand. He spent a great deal of time there when he was at home, and would remove himself every evening when they had finished their coffee after dinner, unless there were guests.

This morning he had some important telephoning to do: the fact that it was Saturday would not prevent him from obtaining the information he sought. He soon found the relevant file among his orderly papers.

The man he had seen that morning at breakfast at Willow House was, he was sure, William Adams, whom he had prosecuted for rape some seven years ago. Colin remembered the case well: it was one of the last serious cases he had taken before being appointed to the

Bench; the man's appeal had been dismissed – his counsel had alleged that as the victim had received only superficial cuts it was not a severe case and merited a shorter sentence – nor had he been granted parole, but he had been released after serving seven years of the ten–year sentence he had received. The victim was a seventeen-year-old schoolgirl, waylaid at knife point on her way home after spending some hours with a friend. She was small for her age and looked younger; it was an extremely violent incident, and Colin had been pleased that the presiding judge had viewed it severely, for at that time – and even, occasionally, today – some rapists received sentences that were much too light. All the same, Colin still felt that women took risks; hedonism prevailed in contemporary society which seemed, to him, to be hurtling into moral decline, and potential victims should protect themselves. The girl Adams had attacked had struggled to escape, and had been cut on her face and arms. Courageously, she appeared in court and identified her assailant; at the request of prosecuting counsel, she had displayed to the court the scars on both her arms; they could see for themselves the thin white line on her face, a line which plastic surgery might later conceal. What about the scars to her soul, Colin had demanded, in his usual unemotional tones.

What was William Adams doing, staying at Willow House under a false name? The man was an evil villain, the epitome of wickedness. Colin knew the police suspected him of carrying out other attacks on women, but they had no evidence, and he had confessed to no other crimes, not even in prison, where sometimes inmates revealed further offences.

But he would have received no sort of remedial treatment; he would not have been encouraged to examine his conscience. Now he was free to commit fresh attacks upon defenceless young females who should be able to walk to their homes unmolested.

Some wicked men, the judge knew, were kind fathers and affectionate sons; they kept canaries or pigeons, collected stamps, loved their wives and their children; others were wholly bad, without a saving grace. Adams, Colin was certain, came into this category, and while he was at large, every woman he came near was at risk.

He did not know that at this very moment the man was sitting outside in his car, watching the house.

Adams had to get rid of the Sierra. The judge – he had heard of the appointment while he was in prison but did not know where he sat – might recognise it, for he must have seen it outside Willow House.

He made an arrangement by telephone with his contact, and they met on Saturday night at a lay-by on the A1. His acquaintance was waiting there in an old Vauxhall, driven by another man. In minutes a wad of notes changed hands, new number plates were fixed, and the two cars drove away.

Adams walked back to the road to thumb a lift. He spent the night in a motel beside a service area where the lorry driver who had picked him up stopped for a meal and petrol. The next day he travelled to Titchford, all his belongings packed in two soft zipped bags. He was going to harass the judge, hound him, make the old man suffer some of the grief he had experienced from being locked up. He must have something to hide, after all: why else should he use a false name?

He had plenty of cash now, but he must have transport.

Titchford was quiet on Sunday. He found digs in an old Victorian terraced house on the edge of the town, and, advertised in a shop window, he discovered a Fiat 127 for sale. It would soon need an MOT test, but it was licensed for two months, which should be long enough; constant change was essential to keep ahead of anyone who might want to check.

There was no need to look for a job. If things got rough, he could sign on, but the less he had to do with officialdom the better.

On Sunday night, lying in bed, he thought about ways to get back at the judge, ways that, in the end, could be lucrative, for surely he would pay up to keep his little secret?

Emily was very precise in all that she did. When they stayed with Stephen's parents she liked to discuss with the judge some legal point Stephen had picked up by reading the law reports in the preceding week. Had he agreed with such and such a decision? What about that particular sentence? Could he explain a certain point of law? Did he agree that parents should be called to account for the offences of their under-age children? And so on.

He would reply patiently, ready to give her information, impressed by her clear thinking but not alarmed, for Emily's demeanour was always respectful, not challenging. He would never give an opinion about another judge's sentence, remarking that as he had not been in court, nor seen the papers, he did not know what had come to light which had caused his colleague to pronounce whatever judgement had been delivered. Newspaper reports, he added, seldom revealed what really went on, pared down as they were from hours of testifying. He enjoyed answering questions, but he always stated both sides of any controversy most fairly, rarely coming down in favour of either. He enjoyed these talks with his daughter-in-law, who would look at him solemnly, her large brown eyes beneath her straight fringe almost unblinking. She would declare views of her own but was always ready to defer to his wider knowledge. Since marrying into the family, she had become interested in legal affairs and now always watched television programmes which alleged miscarriages of justice.

The police had had a bad press lately; it seemed to Emily, reading about confessions extracted, it was suggested, by threats and intimidation, that more than a simple statement of guilt should be required before a person could be convicted. Supporting evidence must be supplied, she declared: didn't the French do these things more fairly, with their inquisitorial system of justice?

'I've had tranquillisers myself,' she admitted once. 'I know that sometimes I've been a little woozy and I can see that one could become muddled about times and dates, and even uncertain of what had actually happened.'

Colin was, himself, unhappy about some instances that had been disclosed in recent years. He knew that it was tempting for a detective to look for facts to prove a theory, rather than fit the theory to the facts, but he was not prepared to be quoted as having these views and would equivocate when Emily spoke of such things, though he always listened with interest to what she had to say.

So did Felicity. She would reopen the subject when alone in the kitchen with Emily, preparing the next meal. She began to grow fonder of the stranger who had become a member of the family, and to find her company stimulating.

The letter arrived on Tuesday morning.

It was addressed correctly, in black print, to Mrs Drew, Waite House, Rambleton. The envelope was a plain white one of a kind available in any stationer's.

Felicity picked up the post from the mat, as usual, and as usual the letters were nearly all for Colin. There were two for her: one was an invitation to a coffee morning in aid of wildlife. She opened the second and took out a small sheet of paper.

WHERE WAS THE JUDGE ON FRIDAY NIGHT? she read, in the same neat capital letters as those on the envelope.

She stared at it, bewildered. She knew that Colin occasionally received unpleasant letters from aggrieved offenders or their families, but such mail was usually sent to the court and dealt with there; he did not talk about it. He had received one or two unpleasant letters at home, since their address was in *Who's Who*, but it had never been a serious problem for him. This was the first anonymous letter she had ever received.

She crumpled it up and threw it in the wastepaper basket. That was the place for rubbish. On Friday night Colin had been in the West Midlands attending a trustees' meeting and had stayed away, as he sometimes did, with one of his fellow trustees. She thought it a sensible plan; the drive back, on a winter's night, was tiring, and this arrangement meant he could have a pleasant dinner with his colleagues, then travel home in the morning.

The mail arrived early in Rambleton, one of the advantages of living in the town, close to the post office where the final sorting was done. That morning, Colin slit his envelopes open, looked quickly at the contents as he ate his muesli and drank his coffee, and sorted them into heaps of more or less urgent as he did so. Felicity watched him. Where could he have been but with his colleague, as he had said? He had first stayed away on a very foggy night some time ago, perhaps three years, she thought, when she had been staying with Stephen and Emily in town soon after they were married. They had brought her back with them on the Saturday; she had gone up then for a special viewing at the gallery where Emily worked. He had told her that he had been forced to stop on the way home because of the fog, and that he had decided, since the meetings were always on Fridays, that he would no longer attempt to get back the same night. He had received invitations to dinner before, he said, but had turned them down because of the journey, and he was certainly not going to drive after even a couple of drinks; a judge had to have a reputation like Caesar's wife. She had said that she thought it a good idea if he stayed overnight; the truth was that she enjoyed her few Fridays with supper on a tray in front of the television.

But perhaps he did not stay with his colleague?

She asked about him – a solicitor, who lived in an agreeable house

54

in the town where the trustees met. Colin said he was well, and his son had just joined his firm, which gave him great pleasure. This was true; why lie? He had wondered what to say if she asked for the address or telephone number of his supposed host, but she had never done so. He refused to consider a possible emergency in which she might need to get in touch with him. She knew of the man merely as Peter; Colin had never revealed his surname. There were advantages in not talking about your work at home.

When he had gone, Felicity could not get the message out of her mind. If he had not stayed with Peter, then where was he? In books, women searched through their husbands' pockets seeking incriminating hotel bills. Feeling ridiculous, Felicity did the same thing, going through all his good dark suits, which he wore in rotation. She was scarcely surprised to find no circumstantial evidence of any kind, in fact nothing at all in any pocket; Colin did not want to spoil the hang of his jackets by loading their pockets with even a handkerchief when they were not on his body. She was certainly not going to hunt through his desk. It was impossible to think of Colin spending an illicit night with some woman; perhaps he had been greyhound racing with Peter, or to some low club?

She could not believe it. Colin was the least likely man on earth to behave with indiscretion; however, it was true that extraordinary things could happen: men of high reputation, as old or older than Colin, could become involved in scandal. But not Colin. This was some sort of practical joke.

All the same, she retrieved the letter from the wastepaper basket, and the envelope in which it had arrived. The postmark was blurred; she could not make it out: in fact, Adams had driven to Newbury and mailed it there. Felicity put them both in a large envelope in which a circular had arrived, and placed that in a drawer of the desk in the drawing-room which she used for her own correspondence and the accounts about which she had to be so punctilious.

Late that afternoon, the telephone rang.

'Ask him who Mrs Kent is,' suggested a strange, hoarse voice, without preliminary.

Then came the dialling tone.

7

Adams sat on the bed in his small rented room and counted his assets.

He had seven thousand pounds in cash, a shabby but more or less reliable car, and an opportunity for blackmail. Chasing that up would be his next operation, and if he continued to harass the judge, he might be deflected from looking for vulnerable women on dark nights in deserted streets.

He had proved for himself how easy it was to con people: the estate agency racket had been so simple to put into action and had ended well for him. If customers were complaining now that they had lost their money, because he had stopped after two operations and had covered his tracks when he left, he was safe enough; the police had more important matters to keep them busy. There were so many things you could do to part fools from their cash. You could pose as a council official and get hold of pension or savings books; you could sweet-talk your way into people's houses and pick up anything useful that might be lying around; you could even get women to fall for you, and spend money on you. Such short-term measures meant there was no need to seek a regular job, no need to grind away at a boring routine.

He'd had no sexual contact since coming out of prison. His mates from inside wouldn't believe that, if he told them; it was top priority on most men's lists when they were released, though some of them managed to get themselves organised while at the open prison. The recurring notion of equipping himself with a conventional partner still had its attractions, and at the back of his mind he retained the theory that to do so could stop him from attacking a girl he might see by chance. It hadn't before, of course, but time had passed since then. There were moments when he knew that what he had done was horrible beyond all excuse, but when he embarked on such an attack, he was filled only with a wild urge to hurt and humiliate a woman in vengeance for the rejections and slights that he had sustained. If the opportunity to do it again came along, he knew he would find it difficult not to succumb.

In a pub, he might meet someone who would do. There were

always tarts to be had, after all, if you weren't fussy; the trouble was that he liked a nice type of woman, one who was clean and took trouble. Even his victims were like that, pin neat and smart. It shouldn't be too difficult, though, to find a female with whom he could develop a relationship adequate to keep him out of further trouble; perhaps his problem was that he'd never found Miss Right.

He met June Phillips at a club for the divorced and widowed, after seeing an advertisement for their weekly meetings advertised in a local paper left by someone else in The Grapes, where he sat alone in a corner drinking a shandy. The small amount of alcohol in that would not do more than give him the courage to make an overture if a likely woman came into the bar.

He tore the piece from the paper. Their meetings were held, he read, in a hotel in Brewer Street, Titchford. Gentlemen must wear ties.

Before he went there, he telephoned Mrs Drew again. She was out the first time he tried but at the third attempt, she answered.

'Ask him about Witherstone,' he said, and hung up.

While diverting himself in these ways, he explored Titchford. His rooms were in a side street near the football ground. There was a junk shop along the road; a barber's where he went for a haircut and had his moustache neatly trimmed; a betting-shop; and a second-hand clothes shop. He came and went without meeting other lodgers. Breakfast was not provided, so he bought bread and margarine and apricot jam, and made tea, catering for himself; there was an electric kettle for the tenants' use on the landing. The contrast between this place and his night of comfort at Willow House was extreme; he need not stay here, of course; he had money enough to go somewhere better, yet he hesitated to move too fast; this was an anonymous sort of house with, he discerned, occupants too intent on their own affairs to be concerned about those of anyone else. He suspected he might not be the only man there with a record.

On one of his walks round the town, he went past the Crown Court, a well-designed new building with the Magistrates' Court at the back. There was parking space for a number of cars and he saw the Volvo which he had followed for so many miles, parked tidily beside a Rover 3000. That would be a brief's car, he decided, or perhaps it belonged to a villain who was in the dock being charged with fraud or theft on a grandiose scale. He was happy, himself, to drive about in an unassuming vehicle which would be unlikely to attract attention or appeal to car thieves.

In the centre of the town, there was a shopping arcade with Boots, Marks and Spencer, Dixons, and branches of the other multiples to be found throughout the land. The Body Shop attracted him; this was something new: he entered the door and soon turned back, repelled by its adherence to what its name implied; every item it sold was for use on the human form, and Adams did not like to think too much about his. He left and entered the safer portals of a newsagent's, where be browsed for a while among the magazines but bought nothing, though he had read a lot while in prison. Since he had been outside, he had not been able to concentrate for long on any one thing.

Other streets offered shoe shops and a department store, music and videos. He had never gone in much for music, though he had quite liked singing at school and had even once fancied himself as a choirboy, but that had not lasted. He'd worked hard in those days, but it had all started to come apart after he left school. He'd done well there, and much had been expected of him, but in vain, though he'd had jobs, some of them good ones in offices, and once with a travel firm, but he could never stick to anything long.

Then a girl he was seeing threw him over for someone else, and because he wanted revenge, he attacked another girl he saw walking through the park alone one dark night. The assault stopped short of actual rape because she broke free and ran off, and of course it had been the fault of the first girl. He did not attach any blame to himself. If the victim reported what had happened, he never knew, and it was six months before he did it again, stalking the streets, a respectable-looking young man watching for girls on their own. One he attacked hit him in the stomach with her elbow, screamed loudly and ran away, leaving him winded. After that he armed himself with a knife, and by then he had a car.

The singles club meeting took place in a long, dimly lit room with a curtained stage at one end and a bar at the other. A small patch of parquet floor was exposed for dancing, and a gentle beat throbbed through loudspeakers high on the wall. Groups of women were seated at tables dotted around the room; all had glasses before them. Most of the men stood at the bar. Adams joined them and bought a beer; he would need it, and maybe another, if he was to get anywhere tonight. He surveyed the available talent and was not encouraged; the women ranged in age from about twenty to over sixty, though few were as old as that. Most looked painfully self-conscious, ignoring the assessing stares of the men who glanced their way when not too busy preening themselves. Adams stood alone, drinking his beer and waiting for something to happen. In his grey suit and plain tie, his estate agent's disguise, he looked safe and conventional. Though all the men, as instructed, wore ties, some displayed vivid patterns above boldly striped shirts, signalling Look at Me, and three were in jeans. There were others in suits, and several in flannels and blazers; like the women, they varied in age. More people drifted in and divided themselves by gender.

A middle-aged man in charge of affairs called out, through a microphone, that couples should take the floor for a waltz; he changed the tape and turned up the volume; the evening, presumably, was about to get under way.

June Phillips, a divorcée who had never been to the place before, was wishing she had not come now, but she had accompanied a friend, more recently separated, who was weary of her lack of a social life. Adams noticed June when he saw her go by in the arms of a stout man of about fifty who was already perspiring freely; when he rescued her during a break in the music, June felt thankful. At first glance, he seemed quite attractive: not very tall, with large dark eyes and a soft moustache, and thick brown hair. His face was pale and thin.

He told her that he had recently returned from five years in New Zealand and was living in digs and looking about before finding a new job and settling down.

'And you?' he asked, not really interested but aware that he must listen; besides, she might tell him something which he could use to his own advantage.

She had told him she was a dental nurse, and about her divorce – she and her husband were incompatible – her three children aged thirteen, ten and eight, with whom she lived in what had been the family house, though she was afraid it would be sold and they might have to move to a flat. Her ex-husband lived in a maisonette on the other side of the town and he saw the children each weekend, on either the Saturday or the Sunday. There was no room in his flat for an overnight visit. Sometimes he took them to spend the weekend with his parents in Wales. He had a new girlfriend, the children said, a librarian.

He escorted her home – she had come in her friend's car but the friend seemed to have plans for the rest of the evening – and he lurked in the shadows while she said goodbye to the baby-sitter, an elderly woman who met the younger children from school and looked after them in the holidays. June had told him that.

Now he knew where she lived. He called the next day with a bunch of flowers – he knew what to do to give someone the rush – and invited her out to dinner. A week later, officially described as the lodger, he moved into what had been Amy's bedroom and she doubled up with her sister. He remained merely the lodger until the weekend, when the children went to visit their father.

June had been very lonely. There was a big gap in her life, and though she did not want her actual husband back, because the rows they had had were so destructive, she felt a little adrift, unpartnered. Adams – he told her his name was Brian Cotton – as a lodger seemed a good idea as a temporary measure. They might grow close, she thought, or it might not work out, in which case he must go. She was not quite clear how it had come about so swiftly that he moved in; she did not remember suggesting it; it seemed to be decided without any discussion after some gentle, passionless kisses, when he had said his digs were unsatisfactory. He offered to pay her what it was costing him there, with a little over the top, or so he said; it didn't seem a great deal, and she would be feeding him, but it should help provide a holiday for herself and the children.

He was impersonal as a lover: disappointing, in fact, but you couldn't expect wonders to start with; when they knew one another better, things might improve. Besides, with the children under her roof, she must be discreet; she did not want them to understand what was happening, and Rose was quite old enough to work things out, given half a hint.

Adams did not mind the restrictions June imposed; although, in theory, he wanted to achieve a normal relationship with her, he had no wish to practise it more than occasionally.

The judge's wife sat at her desk in the classroom where she was learning Italian. She was supposed to be having a conversation with her neighbour using phrases they were expected to have learned by now.

They asked each other their names, where they lived, and the way to the post office. Felicity's partner, an earnest young woman whose toddler was safely parked in the crèche at the centre, had a far better memory and was soon telling Felicity what she had bought at the shops. Felicity floundered along, determined to confound Colin with her grasp of the language.

Instead of concentrating on the vocabulary, her mind kept returning to the telephone calls. She ought to tell Colin about them and show him the letter. He would soon dismiss them all as merely a nuisance and declare that he knew no Mrs Kent, or, if he did, explain her perfectly straightforward place in his life. She could be some clerk, or a past client, or someone against whose husband he had made an injunction; there could be any number of innocent reasons why he should know such a person. He would call the police, have their telephone tapped, or do whatever was necessary; perhaps have them go ex-directory, as most judges were. But what if he showed some reaction, looked shifty and prevaricated? She had never seen him look ill at ease, even when forced to take to his bed with flu, and the mere notion was enough to make her want to laugh. At once she felt more cheerful. She chuckled, and her companion asked her sternly, *'Che cosa fa?'*

'Piacere, mi scusi,' replied Felicity fluently. It was a convenient phrase to have off pat, and she was constantly forced to use it to apologise for incompetence or inattention in class. If Colin knew what an inept pupil she was, he would suggest she abandon her lessons because she was doing herself, and so by extension him, no credit. But she thought none of her fellow pupils knew who he was. She kept quiet about her own life, during the coffee break; others were ready enough to talk about their families and interests. She was sure the teacher had already marked her down as a frivolous, indolent pupil, though in fact she always did her homework.

Colin had taken calmly her remarks about Friday night. She should forget about it, put it out of her mind: it was nonsense.

Walking home, she decided that if the letters and the telephone calls were malicious, the instigator would not leave it at that. Something else would happen: there would be other calls or more letters, and if there were anything sinister in what was implied, she would soon discover what it was, for such a campaign, if that was what it turned out to be, must have some purpose.

What could that purpose be?

8

Colin could not understand why Felicity had asked about Peter, the colleague at whose house he had, allegedly, spent Friday night. She was never curious about his trustees' meetings; he had trained her not to be inquisitive about his work, for there was no need for her to become involved. What had suddenly made her now, on the one occasion when he had had the weird experience of recognising William Adams, ask questions?

It was coincidence. He was jumpy, because it had startled him to see the man there, brought back recollections of the sad case for which he was sentenced, of the victim who, when last he heard about her – for he had made enquiries over the years – was unmarried and was frequently out of work because she lacked the confidence to face the world. She had shot her bolt of courage during her court appearance, it seemed.

If Felicity were ever to discover that he stayed not with Peter but at Willow House, how could he explain why he did so? He did not understand it himself. When he went there, it was as though he sloughed off several layers of acquired identity and became simply an individual, unmoulded by training and habit. At Willow House, he was not expected to deliver an informed opinion on anything: he was not a judge: he was not a father: he was not a husband. He was Desmond Baxter, a paying guest, and his hostess, Mrs Kent, never asked him a personal question.

He had asked her several. He knew about her doctor husband and had seen his photograph on the desk in her sitting-room where she receipted the bills. He had been shown photographs of her family and usually walked round her garden to see how well, or how ill, various plants were faring. She mentioned a scheme by a builder to put up new houses which would mar her view in the field beyond the paddock; she feared there would be no way to defeat it. She was always very correct in her manner, but she was not reserved nor turned in on herself. It became clear to him that her marriage had been very fulfilling. Although her husband had worked long hours and been subject to calls in the night, they had enjoyed things together when he was free, and had given each other confidence to embark alone on what could not be shared. She had dealt with schools for the children, village committees, church work, and had sung in a choir; he had had his practice, which had grown during his time in Witherstone and eventually occupied a modern, well-equipped health centre; he had worked at the cottage hospital, soon, alas, to be closed. On days off he had played golf. Holidays had been precious, at first with the family, but as they began to go their own ways, the parents alone. They had hoped to travel more widely after he retired, go to India and Australia. They had been to New York and to the Canadian Rockies, to Italy by car, to Sicily and to Greece.

'It's not easy to do that sort of thing alone,' she had said. 'The impetus isn't there. I doubt if I'll do much travelling now, unless it's to visit the children in their far-flung locations.'

She had become distantly friendly with a few other regular visitors, but there was something about Mr Baxter which made her regard him as different; she felt concern for him. He had some serious problem. If he wanted to tell her about it, no doubt he would at last, and she would listen. If he had been recently widowed, he had had the chance to say so when she talked about her husband; she did not think that was the trouble. Over the months that he came, however, she noticed that he grew more relaxed. His brow at breakfast was no longer furrowed; he smiled when he arrived and had taken to bringing her a bottle of very good sherry, a small thank you, implied, for the brandies she sometimes offered him. At first, he had never said more than a few formal words of greeting; later, when he knew more about her, he enquired for her family and then began the custom of the half-hour in her sitting-room before he retired. When he left in the morning he looked as if he had shed several years overnight, some of the creases in his face ironed out, and he always said he had slept well. She assumed, because of his beautifully tailored suits, that he was on the board of some big company and preferred staying in guest-houses to large hotels. He always paid by cash, which was unusual, but why not? To him, such an amount was no doubt a very small sum.

His modest Volvo did not support the theory of big business, but tycoons could be self-effacing, see no need to impress. He was an enigma, a puzzle she might never solve.

When he advised her not to accept another booking from Frank Brown, if he came again, she was astonished, but because he said that the man had been in prison, she must comply.

63

Colin, glad that he knew what the man was calling himself, resolved to ask the police to run a check on the Sierra which he had been driving. He had noted down its number before the man drove off. He did not contact the local force, but telephoned Superintendent Manners, of the Met., whom he had known when the officer was a mere sergeant. He learned that it had been legitimately hired by one Frank Brown. At the time Colin made the enquiry, the car had not yet been stolen, and, when its loss was notified, no connection was made with the original request for information.

Brown, né, Adams, could not have been in touch with Felicity, causing her to become curious about Peter. It was Colin's own sense of guilt which was making him attach importance to what was merely an idle remark. He must banish such ridiculous thoughts. But why was Adams in Witherstone? What was he doing at Willow House? Colin had told Superintendent Manners that he had recognised the man while driving through the town, where he had gone to visit a pottery to buy a present for his wife. He had lied about that, too, though a card advertising the pottery was in guests' rooms at Willow House. Colin suggested that Manners might care to inform the local police that Adams had been seen in that area; it might alert them if anything suspicious happened in the district. The man's car could be stopped on any pretext.

It never occurred to the judge that he had been followed home.

Felicity sometimes had to go out on one of Mrs Turner's mornings, though she much preferred to be at home then and would do the ironing, check her accounts, or, if she had no other jobs about the place, keep out of the way by reading. She was a constant visitor to the library and was a keen reader of modern fiction ranging from Frederick Forsyth to Iris Murdoch, and stations in between. Colin owned most of the classics – not Jane Austen, though. They were kept in a glass case in his study. Felicity always intended to tackle Dickens and Trollope but had not yet borrowed any of Colin's volumes; there they were, in reserve.

One morning, while she was at a committee meeting about a Christmas bazaar to be held in aid of a children's charity, the telephone rang. Mrs Turner was quite used to this and enjoyed leaving a clearly written message for Felicity when it happened.

This time, before she was able to speak herself, a voice said, 'Ask the judge about Mr Baxter.'

'What did you say?' Mrs Turner said, but the line was already dead.

She wrote down the message, looked at it carefully, and wondered what it meant. Perhaps this Mr Baxter was coming before the judge in court, or was lodging an appeal, or figured in some other way in the judge's working life. 'No name given, rang off immediately. Man's voice', wrote Mrs Turner in her clear round hand, and the time of the call.

She had gone by the time Felicity returned. There was another message, too, cancelling the judge's routine dental appointment because the dentist had to be out of the surgery that day. Felicity's irritation at the problems she foresaw in making another at a time convenient to Colin was swallowed up by her alarm about what must have been another of the mystery calls.

She told Colin about it when he came home, and showed him the pad with Mrs Turner's message.

'I see,' was all he said.

That night at dinner she asked him who Mr Baxter was.

Colin dabbed his lips with his napkin. He dreaded being unaware of small messes about his mouth.

'Let me see,' he said. 'It's quite an ordinary name. I expect I've met several in my time. Now, was there a barrister – ?' and he went off into some story about a colleague.

'But Mrs Turner's message?' Felicity prompted him.

'It must have been a wrong number,' he answered. 'It meant nothing to me.'

'But the message said, "Ask the judge",' Felicity pointed out.

'Mrs Turner may have got it wrong,' said Colin.

But Mrs Turner did not make mistakes of that kind; she was neither careless nor vague.

Felicity got up to clear the plates, muttering under her breath as she went into the kitchen, 'Mrs Kent met Mr Baxter in Witherstone. He said to her, "Do you come here often?" '

While she was out of the room Colin poured their wine. A bottle lasted them three nights; he had one of those gadgets which extracted the air so that the wine remained in good condition.

Adams had telephoned the house. That was a fact, and it made him very uneasy. The man could have discovered where he lived without too much difficulty; perhaps he had been unwise in listing his telephone number and in putting his home address in *Who's*

Who. Yet what could Adams really do to damage him? If he tried blackmail, the judge would know how to deal with that.

Or would he?

What he had done was such a small deceit; royalty and show business people often travelled under false names for security reasons; was what he had done so different? Yes, because there was no justifiable need for the lie, and he had not understood why he had told it.

When Felicity returned with the lamb chops, he distracted her by suggesting they might have a night in town and go to the theatre. She agreed at once. It was over a year since he had taken her to the theatre, though she had been with Stephen and Emily on one of her visits. She wondered if he would consult her about what they should see and how long it would be before the outing took place: months, she resignedly decided.

Adams enjoyed making the telephone calls, imagining the consternation they must cause at the other end of the line. He had made them all during the daytime, when the judge would be in court and his wife would be in the house alone. This time, he had used June's telephone. Why pay, when he could get it for nothing?

He was painting her kitchen. When he saw how marked the walls were, with stains round the sink and stove, he had offered to do it, and he felt quite domestic, setting about his task while she was at the surgery and the children were all at school. When she came home, he would have the kettle on, ready for tea, and the children would all be in the sitting-room watching television. Their minder, Mrs Downes, got on with the ironing while their times overlapped; she was paid to stay until June returned and she was not going off leaving the children with some strange man, in spite of his suggestions that she need not linger.

They had bought the paint together on Saturday, using June's Access card because Adams had no cash on him; anyway, it was June's house, so why should he pay? He was giving the labour free. He whistled while he painted, finding the work satisfying. It had taken him all the previous day to wash down the surfaces and fill up the cracks. He wanted to finish the walls today; then he could gloss the doors and the window tomorrow. June had mentioned that it might be better to leave the windows till spring, but he had found some quick-drying, one-coat paint in the store and said that would do the trick in a few hours. It was marvellous what you could get these days; stuff like that hadn't been used by prison working parties; it was too expensive.

As he worked, he wondered about the judge's wife and her state of mind. Would she tackle the judge and ask him who Mr Baxter was? To prod her, he'd send her another note soon, but this operation was a slow one, with no specific goal or deadline. He did not yet know how he was going to move it onwards. Meanwhile, he had a new scheme.

While he was in Witherstone library, studying newspapers, he had had another idea. It wasn't original; others had done something along those lines before and he had seen a television programme exposing such a venture. He would advertise slimming powder, write a glowing advertisement mentioning something magical, with false testimonials from delighted customers, and offer a post-free trial jar for ten pounds. There were always some suckers who could be enticed by a few slick phrases. He would have to find a holding address for the mail when it arrived, and open a bank account in the name of the bogus company he would invent. He could send the applicants tiny packets of Epsom salts and show a good profit, or he could simply send them nothing at all.

It might be wise to have the holding address in another district, in case someone decided to investigate if the product did not arrive. He would not be too ambitious: that was where schemes like this came to grief; he would use only provincial papers, and run the operation for a very short period, winding it up before dissatisfied customers started to make a fuss. He might set up his mailing address in Witherstone; there could well be a small shopkeeper there who would be glad of what he would pay for the service.

He might stay with Mrs Kent for a second time.

9

Mrs Turner had flu and could not come to clean.

'I'm not too bad,' she said on the telephone. 'But I don't want to give it to you or the judge. I'll be all right by Thursday.'

But on Thursday she telephoned again to say that though she was much better, she had a nasty cough and had been to the doctor who had prescribed antibiotics and advised her to stay indoors and take it easy.

'There's a lot of it about,' she told Felicity. 'They were all coughing like ghouls in the surgery.'

Felicity enjoyed this description.

'Take care,' she said, and asked if Mrs Turner had everything she needed. A neighbour, it seemed, had shopped for her.

Felicity vacuumed the house and dusted round. Everything gleamed from Mrs Turner's constant attention and regular applications of polish; there was no need for her to do more. She went into town and bought some grapes and a bunch of freesias, and set off for Mrs Turner's bungalow. Colin could not begrudge these expenses when she declared them.

Mrs Turner's bungalow was on the town's outskirts beyond the health centre. Felicity had been there recently to inspect the new curtains in the living room, a present from Betty, and to see Mrs Turner's new dress, bought for her trip to New York with her friend Mrs Jones, who had won the holiday in a competition. Mrs Jones spent a great deal of her time competing for extravagant prizes and subscribed to a magazine which aided this pursuit. She had won a microwave oven and a case of wine in previous tests of her skill and cunning. Felicity had envied Mrs Turner her New York adventure; she and Colin had never been across the Atlantic.

The bungalow, number three in the road, had the name *Balmoral* on a plaque clamped to the wall. In the living room there were photographs of the Queen and her family at various stages in their lives on every available shelf and wall, far outnumbering those of Betty and of Mr Turner. A picture of the original Balmoral hung above the fireplace, and a print of the Annigoni painting of the Queen, when young, in Garter robes, was on one wall. Mrs Turner had albums of clippings of royal occasions stacked in a bookcase. Her own hairstyle, Felicity had recognised early in their acquaintance, was modelled on that of the monarch, though the smooth waves were a pepper and salt shade; Mrs Turner must have been a striking redhead in her youth.

When Felicity arrived, she was watching a video of a foreign tour the Queen had made; she recorded all the televised tour programmes and state occasions, watching them again and again in the way others reread favourite books.

For the umpteenth time, Felicity wished that Colin would get a video recorder. Good films were shown late at night; they could tape them and watch them at a more convenient time – or she could: Colin was not interested. Sometimes she sat up late to see them; when she went upstairs he would be asleep, a large quiet hump in the second bed. He rarely snored, unlike, as she had learned, the husbands of most of the women she supposed were her friends, who complained of foghorn noises keeping them awake.

After she had enquired about Mrs Turner's progress, they settled down, with cups of tea, to chat, and Felicity asked about the man who had telephoned and mentioned Mr Baxter.

'He gave me no time to speak,' said Mrs Turner. 'At least, I asked him to repeat the message, but he rang off. He could not have heard my voice. Perhaps the line was broken.'

'Perhaps,' said Felicity. She decided not to tell Mrs Turner about the other calls. 'The judge didn't seem to know what it meant or who Mr Baxter was.'

'Well, I suppose important people must expect that sort of thing,' said Mrs Turner. 'Could it have been someone the judge sent to prison, wanting to worry you?'

'I suppose it could,' said Felicity.

'If it happens again, you could tell the exchange and they'll intercept your calls for a couple of weeks,' Mrs Turner suggested. 'That usually makes people give up.'

It had happened to Betty and Zoe. Really spiteful, some of the calls were, and they had to change their number and have two lines, with the shop separate from the flat.

'Yes,' said Felicity. 'If it goes on, I suppose we'll have to do something about it.'

But the next thing was another letter.

WHO'S A NAUGHTY JUDGE? was all it said, in the same capitals as the first one, and the postmark was Northampton.

Felicity put it away with its predecessor.

Adams had sent the letter as a reminder that he was still out there, the unknown vigilante watching what the judge was doing. Had his wife challenged him? Were there daily quarrels, accusations of adultery, anger in the air? He hoped that there was fear, for that was the real destroyer, fear which made you tremble, sent away your power to order what you did: fear was what he caused in his victims; fear was his revenge.

He liked the thought of reducing the judge to fear. What was he like on the Bench? Implacable, authoritarian, dogmatic, naturally: he had been all those things as counsel, swaying to and fro a little as he spoke, glasses on his nose, jaw jutting forward, never letting up. What gave him the right to dispose of the fortune of others, except an accident of opportunity? Given his chances, Adams, too, could have been a man of consequence. Thinking thus, Adams ignored the need for effort.

Plaguing the judge's wife while he thought of ways to torment the judge himself, maybe somehow bring him down, was no more than a prank at present. When he had time to make a proper plan, it would be a good one; tipping off the tabloids was one way it could be done, or, perhaps, writing to the top judge of all, the Lord Chief Justice, was it? That would cause a lot of trouble. Meanwhile, Adams was enjoying life at June's, where he had certainly fallen on his feet. He hadn't thought about prowling the streets at night since he'd been there.

But in the past he had gone for months at a time without such an urge; when it happened, it came on him suddenly and he was overwhelmed by a furious rage, a wish to avenge himself for everything that had gone wrong in his life and for which he blamed others, not himself. Now, with things going smoothly, he was free from anger.

June was a good cook. Every evening they ate well – casseroles, fish pie, spaghetti bolognese. She prepared the meal as soon as she came home from work, and they sat round the table for all the world like the family in the Oxo advertisement. Sometimes, before she left in the morning, she peeled potatoes, scraped carrots, put things ready; she was a good planner. While she was at work, and when he had finished the painting – a scheme to do the sitting-room had not materialised, he'd lost the urge – he watched a lot of television, sprawling on the sofa eating bread and cheese for his lunch, or what was left over from the night before, with one of those Australian serials where it never seemed to rain on the screen.

Apart from Rose, the children had taken to him. He knew some card tricks, and the younger two enjoyed learning how to do the simpler ones. Rose, however, avoided him; she spent a lot of time in the bedroom which, since he had moved in, she now shared with her sister. She resented having Amy in with her, taking up space; Adams thought she was a spoilt, silly little girl, but he would win her round with flattery or gifts of whatever girls her age liked – records, was it, or perfume? She pointedly avoided sitting next to him at meals or if they went out anywhere. In the Fiat, the three children had to sit in the back where, because the car was small, they were cramped, but they enjoyed the excursions he took them on – to a wildlife park, where it was very cold and damp, and to an amusement park. She edged away from him whenever there was an occasion for them all to sit down.

June was embarrassed about her elder daughter's scarcely veiled hostility.

'She's at an awkward age,' she excused. 'And she's very close to her father.'

'I'll win her round,' said Adams, but he failed.

In those weeks, June blossomed. Struggling alone had been so hard, and it was nice to have someone around who wanted to help her. She knew something bad had happened to him; some tragedy; perhaps his wife had died while he was abroad. He never talked about the past, but he would one day, when he felt more confident with her. Meanwhile, he had done a few little jobs about the place, things she could manage but had put off tackling, like repairing a curtain rail that had come adrift, and the kitchen looked lovely, painted a soft primrose yellow. She was content enough with the arrangement, though the sex part continued to be disappointing. It was almost as though it was an exercise, and as if she wasn't there; but she told herself that was because they were new together. She was out of practice, and both of them were shy, or so she thought.

He had gone away one night.

'Oh,' said June, when he told her. Was it over so soon?

'It's a business thing. I'm going for an interview. It's in the north.'

'That means you'll be moving out.'

71

'Maybe the job won't suit,' he said. 'I can afford to pick and choose.'

'What is it?'

'Oh – selling things,' he said. 'I'd be on the road and I'd have a company car. It's not quite what I had in mind, but it's worth following up.'

'Yes, of course,' said June.

He was pleased with his idea of becoming a sales representative. It would explain absences, if he wanted to move around, and he could keep her place as a base between operations. He liked the idea of that: somewhere to return to: some stability in his roving life. And he meant to win Rose round, get her to like him.

If he decided to tell June that he'd got the job, he'd need a better car. No sales representative would be going round in an old Fiat 127.

He took a cross-country route to Witherstone, passing through Bicester on the way, then Northampton, where he posted a letter to the judge's wife. The town might suit his purpose; it was quite large, and there were areas radiating from the centre where he might see what he wanted. Then he found it: a small corner shop selling newspapers, sweets and cigarettes. It did quite a line in soft porn, he saw, noticing the titles arranged at eye level among the magazines. Such stuff had no appeal for him; in prison there were no girlie pictures pinned to his wall. He put on a tweed hat and a pair of glasses before entering the shop, where he soon came to an understanding with the shopkeeper who would accept mail for the postal business he was starting and which he would collect at intervals. Adams paid a good deposit and promised more each week; if you wanted such a service, it had to be made worth the supplier's while.

Then he went to the library to complete the advertisements which he had already drafted out and typed on June's typewriter while she was at work: all he had to do was print the mailing address. He had decided there was no need to register his company: who was going to check on the sort of advertisement he was sending out? It would not appear in the quality dailies, only in small provincial papers, a few of which were syndicates which he had already marked down. He could open a bank account in the company name and write himself authorisation in the coming week.

Afterwards, he drove to Witherstone.

It was dark when he drew up at Willow House. He still wore his hat, though he had removed his glasses.

Since the warning Mr Baxter had given her, Judith Kent had wondered if she would know the man again, but she would certainly recognise his car, as she had noted its number. The man, however, was inconspicuous – medium height, slim to medium build, sharply smart and with brown hair and a soft, dark moustache. But she need not have worried. As soon as she opened the door and saw him there, she recognised him, and told him that unfortunately she was fully booked that night.

'I'm so sorry,' she said, holding the door firmly, ready to close it in his face, though she didn't know what she expected after Mr Baxter's warning.

'Too bad,' said Adams, whom she knew as Frank Brown. Thwarted and annoyed, he turned away. He had meant to taunt her in some way, make some remark about the judge, trusting to inspiration on the moment. Now he was frustrated, and, deprived of action, angry.

As he departed, Judith saw that he had a different car, quite a shabby one, and small; a Fiat, she decided. She memorised the number and wrote it down at once.

That night a young girl was attacked in a road in Banbury. She fought hard and screamed, and her attacker ran off, though not before she had scratched him. He had a moustache, she said, but she had not seen him clearly as he had come up to her from behind and jumped her. Since she had escaped with nothing worse than a serious fright and some bruises, not much was made of the incident and it was not reported in the press.

Adams drove back to June's tense and in a rage. She was in bed when he returned, but he had a key and let himself in. She heard him and came down in her dressing gown.

'You're soon back,' she said.

'Well?' he snapped. 'Why not? Do you mind?'

'Of course not. I'm very pleased,' she said. 'But what happened? Didn't you get the job?'

Job? What job? What was she talking about? Then he remembered the story he had told her.

'It was for peanuts,' he told her. 'I turned it down.'

She made tea and offered him some cake. He discovered that he was hungry; he had not had an evening meal.

73

June, joining him at the kitchen table, saw the scratches on his face.

'What have you done to yourself?' she asked him. 'You look as if you've had a tangle with a cat.'

He brushed crossly at his cheek. He had not realised the girl had marked him.

'I did,' he said. 'It jumped at me when I was walking to the car.'

'How very unpleasant,' she said. 'What an odd thing to happen.'

She was somewhat thrown by his bad mood, but of course, if he had been on a wild goose chase, he was annoyed. After all, most people had bouts of ill-humour; her husband had them frequently, and she was not always sunny.

He seemed to mellow after the tea and cake, and eventually she went up to bed, leaving him alone downstairs. He said he wanted to watch the late film on television; this was nothing new; he often stayed up after midnight.

Some time afterwards she heard him go out again, but she did not hear him return.

Everything was normal in the morning. June set off to leave the younger children at their primary school on the way to work; then she and Rose went on together to their separate buses. Rose went to the comprehensive school on the far side of the town.

'How long is Brian staying?' Rose asked her, when they had parted from Amy and Sebastian.

'I'm not sure,' said June. 'He's looking for a new job.'

'Well, I wish he'd get on with it and go away,' said Rose.

'Now that's very unkind,' said her mother. 'He's done a lot for us – painted the kitchen – mended the ironing board and several other things – and he's very good to you all. Look how he plays games with the other two.'

Rose set her lips mutinously.

'Well, I don't like how he looks at me,' she said. 'I think he's a creep.'

As she spoke, she turned away towards the waiting bus and June was not certain she had heard her correctly. What nonsense she was talking, though: there was nothing wrong in Brian's manner to any of the children, or to herself. Rose was being irrational. All the same, what right had she to impose upon the children the company of someone they disliked? But the other two liked him; this was simply

Rose, who was at an awkward age, and, no doubt, annoyed because Amy was now sharing her bedroom. June worried about it all the way to work; then it had to be tucked away at the back of her mind for later examination.

The surgery was in a pleasant Victorian house near the city church in a square with a patch of garden in the centre. Here, in summer, workers from offices in the other houses, once private dwellings, and a few now converted into flats, ate their sandwiches at lunch time. The sparse trees had shed their leaves and the grass beneath was limp and pallid. Daffodils bloomed there in the spring; June liked the garden.

Late that afternoon, after the court adjourned, the judge kept his rearranged appointment in that same surgery, where his teeth were scaled and a small rough edge made smooth. He had two gaps at the back; his teeth were all his own. He took no notice of the dark-haired nurse in her blue uniform who filled the glass with mouthwash.

When June returned home, Mrs Downes asked if they could speak privately.

'Yes, of course,' said June.

Adams, known to her as Brian Cotton, was in the living room watching television – some game show was on – and she sent Sebastian and Amy to join him. Rose was upstairs in her bedroom. Then she turned to face the woman on whose reliability depended her existence. Without Mrs Downes as stopgap, June's ship would sink, and it was obvious from her tone that there was trouble.

'You won't be wanting me to continue,' Mrs Downes said, in a flat voice.

'Why ever not? I can't manage without you,' June said, dismayed.

'Well, he's here now, isn't he?' Mrs Downes jerked her head in the direction of the other room. 'Hardly needed, am I? He as good as said so.'

'He's only here for a short time, Maisie,' said June. 'Till he finds a new job and that could be anywhere in the country.'

'That's not what he said to me,' said Maisie Downes, standing foursquare in the kitchen beside a pile of neatly ironed school shirts. She'd done none of that fellow's ironing; that was not what she was paid for; let him get on with it himself instead of idling about all day using June's electricity and heating. He'd soon given up on the jobs about the place which he'd begun with such apparent keenness.

'Oh, dear. Well, I think you must have misunderstood him,' June declared. 'Why, he went off for an interview only last week. It wasn't any good, but there'll be something else soon.'

Maisie Downes looked at her sharply. She understood the sleeping arrangements in the house, but that proved nothing. June was obviously involved in some way with the man, or he would not be here.

'There's nothing between you then?' she asked. 'Not that it's any of my business, except where my job's concerned.' And I care about the children, she could have added: a blind man could see that Rose disliked the so-called lodger.

'Even if there was, it wouldn't affect your job,' said June smoothly. 'Because he'll soon be out all day too, if he gets a job in this area and stays on.'

She'd said it; she'd faced the possibility that he might remain there; June could utter the words, but she could not sort out her own feelings on the subject.

'Well, if that's so, then of course I'll stay,' said Maisie Downes. 'But if it isn't, then I'll be finding somewhere where I'm really needed.'

Only half-mollified, she went off without saying goodbye to the children, something hitherto unheard of, and June saw that she would have to be coaxed into accepting the situation until Brian's plans were made.

There was nothing to be gained by worrying. She wasn't going to throw him out, whatever Mrs Downes or Rose might feel. It was nice having someone there in the evenings, a man about the place.

Wasn't it?

PART FOUR

1

The boy had been sent away to school after his grandmother's death. He did not mind, except that he missed his mother: it got him away from the man. During one long summer holiday he went to a holiday camp, which was housed in a boarding-school in Wales, where grey-green mountains soared up at the back of the big granite building and the sea was not far off. It rained a good deal, but the boy was not unhappy. He was no good at competitive sport, but to some extent the children were allowed to select their own activities, which depended on the talents and interests of the staff; he learned something about photography, and messed about with clay in the art room, not for enjoyment of what he was doing but because the conditions were peaceful. The supervision was good and the children were organised most of the time, so that opportunities for bullying were limited. They went on climbing expeditions and sailed on a lake, and although he capsized his small boat, he came to no harm and was not mocked, for most of the other boys did the same thing in their turn. At night he slept in a narrow iron bed on a thin mattress, beneath a red blanket, and counted each day as another one passed without catastrophe.

He went home a few days before the new school term began. There was no one at the station to meet him. He had not been instructed to take a taxi, and he did not know what hiring one would cost; he might not have enough money left from his holiday allowance, and his mother might not be able to pay when he arrived. He caught a bus, just able to manage his luggage, stowing it under the stairs.

He never forgot the walk from the bus stop up the road to the house, and what happened then. It was a fine day, warm and sunny, and he thought about greeting his mother and how pleased she would be to see him. Perhaps she had been late home from work and that was why she had not met him. The man would not be home yet.

He always thought of his stepfather as The Man, never by name, and when he was old enough he would drop the hated surname he had been forced to use.

He imagined how it would be: the door would open and his mother would tell him how happy she was that he was home again. Perhaps she would have made a cake today, to celebrate, and they would have tea together while he told her all about the camp, making it sound fun, letting her think he had made lots of friends and had had a wonderful time, just as he did about school, for he wanted to spare her worry on his account, make her think that he was doing well in every way. She never had much to say after one of their separations, but he knew she missed him; he was safe, however, when he was out of the house, and that mattered to her; it had never been discussed between them, but he knew. He believed things were easier for her in his absences; the man had less excuse to get annoyed and start ill-treating her.

She would be watching for him to come up the path. She would open the door as he turned in at the gate. He was almost there, and the excitement he felt was a sort of agony in the area around his heart; he could hardly contain his joy.

But she was not at the door, and when he rang the bell, she did not come.

She might be in the bathroom. He rang again and waited, then a third time. Not a sound came from the house. He looked at the neat brick facade, not a plant allowed to climb on it; at the closed windows. Nothing stirred. She couldn't be at home. He pushed open the flap of the letter box and called through it, but there was no response. He could see part of the tidy hall, the rise of the staircase with its worn brown carpet.

She always kept a spare key hidden in the shed in case she locked herself out of the house, as had happened once. He had never used it; perhaps it was no longer there: he decided to go and see. He walked round the side of the building, brushing past the row of asters she had planted in the spring; they were blooming now, blue and mauve and deep red. He peered in at the windows as he passed. Everything was orderly, as usual; she was very tidy, forced to be because at the least hint of untidiness the man would complain, shout, and might even hit her. The boy did not look in through the kitchen window because he did not pass it on the way to the shed, so he had no warning.

The key was there. He opened the door, smelled the fumes instantly, and found her on the kitchen floor, the oven door open and the gas full on.

Coal gas, before natural gas from the North Sea replaced it, was *more swiftly lethal than the build-up of carbon dioxide which makes methane gas ultimately fatal. The boy rushed, coughing, towards her and caught her legs, pulling her through the hall out of the door and over the step into the fresh air. Then he began slapping her face and shaking her, crying aloud, but she was already cold.*

A neighbour who had seen him walk up the path and ring the bell in vain soon saw he was in trouble and came round. After that what happened became a blur of horror.

She had left no note, and, though the boy did not know it at the time, there was some difference of opinion as to whether she had taken her own life or her husband had killed her and made it look like suicide. Some neighbours testified to her love of the boy and said she would never have created a situation where he would be the one to find her, and they said the couple were known to be on bad terms. However, there was no evidence to warrant a case against the man and a verdict of suicide while of unsound mind was returned. It was decided that she had forgotten about the key in the shed. The boy would never know the truth, and he could not bear to think that she had not waited to see him again but had taken her own life without saying goodbye.

He would not stay in the house with the man. A neighbour took him in until it was time to return to school. After that, he had no home, but lawyers appointed as trustees took care of his fees and made holiday arrangements for him until he was old enough to look after himself.

2

The scratches on his face had healed; they were only superficial, but the girl had fought like a tiger and her language had been foul, which shocked him. Kids had no refinement these days; even Sebastian used words which, while commonplace in prison, would have led to Adams having to wash his mouth out with soap and water at the same age. June always rebuked her son, but half-heartedly; she said the boy did not know what the words meant and would grow out of such playground talk. Playground talk indeed!

Last night, he had gone looking for another girl. June had got at him after the children went to bed, saying she didn't want Mrs Downes upset and could he be tactful with her? He'd been the soul of tact, he'd said, and June had soon crumpled, walking away, looking wounded. Adams had been angered by the conversation; it threatened his security in the house; he liked it here, and did not want to leave until he was ready, whenever that might be.

He'd stayed out for hours, stalking the streets, and had seen a pair of girls walking along, their skirts up to their fannies even on a winter's night, boots on their spindly legs. He had followed them, waiting for them to separate, but they had stayed together, finally entering a building which seemed to be a hostel. He couldn't take two of them on, and he hadn't got a knife. He walked on, looking for another opportunity, but he failed to find one, just as he had the night he returned from the north. Eventually he grew tired and the urge had left him, so he went home. The house was dark; even the porch light was off; not very welcoming, he thought, and had considered going into June's bedroom, teaching her a lesson, but, in the end, prudence prevailed. She was no stick-thin teenager; she might not accept punishment; she was his consolation, not his victim.

He watched Rose at breakfast the next morning. She avoided his gaze and studied her plate, finishing her Weetabix quickly. She was nearly as tall as her mother, with small breasts beneath her dark school sweater, and hair in a fashionable tangle – rather a mess, if you asked him. He liked sleek hair.

He'd keep out of that silly old bag's way when the kids came back from school. He hadn't liked her attitude the previous evening.

She had given the children their usual drink and biscuits – Sebastian always had Ribena and the girls had tea – but had not brought him a cup, nor a slice of cake. He had gone to the kitchen and instructed her to do so, and after some delay Sebastian had appeared with a mug and some biscuits on a plate. Impertinent old cow; after all, she was only a servant. But while she was there the children ignored him, and when he told her she could go home, she said her responsibility was to Mrs Phillips and she was not leaving until the children could be handed over to their mother.

He'd get even with her. He'd get her disgraced and sacked. He only needed to put something of June's in her coat pocket; then, when it was missed, contrive to find it. He'd enjoy fixing that little fit-up. You had to look after number one, for no one else would in this world, and he was on to a good thing here, until its usefulness ran out. Mrs Downes was, at the moment, the only flaw: apart, that is, from his failure to impress young Rose.

For a few days he forgot about the judge, waiting until his advertisement appeared and the eager punters sent their money. He would telephone the holding address and see if there was any mail; there was no point in travelling so far unless there was something to collect.

But he sent a letter to Mrs Kent.

ASK MR BAXTER HIS REAL NAME, he wrote.

Of course, Mr Baxter might not stay there again; it could have been a one-off visit, but such a message would unnerve the woman. She'd had no room for him when he required one; so she deserved something in return.

He typed the letter on June's machine.

Felicity's fund was growing.

She began reading advertisements for flats to rent and was dismayed at what they cost. Perhaps she should go as housekeeper to some elderly widow, to start off with, but wouldn't that be an escape from one prison into another? And in the new one, there would be no Mrs Turner to support her. Of course, she could move on from the first widow to a second, if she chose; she need not remain until death did them part. A job like that would give her a roof over her head and her keep until she had time to arrange a better scheme.

She dreamed of freedom. Apart from her year in London before her marriage, she had had none. Her daughter-in-law, Emily, on the other hand, had been independent for a decade before she met Stephen and still was, keeping on her interesting job because it was part of her life, and the second income meant that they could afford their pleasant little house in Pimlico. The dog went to work, too, sleeping in a basket under her desk. Emily had a good knowledge of the world she worked in and was much appreciated by the owner of the gallery.

Stephen and Emily would be horrified if she left Colin. Such things did not happen in the parental generation. Colin could engage a housekeeper. A man in his position would have no difficulty in finding someone suitable. He would have public sympathy as well, while she would attract only condemnation. Maybe Mrs Turner would take care of him, coming in each day; she could easily do whatever he required, and knew his ways.

She had shown Felicity the photographs she had taken on her New York trip with Mrs Jones. They had sailed round Manhattan Island in a boat, and had been to the top of various tall buildings; they had seen *Phantom of the Opera* on Broadway – part of the prize – and had visited the Metropolitan Museum. The noise and bustle amazed Mrs Turner, who was glad she did not live there, but she said it was a most exciting city and she was thrilled by every minute of her stay. She had not been mugged, nor seen any overt violence.

'You could be mugged in Rambleton,' she said. There was plenty of petty crime in the small town, though violence was unusual. There had been a nasty set-to with some lager louts not so long ago, quite well-off young men who had started a minor riot, worse than the occasional Saturday-night affray, but not really serious. 'Anything can happen anywhere,' she added.

Felicity agreed.

Then one day the strange voice rang again, this time bidding her to ask the judge about Willow House. Once more the line was cut before she could utter a word. She noted the date and the time, and tried to remember when the other calls had been made. She was able to track down the one Mrs Turner took because it was on a day when she was at a meeting, but she was less sure about the first; then she remembered that it was soon after the arrival of the original letter; she could date it from Stephen and Emily's visit.

That evening at dinner she raised the subject.

'Did you remember who Mr Baxter was?' she asked Colin.

'Mr Baxter?' Just for an instant, Colin's face took on a wary, hunted expression she had never seen him wear before.

'There was a telephone message about or from such a person a little while ago. Mrs Turner took the call,' she reminded him.

'Oh yes. It can't have been important, or there would have been a further call,' Colin temporised.

But there had been other calls, and the letters: Felicity did not understand why she had not mentioned them to Colin; perhaps she was afraid of learning something she would rather not know. She did not do it now, but neither did she let the matter rest.

'Don't you think you should go ex-directory?' she said.

She was right. The nuisance must not be repeated, but it was not Colin's way to make decisions without careful thought. Silently, he dissected his rainbow trout. Felicity watched irritably; he was so finicky about these things, always so precise. He hated mess of any sort and would be most upset if he got a fishbone in his mouth, or, worse, choked on one, not because of the discomfort but because he had been a careless filleter: a hang-up from all those legal dinners he had had to eat when he was young and less confident, she supposed.

'I think you may be right,' he conceded at last. 'I'll see about it in the morning.'

'Can't I deal with it?' she asked. 'I'm sure you've got enough to do already.'

'Oh.' He considered for a moment. 'Very well,' he agreed. 'I don't see why not. Thank you.'

It was a little victory. He had acknowledged that this simple operation need not be controlled by him.

After dinner he went off to his study to read papers concerning a pre-trial review in the morning, and Felicity took out her Italian homework. Ironically enough, her lesson was concerned with making telephone calls.

Why shouldn't he splurge some of his money on a slice of the good life?

Adams, expecting more as soon as his advertisement bore fruit, asked June if she would like a week in Tenerife? He had not got a passport, but he could get a visitor's one quite easily, he thought, without disclosing details of his past.

'It would be lovely,' she replied. 'But not just now. Not with the

Christmas holidays coming up. Maybe at half term, in February. A break would be nice then, only wouldn't it be very expensive for five of us?'

'I meant just you and me,' he said.

'Oh, but I couldn't go away without the children,' said June.

'Couldn't the kids go to their father?'

'Not really, midweek,' said June. 'He's working, remember. Anyway I've no more holiday to come until next year.'

Meanwhile, she had a difficulty. Mrs Downes was becoming more unsettled. Brian had stopped clearing up his lunch things at midday and now left them in the sink, or even on the kitchen table, for her to wash up when she came in with the children. He had lost interest in decorating and continued to idle the time away when June was out.

Maisie Downes regarded June as a friend as well as an employer, and was some ten years older; she had decided she must speak again.

'June, he's not working. Why should you keep him?' she said one day when he was in the sitting-room with Sebastian watching television. Rose was in her room, and Amy was at a friend's house.

'He's been for another interview,' June said. He had gone off again for a day, returning late, but this time in a good humour, though without accepting a post he said he had been offered. 'He is my lodger, Maisie. He pays rent.'

'I know, dear, but he is a stranger, really, isn't he? Not family.'

Mrs Downes was now aware of the true situation, discreetly though things were conducted. She had taken a dislike to the man because of his manner towards herself at first, but then she became convinced that he was taking advantage of June, who wasn't so hard up that she needed what he paid her. He was costing, in terms of food, light, heat, not to mention washing. Who ironed his shirts, since she, making a silent statement, did not? June, of course.

Here she did the man an injustice, for he did them himself; he had always liked being clean and neat, and one of the joys of liberty was to wear his own things, freshly pressed, not prison clothes from stock.

'Leave it a bit, Maisie,' June said. 'It'll work out, you'll see. He'll be gone soon.'

He didn't seem to be seeking local work. She was surprised, because there was plenty going in the area. Of course, she did not know what his line was; he had spoken generally about controlling finances, but had avoided any direct description of past jobs, saying he could turn his hand to most things.

She paid Mrs Downes and saw her off, for once relieved to see her go. Her attitude to Brian made June feel uncomfortable; there were things about him which she preferred not to think about, and they were just the points which Mrs Downes had mentioned.

3

Colin knew that Felicity's suggestion about going ex-directory was a good one but he had always prided himself on being accessible, and until now it had not been a problem.

The possibility of further annoyance should be prevented if Adams could not get through on the telephone. He would not dare approach the house, for if he attempted any personal aggravation he would be arrested instantly, and would know that the word of a judge would prevail in any argument against that of a convicted man.

Had he been in touch with Mrs Kent, started annoying her? It was possible, though the judge must be his target. It seemed he bore a grudge which might have lain dormant but for their accidental meeting and the chance it gave Adams to exploit what he had stumbled on.

He might try writing letters.

Felicity would tell him, if any came addressed to her. Wouldn't she? He frowned, not certain. What if there had been other calls, apart from the one referring to Mr Baxter?

He dared not ask her, for if it had been an isolated incident, she would be curious and wonder what had provoked his question.

How easy it would be to dismiss all this if the call had been, in fact, meaningless. As it was, he couldn't.

Meanwhile Felicity, too, was wondering at her own reticence. Why had she not told Colin everything, shown him the letters? Was it because she knew he was being evasive and that the anonymous correspondent and caller might reveal something in Colin's life to his discredit? Either it was all a nonsense or Colin knew a Mrs Kent, a Mr Baxter, and a Willow House which, most probably, was in Witherstone. She had looked the town up on a map; it was a little way off the route Colin would take when he went to his trustee meetings and stayed with Peter.

Or did he stay with Peter?

She could not telephone Peter to enquire; she knew neither his surname nor the name of his firm. It would be difficult to track him down, impossible without asking Colin about him and why should she do that now, so suddenly, after all this time? Besides, the idea of spying on her husband was repellent.

She decided to keep her secret. With the telephone number changed, they would be protected from more calls, so the man would have to write, if he meant to make more mischief. If another letter came, she would think about telling Colin.

The next few days were uneventful. Colin came and went to court as usual, leaving home early to attend meetings with probation officers before the court sat, never back before six because he was not one of those judges who rushed off at the official closing hour of four o'clock; if a case could be wound up, witnesses sent home instead of staying overnight, under Colin's jurisdiction, it was done.

Mrs Turner had to be told about the telephone and given the new number. She was pleased about the arrangement; anonymous calls were unpleasant, even when not lewd. Felicity had explained that there had been others besides the cryptic one about Mr Baxter.

'You can't be too careful,' Mrs Turner said as they sat together at the kitchen table cleaning the silver. This was a monthly session they both enjoyed when Mrs Turner would relate the latest gossip from the town, and the news of Betty in her salon. An actress who appeared in a television comedy series had become a regular client, which was good for business; she wore her hair cropped short at present, rinsed a brilliant copper colour, and came in each week.

'She used to live on a council estate not far from where they are, until she hit the big time,' said Mrs Turner, polishing away. 'You never know your luck.'

'Up one minute, down the next, isn't it, in that world?' Felicity said.

'Unless you're that Meryl Streep,' said Mrs Turner. 'She's always up.'

Felicity was not sure if she had seen her perform. She seldom went to the cinema, and never with the judge. Mrs Turner thought it was dreadful that there was no video in Waite House, but neither was there a microwave, and only a small freezer on top of the fridge. And no dishwasher, either, though if they had one of those, Mrs Turner would not be asked to help on dinner party nights, and that would be a sad deprivation for her. All the same, the judge must earn a lot of money and should be able to provide his wife with these modern assets, all of which Betty and Zoe had in their flat.

Mrs Turner thought that there would be every modern aid in the Queen's various residences, though she would hardly need a personal microwave, unless she and the Duke had cosy snacks together on an informal evening. It was unlikely, she supposed.

She was sorry for Felicity, and yet wondered at her pity, for the judge's wife lacked nothing you could call essential. She wore nice clothes; they ate good food; she had a lovely house and pretty garden in which Joe Green, with whom Mrs Turner had walked out before meeting Mr Turner, worked for a day a week and more when it was needed. In winter he was paid a retaining wage, and sometimes washed the car or swept the yard.

Mrs Turner came to help when Felicity had to take her turn at entertaining groups of ladies to luncheon, and always admired how calmly her employer took these occasions; in her turn, Felicity was fortified by the knowledge that she had the support of Mrs Turner in the background, and because of her early training, she knew that the food would be as good as any produced by rival hostesses. Mrs Turner enjoyed hearing the conversation as she bustled round collecting plates. She had been known to wait at table in the evening, when the guests were those the judge had wanted asked. Then she had worn a plain black dress and a muslin apron, and had looked extremely grand.

'Your help's so regal, Felicity. Aren't you terrified of her?' one of Felicity's acquaintances, married to a marketing executive, had enquired.

'Not in the least,' Felicity had answered, with some hauteur.

Her questioner shrugged. Felicity was an odd woman, rather prickly and very reserved. She never joined in gossip about people they all knew – who was ill, whose child was not doing well at school, who had moved in with a lover or was getting divorced, whose husband was suspected of an affair – which formed much of their conversation. Political discussion often led to argument, and mention of incomes was taboo, but they discussed local planning decisions, which were often incomprehensible, plays they had seen, who was building a conservatory and whose parents were ill, requiring care. It seemed to Mrs Turner that Felicity never had people to the house because she liked them and enjoyed their company; there was always some purpose behind these gatherings.

'Who would you be friends with, if you could choose?' Mrs Turner asked her one day. She knew that after so much time together in their working relationship, this was not a liberty.

'What a strange question!' Felicity looked in surprise at Mrs Turner, who sat rubbing away at a silver box which Colin had been given when he left his chambers to become a judge. 'Who would you?' she countered.

'Oh, I do choose my friends,' said Mrs Turner comfortably. Her hair was looking particularly smooth and even today, waved symmetrically back from her forehead. She had told Felicity that Betty was always trying to persuade her to have it restyled in a more modern manner, but she would not agree. The Queen and she had both chosen this style in their youth and both were sticking with it now. 'There's Doris Jones, for instance, who I go away with, and Mary Plumb, and the Fosters – ' She ran off a list of people she had known for years. 'Some of us were at school together,' she said. 'That's what comes of staying in the same neighbourhood most of your life. There's plenty of folk about. You don't have to bother with those you've got nothing in common with – not unless they're family. You can't choose them, of course.'

'True,' said Felicity.

'You and the judge don't get that freedom,' Mrs Turner observed. 'Seeing who you are. You can't be having just anybody in for a meal.'

'Why not, if I liked them?' Felicity challenged, smiling.

'Well,' Mrs Turner contemplated a silver photograph frame surrounding a picture of the judge's mother. 'Pretty, wasn't she?' she said, at a tangent, and then went on, 'Oil and water can't be mixed.'

'Well, I don't suppose the judge would be too pleased if I asked a few ex-prisoners in,' said Felicity. 'But you wouldn't be doing that, either.'

'Not knowingly,' agreed Mrs Turner. 'But who's to say what folk have done long ago? I wouldn't have any of your murderers and that, but we've all scrumped apples in our time, haven't we? And you've got to start trusting them some time, if they're ever to go straight. The thieves, I mean, the petty criminals.' She told Felicity about some cases she knew of in the town, a man who had failed to pay a fine and so was gaoled, and another who was a bigamist. 'He couldn't bring himself to upset either of them by telling them about the other.' She was laughing as she spoke. 'One lived here, and the other one lived in Dorset, where he went for weekends.'

'How complicated,' said Felicity. 'You'd think they'd get suspicious.'

'Yes, you would. He was a commercial traveller, a rep they call them nowadays. I suppose that was how he got about. He was caught by some tax check, I think,' said Mrs Turner. 'We've all got so many numbers now, no one can get really lost.'

She enjoyed making Felicity laugh during their conversations; she laughed too little, Mrs Turner thought. Yet how could she be unhappy, with so much to enjoy and the judge, though a bit stiff, always polite. Mrs Turner thought he could never have been very dashing, even when young – not a patch on the Duke, for instance, who was still a fine-looking man – and you'd never take him for what he was if you met him just anywhere. You'd think he was a bank manager, perhaps; something responsible, but hardly someone important.

After Mrs Turner left, Felicity thought about the bigamist she had mentioned, with the wife in Dorset and the one in Rambleton.

Colin couldn't have a wife in Witherstone, but Mrs Kent could be a mistress. Unlikely as it seemed, such things were possible. But who was Mr Baxter? And who was the mysterious caller?

If she could drive and had a car, she'd go to Witherstone and investigate. The place itself was real enough. Perhaps Directory Enquiries would tell her if a Mrs Kent lived in Witherstone.

What would she do, if that proved to be the case?

She decided to put it to the test.

First, she asked for a Mr Baxter in the area. She could provide no address apart from Witherstone, and Enquiries came up with two Baxters, one a butcher and one a private person. Felicity wrote down the details. Then she tried asking for Mrs Kent, possibly of Willow House, and straight away Enquiries gave her J. Kent, of that address. Procrastinating, because amazed, her heart thudding, blood pounding in her temples, Felicity asked if there were any others, and was told of M. W. Kent. She dialled the number for Willow House but there was no reply.

Having got so far, she could not leave it there. She dialled the other number, and a man replied.

'Is Mrs Kent in?' she asked calmly.

'Yes,' said the voice. 'Who wants her?' It was not the voice of the man who had made the telephone calls; she was sure of that, listening intently.

'I wanted to speak to her about holding a Tupperware party,' said Felicity, amazed at her own invention.

'Sorry, love. She won't be interested,' said the man.

'May I speak to her?' Felicity persisted.

'She's making the Christmas pudding,' said the man. 'She can't talk now,' and he hung up.

This, she knew, was not the relevant Mrs Kent. She already had her proof that the caller was correct about something. 'Who's a naughty judge?' the last letter had said. She read it again. If it did not imply sexual misconduct, what did it mean?

Members of the judiciary sometimes indulged in less than prudent behaviour. Everyone was fallible. There's no fool like an old fool. Various clichés ran through her mind.

She tried the Willow House number again, but there was still no reply. Even if the woman answered, and Felicity asked her if she knew Colin, she would deny it if the pair had anything to hide.

Where now? She did not know.

Felicity went to London on a Christmas shopping trip, an annual event, and since Stephen married she had spread it over two days, staying with him and Emily in their beautifully furnished little house. Emily had a History of Art degree and was knowledgeable about china and glass, as well as paintings. In her company, Felicity felt dissatisfied with her own amateur talent for picking up a modest bargain. She considered herself only half-educated, and the efforts she had made to fill some of the gaps had been undertaken more as a means of keeping occupied than because she felt a desire to learn about the particular subject.

She met some friends for luncheon on the first day. Maintaining contact with her former flatmates and other youthful companions was not easy; their lives had diverged with their marriages or careers, and these infrequent reunions, which at the time she enjoyed, were of only superficial value. After leaving them, she did some shopping, carefully listing what she bought, for whom it was intended, and its cost, and keeping the receipts in a special compartment in her purse. Then she met Emily at her gallery and they travelled home together in a taxi, for which Emily paid.

Felicity made no effort to forestall her. Her budgeting, accountable to Colin, covered taxis only in emergency, and some of her cash for this excursion had come from her store beneath the floorboards.

Ferdy sat on Emily's knee, depositing white hairs on her scarlet pleated skirt. She wanted to know what Felicity had bought, and could not be told as it would be disclosing Christmas secrets. They arrived at the house in high good humour.

'My two favourite women,' Stephen said at dinner, beaming at them both in the candlelight in the tiny basement dining room. Everything in the house, apart from solid Stephen, was so small; Felicity wondered how he managed to move around without smashing things. She felt large and clumsy and went cautiously past little tables bearing precious figurines; at each visit, she always stepped on Ferdy.

Felicity knew they had put the proceeds of their two flats into buying the house, but Colin had given Stephen a considerable lump sum as a wedding present. He had not wanted Stephen to be at a disadvantage, living in a house financed in greater part by his wife, for Emily's flat raised much more than his.

'We love you too,' Felicity said now, astonishing herself by this bold declaration. Sentiment had never been a feature of life with Colin, and hugs and kisses had gone by the board with Stephen at an early age. She had had a large gin and tonic before dinner — stronger than she realised — and several glasses of wine with her meal. Gin was rarely consumed at Waite House: sherry before dinner was the pattern; but Emily's parents were livelier souls, and it was she who had pointed out to Stephen that Felicity was never really relaxed in the judge's presence. She had determined that on her visits to them, Felicity should enjoy herself.

'He puts her down, certainly,' Stephen had said. 'They married when she was very young, and he's so much older. I suppose he's never really built up her confidence.' He had gazed at Emily as he spoke. 'It's different with us,' he added. 'You've done wonders for me.'

Emily knew, with satisfaction, that that this was true; he needed encouragement: space to grow: everyone did. She had also known that she would not find a man her age or older to marry for she did not attract the sort of man who might appeal to her; experience had taught her this. She wanted to get married, for she found many aspects of life alarming and did not want to go through the years facing them alone. She loved Stephen, who was gentle and calm, and totally dependable. Fireworks between partners existed, she was aware, and were sought by many, but she preferred to warm herself at a gentler fire. At college, she had seen her friends in the throes of wild emotions and decided that the ecstasy they appeared to feel was not worth the woeful agony which so often followed. If you expected less, you were less likely to be disappointed, and might even have some unexpected joy.

'What have you been doing at home, Felicity?' Emily asked her mother-in-law. They had not met for nearly two weeks; she and Stephen had spent the previous weekend with Emily's parents.

What would they say if she told them that the judge had some secret in his past which was causing present persecution? They knew that there had been a tiresome telephone call; that had been the reason for the new number; but they did not know about the letters. No one did, except herself.

'I've helped run a bazaar for the NSPCC at which we made nearly a thousand pounds,' she said. 'And I've bought some small objects and bits and pieces and sold them at a profit.'

'No! Have you? What sort of objects?' Emily asked, interested immediately.

Felicity was already regretting her indiscreet revelation.

'Nothing much,' she mumbled. 'Just a few things I picked up at a junk stall in the market.' Then, in a rush, she added, 'Don't tell Colin. He doesn't know.'

'Of course we won't,' said Emily. She didn't ask why not; she guessed there were several reasons.

'But surely he couldn't object?' said Stephen. 'After all, it's a perfectly respectable thing to do. Why mustn't he know?' He refilled her glass. 'Tell us,' he prompted. 'We're grown up now.' As he spoke, he glanced across at his wife and in that instant Felicity saw that what seemed to her their extraordinary union worked. They understood and supported each other. She and Colin supported one another in the front they presented to the world, but they did not understand one another at all, yet they had been married for nearly thirty years; Stephen and Emily had been together not much more than thirty months.

'He'd wonder how I got the money together to start,' she said.

It came out then. Felicity made light of it, emphasising that he had always been generous, she had lacked for nothing, but every last expenditure had to be not only accounted for, but justified.

'Maybe that's why I became an accountant,' Stephen said.

'Watching you count the pennies while I was small. I remember how you always wrote things down in a little book.'

'I had to do that, otherwise I forgot what I'd spent,' said Felicity. 'I cooked the books sometimes,' she confessed. 'When things didn't balance. But it was difficult to get away with that as I had to produce receipts unless it was quite impossible.'

'Train tickets?' suggested Emily.

'Yes, but those amounts could be checked. So I have to make some money of my own, you see,' said Felicity. 'I'm too old for women's lib and all that.'

'You're not. Yours is the generation that got it going,' said Emily. 'It's because you married so young, before you'd achieved your own independence. You'd just had that one job, hadn't you, and a few months in France?'

Felicity hung her head, as if it was something to be ashamed of; at the time, marrying so young had been considered an achievement.

'You can make up for it now,' said Emily. 'You should open a shop. Why not? As long as you sell really respectable stuff, it couldn't be bad for the judge's image.'

Hearing her talk, Felicity realised that she was closer in age to Emily than to Colin. She could benefit by association with her daughter-in-law's clear thinking.

'I'd never find the capital,' she said. 'I think I'm better carrying on quietly, doing my own thing. I spend some of my profits,' she added. 'For instance, today I met three women I used to know for lunch and I don't have to tell Colin about that.'

Stephen was shocked by what he was hearing. How could his father be so mean?

'I could make the money work for you, in the City,' he said.

'It would be complicated with tax and things,' she answered. 'Your father would have to know. You won't tell him, will you? Either of you?' Anxiously, she repeated her plea.

'Your dread secret is safe with us,' Stephen assured her, and Emily rose to make the coffee, breaking the thread of conversation and enabling Felicity to regain her equanimity.

'Poor thing,' she said to Stephen, in bed that night.

'I've always thought they got on quite well,' said Stephen.

'I think they do, in a negative sense,' said Emily. 'They avoid conflict. Your father goes off to his study and buries himself in his papers and those enormous tomes. What does she do? Reads and watches television. She's very lonely.' And, thought Emily, with a pang of remorse, she'll never have grandchildren to compensate. Her own mother, much older than Felicity, got great delight from three grandchildren provided by Emily's brother. 'She's not yet fifty, is she? I wonder she hasn't broken out.'

'Oh, I don't think she's the type,' said Stephen.

But who was the type, wondered Emily; these things happened, or did not.

'We'd better keep more of an eye on her,' she said. 'Have her up more often – he doesn't seem to mind that – and ask people in to meet her. That sort of thing. And I could look at the pieces she's got and see if she's doing the best she can for herself, under the circumstances. If only she drove.'

'Why?'

'I've a friend with an antique business in Swinbourne. That's only about thirty miles from Rambleton. She might have given your mother a job. Even a day a week would be something.'

'We could give her driving lessons,' Stephen said. 'I wonder if she'd be able to learn, or is it too late?' His father had paid for him to learn, and had taken him out in the family car to practise. Being such a steady individual, Stephen had passed his test first time and had eventually bought a small car. His father had instilled care and caution into him: a car, he said, was a lethal weapon and must be treated with respect.

'It's a marvellous idea,' said Emily. 'Let's give them to her for Christmas.'

'We won't be able to give her a car, if she passes her test,' he pointed out. And if they did, how would she pay for the petrol? Why, with her salary from the job with Emily's friend, of course.

'No, we couldn't,' Emily agreed. 'But you could work on your father – get him to give her one for her fiftieth birthday, if she can pass by then. Couldn't we make it difficult for him to refuse?'

Stephen wasn't sure about that.

'We could try,' he said. 'I'm sure he could find the money. He's very shrewd, and he has contacts. He's made investments, though Waite House cost a lot more than the house they sold to move there. A little Metro: something like that. It needn't be new. One careful owner.'

They hugged each other, delighted with their plan, while Felicity, in the spare bedroom, scolded herself for telling them things she should have kept secret.

She was slightly hung over the next day, but able to finish her shopping, and catch her train home.

4

While Felicity was in London, Colin drove up to Witherstone, but he did not book a room. This would be a hurried, flying visit.

He did not get away from court until after five, when a fraud case he was hearing ended. Even this was earlier than usual, and his prompt departure surprised the clerk and those who thought he would, as usual, attend to matters in preparation for the following day.

Judith Kent was alone when he arrived; her guests were all out at dinner.

'Oh, Mr Baxter – what a surprise,' she said. 'I'm terribly sorry – I haven't a room free. Would you like me to ring The White Hart?'

'No – that's all right. I was just passing and called in to bring you this,' he said, proffering a potted azalea which he had bought on the way into court that morning and which he had concealed in the boot of the car. 'Happy Christmas,' he said, somewhat sheepishly.

'How very kind. It's lovely,' said Judith Kent. 'Won't you at least come in and have a drink?'

'Thank you.'

The judge entered the familiar, friendly house. Why did he like it so much more than his own, which was old and more expensively appointed, and should have possessed character? Was it something to do with the woman who lived here, older and more accomplished than Felicity? He did not care to entertain disloyal thoughts about his wife, and shut off that line of supposition.

'I hope I'm not interrupting your dinner,' he said.

'I've eaten,' she said. 'I always eat early. The guests start arriving any time after eight, as a rule, though it's usually nine or later by the time they've waded through several courses at The White Hart or one of Witherstone's restaurants.' She led the way into the sitting-room, and only at that moment remembered the anonymous letter, with its allegation that Baxter was not his name. 'I've got two reps coming,' she told him. 'They come regularly and are always exhausted after driving for miles keeping appointments that have been too closely booked – the more, the more profit, of course. Brandy or whisky?'

'Could I have coffee, please, as I'm driving?' said Colin, who was scrupulous about not having more than one glass of wine if he were to drive afterwards. You could never tell when you might be involved in a collision through no fault of your own, and if you were to be found over the limit, much trouble would ensue; a clear conscience was the best defence.

She had cups which took individual filters and soon had it prepared.

'How useful,' he marvelled.

'Haven't you seen these before?' She was astonished. Where had he been all this time?

'No.'

'I get them at Marks and Spencer's,' she told him. 'They're very handy when you just want one or two cups of the real thing.'

That was what she was: the real thing; yet surely Felicity was real, too?

'I mustn't stay long,' he said.

'Your usual night is Friday,' she observed with a smile. There he sat, a pillar, one would have said, of society; of course he was Mr Baxter: who else? Yet he was secretive; she knew no more about him now than when he had first stayed at Willow House on that foggy night.

Colin was wondering how to introduce the subject of Adams, or Brown, as she thought him to be. He needed to know if the man had contacted her in any way, yet he did not want to make it seem important. Perhaps, if he waited, she would reveal whether the man had telephoned or called.

She did. She told him that he had come in one evening and she had turned him away.

'When was it?'

'About two weeks ago – maybe less. I've got the date noted,' she said. 'He was in a different car and I wrote down its number. It was a small Fiat. Black.' She looked at him curiously. 'Why are you interested? Has he done something wrong?' Then she had a sudden idea. 'Are you a policeman?' He was rather old for that, she thought, but perhaps he was very senior.

'Not exactly,' he said. 'Let's say I have connections with the police.'

'And that's how you recognised Mr Brown? Your paths had crossed in that way?'

'Exactly. I contributed, in a sense, to putting him behind bars for

100

quite a long rest,' said Colin. 'And Brown is not his real name. It's Adams. William Adams.'

Should she tell him about the letter?

'I've got something to show you,' she said, and went to a drawer in her desk. She handed the paper over.

He read it silently. ASK MR BAXTER HIS REAL NAME.

'It's true that Baxter is not my name,' he said heavily. 'But will you believe me when I tell you that I have a good reason for using it?'

'Yes,' she said. Though what could it be?

Why did he not tell her the truth now? Colin did not know the answer.

'If he comes again, telephone the police and they'll warn him off,' he said. 'He's a dangerous man. Don't let your daughter near him.'

'He's that sort of dangerous?'

'Yes.'

'Oh!' She had gone very pale. 'My God.'

'I doubt if he'll return,' Colin said. 'I've had some harassment, too, but by telephone. I've already told the police that he's been seen in this area. The car he was driving that first time was hired. I'll get them to trace this other car.'

'Why are such men ever released?' she asked.

'It's how the law works,' said Colin flatly.

'Well, he can't be living in this area,' she said. 'If he was, why would he want a room?'

'You're right,' said Colin. 'But I'll make sure that the local police are told he's been seen in the district.' If anything happened in the neighbourhood, a girl being attacked, for instance, he could be hauled in and questioned as a suspect. It was quite wrong that such a man was free to roam the country without supervision.

He finished his coffee and, with a sense of foreboding, left. He knew he would never come here again. His odd little flight into fantasy was over.

Adams had begun to consider marrying June. She would probably jump at it, he decided; why else had she been at the singles club, if she were not seeking another husband? All women wanted to be part of a couple. It would be nice to feel that he had a settled home, a base, somewhere from which he could not be ejected on a whim. June's job seemed to be a secure one, and while her salary was probably not high, it must be adequate for her needs. Their father provided for the children, he knew.

He decided to look for a regular position in Titchford, to show that he had serious intentions; she would view him more favourably if he seemed settled. Meanwhile, he must work on Rose. He could feel the hostility emanating from her. She would scarcely look at him, and if she did, her dark eyes glared at him balefully from beneath her tangle of curly brown hair, which had to be worn tied back at school but which tumbled about her shoulders the rest of the time. He'd like to wipe that smug, superior look off her face: he thought about that, quite a lot.

He found a job in a large store in Titchford, working behind the scenes moving stock and making up orders. It would end after the New Year sales, but by then he might have tied things up with June. He said nothing about his prison sentence, stating that he had been out of the country for years and producing references as to his character. One he had typed on June's machine; the other he wrote himself, in a disguised hand. Both purported to come from New Zealand from a plastics factory where he had allegedly been a storekeeper. He set up headed notepaper, using bought letters and a photocopying machine. It took a few attempts to get passable results and he kept a sheaf of pages for possible future use.

June was pleased when he started work. He did not tell her what the job was, pretending that it was an important administrative position in a factory on the outskirts of town.

Why tell someone the truth? It was much better to keep them guessing.

Rose was alarmed when she heard. Until now, she had consoled herself that his stay was temporary, as her mother had said, until he moved away into some important post. She kept quiet about him at school, where people talked about their fathers and stepfathers and, in some cases, 'uncles'. Now she feared he would never go. The other two were too young to discuss it; they both seemed to like him because he played cards with them and bought them sweets. She always refused any he tried to give her, saying that she never ate them because they were bad for her teeth.

'Miss Goody-Goody,' he mocked her, understanding her perfectly. She would accept nothing from him.

She told her father at last.

'Mum's got this friend,' she said. 'Well, he's called the lodger, but he isn't just that.'

'Tell me about him,' said her father. He found the separation from his children hard to bear, but he was glad to be away from the tense atmosphere which had grown up between June and himself, the constant rows, the lack of communication. He worked in the highways department of the council, some of the time in the office but also outside, inspecting repairs and maintenance work in the county. He liked the outdoor part of his job, and was not over-ambitious, but both he and June had wanted the best for their children. He felt, though, that he had been demoted to second place in her life – or rather fourth place, after all the children were born, unable to concede that the demands of looking after them and the house took almost all her energy and most of her time. He had started to go out on his own in the evening, at first harmlessly enough, to a bowling alley with someone from work, then ending in a pub where there was friendly company. He began to drink too much and came home angry, ready to find fault with everything June did. Their quarrels grew worse and they found it increasingly difficult to make up. He stayed out even more in the evenings, playing snooker, he said; in fact he had met someone else, a divorcée who worked in one of the pubs he frequented. She was the immediate cause of his moving out, but after living with her for a time, he saw that he was exchanging his own family for her two adolescent boys, who resented his presence. Besides, his first euphoric feelings for her had died down, though not his desire for freedom. He found his one-roomed flat eventually, and later Valerie, who was only twenty-three.

Rose still imagined that her parents might be reconciled. She wove dreams in which one of them became very ill and the other rushed to the sick one's side, to be reunited as the doctor pronounced recovery would follow. Sometimes, in these fantasies, the reconciliation took place over her own inert form as she lay in a ward smothered in bandages but able to overhear her parents' hesitant words as they clasped hands across her body. However, in daylight these dreams retreated, and she knew that they would not come true.

The presence of that man in the house contributed to this knowledge. He was sweet on her mother, of course. This was proved when once he brought her some flowers.

It was difficult to describe him to her father, for she did not want to be disloyal to her mother. The children were guarded in what they revealed to one parent about life with the other. Donald Phillips

103

always wanted to know how her mother was; he still felt a sort of love for her, a sense of responsibility, and guilt because he was the one who started playing games away from home. Other people muddled through these things, but once he had walked out and moved in with someone else, it became difficult to swallow his pride and slink home, sheepish and ashamed. Besides, he did not want to return to the old routine of rows and heavy silences, and there was no reason to suppose that things would improve if he did come back. It wasn't easy to live with one person for years and years; you both changed, took each other too much for granted, expected more than could possibly be delivered.

Rose answered his request.

'Well, he plays cards with us,' she acknowledged. 'Or with the others. I don't usually play. I've got too much homework.'

'I see,' said her father, not sure that he did.

'The other two like him,' Rose volunteered.

This conversation was taking place on a walk beside the canal. Valerie was ahead with Amy and Sebastian, hurrying to the lock to watch a barge pass through. Rose, trying to match her strides to her father's, was happy in an anxious sort of way. She quite liked Valerie, but resented her because she had usurped June's position, and while she was around, the chances of getting her parents together could be seen as remote.

'But you don't?' Donald said. 'Why not?'

'I don't know. I suppose he doesn't like me. That's why,' said Rose, unable to explain.

'He hasn't been unkind to you? Hurt you?' Dread surged through Donald; surely the fellow hadn't – no, June would never allow that; it was June the man was after, not a young girl.

'No. In fact, he buys us sweets and he took us to the cinema and to Thorpe Park,' she said. 'With Mum, of course. I just don't want him to live with us for ever.'

It was funny, Donald thought: when you split up, you thought only of your own new start, and trying to begin it without too much grief and aggravation. Maybe you had a new and more exciting partner, but you wanted to go on caring for your kids; you didn't stop being their father. Then the introduction of a new person into their lives created problems. Valerie was very good with the children; she had brothers and sisters, met all sorts of people in her work at the library. He wasn't sure if they'd marry, but if they did, she was young and would want children of her own. Would it all start again –

the demands made on Valerie by a new family, his own sense of exclusion, or would it be easier with her? Different?

These were questions he could not answer, best not thought about. 'Do you really think he will be living with you for ever? This man?' he asked his daughter.

'I don't know. Mum hasn't said anything.' She hesitated, and then said, 'He's sleeping in Amy's room. She's in with me.' Saying this, she blushed.

'Well, there you are, then,' said her father thankfully. 'He's only the lodger.'

He hadn't met the man. At weekends, he waited in the car outside what had been his home till the children ran out, and his conversations with June about collecting and returning them were tense, held at the gate, though getting easier as time passed. He knew that even this was more than some separated couples managed.

June herself was beginning to wonder if she had made a bad mistake in letting Brian move in. The first flurry of flattered excitement she had felt when they met had dispersed. She had gone to the singles club because she was tired of spending all her evenings alone when the children were in bed. She was thirty-six years old and she had not been out for an evening's fun for more than a year, apart from once to a cinema with a girl friend, while Maisie Downes babysat. Then, with Brian, it had all happened so fast: one minute they were dancing; a week later he had moved in. At first it had seemed a good idea, but then he had begun upsetting Maisie Downes, and there was Rose's overt hostility towards him. June was annoyed with her daughter, whose behaviour, she felt, verged on rudeness. Rose snubbed him whenever she got the chance, rebutting any suggestion he made, even to the offer of second helpings when he prepared to spoon more vegetables or pudding on to her plate. When this happened, both he and June were unaware that Rose resented his presumption; this was their house; her mother was the person who should be dishing out the food, or, if help were needed, it should come from Rose, the eldest of the family.

Once, he followed her to school. When she parted from her mother, there he was, on the bus with her, sitting apart from her, just staring at her; she could feel his eyes boring holes in her back. It felt weird, and she got off two stops early to avoid him. She wondered what he had done with his car that day; he always drove off in it to work.

She did not mention the episode at home. Nor did he.

June never spoke of her domestic problems at work. She was on good terms with the receptionist and the other nurse – there were two dentists in the practice – but she felt she had got herself into a difficult situation which reflected poorly on her judgement, and she did not want to hear her colleagues reinforce her fears. Though what she was afraid of, she did not know. He had never been really angry or even the least bit drunk. If she told him to go, he would do so. Wouldn't he?

5

Colin telephoned Superintendent Manners and told him that William Adams was no longer driving the Sierra previously reported as his, but had been seen in a small Fiat, and he gave the number, mentioning the district.

Manners was irritated. The old boy had got a bee in his wig about Adams, and though Manners agreed that such dangerous men should not be at large, or, if released, should be supervised – but not by the police, who had too much to do as it was, catching other villains – he thought the matter of no consequence. He made sure that the judge was not reporting harassment or nuisance, was he? Colin had to reply – because to do otherwise would be to admit his own deception, minor though it was – that no, he wasn't. Mrs Kent's letter was another matter, but it was connected with himself; Adams was not threatening her.

Manners pointed out, respectfully, that alas, he could not reform the law to make Adams more accountable; perhaps the judge was the person to do that. He would have the car checked and would alert the police in the area given as the owner's address, so that they could keep Adams' name in their minds. At the moment, with a serious case of arson and an impending drugs raid on his patch, he could not regard the matter as urgent.

Felicity had returned from her visit to London laden with carrier bags. She presented Colin with a wodge of receipts attached to her list of expenditure. He knew there would be no errors: nevertheless, he went through them all punctiliously, ready for when the bills arrived. For certain approved shopping of this nature, she was allowed to use a charge card. While she sorted the slips, she had wondered what would happen if she bought a diamond ring or some other expensive item which she could then sell, and take off on the proceeds. She knew there was a credit limit but it was high, more than a thousand pounds – nearer two, she thought. Could he, or would he, have her pursued and make her give it back? Not without causing a notable scandal. He would not openly accuse her of theft.

She thought of the problems she heard other women discuss. Sex seemed to be a perennial worry – too much, or else too little, were the complaints. Most of the women she knew seemed to be able to spend at least small sums freely. She had never heard anyone mention that their husbands checked bills minutely or that they were really short of housekeeping money. These women met one another for coffee and lunches in pubs, and were always ready to buy tickets in raffles or for their various functions. But she didn't advertise the restrictions imposed on her, so maybe there were others, also keeping quiet. Very few of the women she met socially had paid jobs, though some spent a lot of time in voluntary work.

Sorting out her shopping, putting the gifts away ready to wrap in the festive paper she had bought from a charity, she began to look forward to Christmas. Stephen and Emily were coming to Waite House this year, having gone to Emily's parents last year. The court would not be sitting, but often there were emergency hearings when a judge was needed and Colin was always willing to step in at such times.

And I don't mind if he gets called out, Felicity thought. It just means he may need sandwiches and a flask of coffee, and he won't be in his study.

She had enjoyed being with Emily and Stephen this time more than ever before: she would enjoy having them in the house at Christmas. Their unlikely marriage was a partnership; they were lucky.

When Stephen was small, Felicity had been happy, or at least content, or so she realised now, looking back; you did not always recognise what constituted happiness until it had gone. He had been a docile little boy who would obediently play any game she suggested or join in building projects with bricks, or complete jigsaws in a good-natured way, as if humouring her interest. He was rarely enthusiastic, but he had the usual small child's immense physical energy, running across the park near where they lived with arms outstretched, an aeroplane, or endlessly parading as a soldier; he had imagination then; she thought it had become obscured at puberty.

Their walks together to and from his first school were a routine pleasure for her; she enjoyed his undemanding company, and, young herself, was not exhausted by her daily tasks, though she was often bored during school hours. Stephen would stump along beside her, feet in sturdy laced shoes, willing each morning to set off but happy, too, to return at the end of the day. He would hug her briefly when she met him at the gate, then resume his stumping walk. She thought of agreeable things for them to do together; everything had to be free or of such an educational nature that she could ask Colin for the money and be sure of his approval. Thus, trips to museums were financed – for even if admission were free, they had to travel by bus or train and eat something during the expedition. Picnics in woods and other more frivolous excursions had to be managed without aid. There was her family allowance; Colin wanted to know what she had spent it on, but sometimes she was able to milk away small sums which they could spend in an illicit manner. Somehow Stephen understood that bus journeys of any length must not be mentioned to Daddy, nor the unexpected ice cream. Evasion became a way of life; he learned that though lies were wrong, there was virtue in discretion. He was devoted to his mother, but in an undemonstrative way; he respected his father but scarcely knew him, since Colin spent so much of his time, even at weekends, in his study with the door closed, reading or working on his papers.

There was a good preparatory school not far away and Stephen went there as a day boy. If he had been a boarder, Felicity knew she would have found her loneliness unbearable, and if she had broken it by finding a job, Colin would have been so angry that she would not have been able to continue in it. She had mentioned working part-time during term, and was told there was no need: Colin provided more than adequately for her: had she not got everything she could want – a comfortable house, plenty to eat, enough clothes? And seaside holidays, appropriate for a family, in Cornwall in the summer. Well, then: and the subject was closed. There were some activities connected with the school with which she helped, but her inability to contribute in terms of what things cost hampered her efforts at coffee mornings and other fund-raising projects. Even baking cakes was a problem, for when she did suggest to Colin that she needed money to buy ingredients for these events, he decided that she was being taken advantage of by the other women and had quite enough to do already. Eventually, she told one friend that Colin, though generous, gave her no spending money and she could spare only her time, and after that she was able to help more generally. The other mothers were not particularly well off, but they had access to ready cash.

When Stephen went away to public school, her real isolation began. She walked for miles, alone; she read five or six novels every week, borrowed from the library; she cleaned the house; she worked in the garden; and she was only in her early thirties. She had no extra-marital love affair because the opportunity never arose. Sometimes, in later years, she wondered about that: was it she who never attracted overtures, or some inhibition in herself that made her subconsciously flinch away from a potential situation? Would she have flung caution – and morals – to the wind, or was she so conditioned by Colin's benevolent despotism that she could not think for herself? She regretted her lack of experience now, and would think back to recollect pleasant men who had come to the house to mend some piece of equipment or to paint a room, and wonder if it was ingrained snobbery that had held her back even from mild flirtation. But such chances would not have led to love affairs and she could not really imagine herself being carried away on a wave of abandon unless for love. After all, she had loved Colin once, or so she had thought at the time, but at nineteen she had really been in love with the idea of romance and marriage.

She had decided that life must be like that for most people, and she should count her blessings. Colin was generous, if only to his own pattern; he never lost his temper, and if he found fault with her, his reproof was gently delivered and excuses found for whatever failure had provoked his displeasure.

He was so controlled, so remote. When she was young, she could see no way to overcome what she understood as she grew older must be some deep repression, perhaps not uncommon in his generation, perhaps not uncommon at all.

It was too late now. She had missed out on passion.

When Colin became a judge, Stephen was still living at home. He had finished at university – he did not get in to Oxbridge, thereby disappointing his father – and was still completing his accountancy training, but Colin felt able to accept the drop in income now, since his son was attached to a respected firm and his career looked, as indeed it proved, to be set fair. Stephen found digs in London, then the flatlet where he stayed till he was married.

During those years, he came home almost every weekend, and Felicity was able to run her life from each Monday by looking forward to the following Friday evening or, at latest, Saturday morning, when he returned. There was always clearing up to be done when he left, and the washing which he collected next time; then the preparations for his subsequent visit. Their routine settled down, the first flood of invitations dwindling as Colin's revealed dullness and her timidity detracted from their social appeal. But he was respected as able, fair, and very conscientious; he never made ridiculous comments in his judgements and could be relied on to punish serious offenders properly. He would not set the Bench alight, in any sense, but no breath of scandal would attach to him.

Colin had fallen short of some of his own targets; nevertheless, he had had a successful career and was still enjoying his profession, with many years of it ahead of him. His home life was blameless; Felicity, a lonely girl who lacked the support of her family, had been nurtured by him for nearly thirty years. His son, whilst less brilliant than might have been wished, was well launched in life and had made a satisfactory if unconventional marriage. Colin could not permit any libellous or slanderous statements from a convicted criminal to prejudice the order of his days.

If William Adams were at large, and if the police made up their minds to do it, he could be picked up on some minor charge and put away for several years. The man was almost certain to be offending in some way; he had, for instance, hired the original Sierra in another name and might have used forged or stolen documents to do so. He could be using still another name as driver of the Fiat.

Perhaps he could suggest to Superintendent Manners that further checks along that line might prove fruitful.

Manners had taken his time about checking out the Fiat; when he did so, he found there was no reference on the computer to it being owned by Frank Brown, or William Adams. It was still listed under the ownership of a dealer. For curiosity, Manners had a constable check whether the original Sierra had been returned by Mr Brown in good condition, and found that it had been reported stolen. Brown had not returned it.

When hiring it, he had given an address in Liverpool; Manners asked the police up there to check it out and soon had the information that it was bogus.

The judge would be pleased to hear all this, he thought: he'd wait to tell him till the Fiat was located. All forces were asked to look out for it.

Manners did not like knowing that rapists were at large; leopards, in his opinion, did not change their spots and a man who had raped once could do so again. There were, he conceded, rapes and rapes:

there was the rape of a foolish or loose-living woman who had got herself into a dangerous situation with a man who might have had too much to drink or who imagined he had been given the green light. Perhaps he had, only to have it change to red, which was the woman's right. But such a man was not in the same category as one who stalked the streets armed, looking for prey: who hunted down the vulnerable and pounced on them in a park or dark street, or scooped them into his car. Worse than both, he held, was the man who picked on children.

Adams came into the middle category, a violent, dangerous man who had raped an innocent young girl at knife point and who was suspected of other attacks, though he had admitted to no more and nothing could be proved. His features were very like a photofit made when a young girl disappeared some eight years before after a disco in a village in the Midlands. People had noticed her talking to a man outside the hall where the dance was held. She had never been seen again.

He might at least be made to answer a few questions about the Sierra, but unless it was found, which was unlikely now, nothing could be proved against him. Manners suspected he had passed it on for money.

When he was convicted, a sad story about his unhappy, persecuted childhood had been told by the defence. Such tales did not wash with Manners, who had grown up in a children's home. You were what you made of yourself, and how you dealt with your misfortunes was what formed your character; adversity was there to be overcome, and doing so was what separated the men from the boys. Manners had got into mischief as a lad; he had pinched the odd apple from a barrow, had even swum in the pool at a private house, with two other boys, as a dare. He had never been caught and he had not turned to crime in later life, but things could have developed differently. He knew that some very good policemen might have gone the other way, and it was because of this that these men knew instinctively how the minds of certain criminals worked. By the same token, sometimes such men overstepped the mark and made serious mistakes.

When the Fiat was traced, the driver could be questioned and if anything were out of order, he could be charged with the offence, however small. Manners advised that it might be in the ownership of one Frank Brown, whose real name was William Adams. What could be useful from the exercise would be discovering the where-abouts of a dangerous past offender, but it was not urgent.

Some days later an alert woman police constable saw the Fiat parked outside 30 Endor Street in Titchford. She walked all round the car and saw no visible defect; the tyres were sound and it was taxed. The report was made, instructions awaited.

That night two officers were sent to the house. It was seven o'clock, a dark evening and raining hard. The men were in plain clothes but they showed June their warrant cards and she saw that they were genuine. They asked if the owner of the Fiat was in the house and she said yes, she would fetch him, but what was it about?

'Just a few enquiries, Mrs Phillips,' she was told. The police had discovered who lived in the house before calling. They did not ask for Adams by name.

'You'd better come in,' she said, and she took them into the sitting-room where Adams was sprawled in an armchair watching television. A small boy lay on his stomach on the floor, playing with a toy car; a slightly larger girl was doing some sort of sewing – craft work, the officers wrote later in their report. 'These two policemen want to talk to you about your car,' she told Adams, without mentioning his name, so they did not learn that here he was called Brian Cotton.

June took the children with her out to the kitchen, leaving Adams alone with the men.

He had stared at them as they entered, and as June said that they were policemen he had seemed to dwindle suddenly, getting slowly to his feet.

While they talked, she wondered what he had done.

After a while, the officers left.

Adams had produced his proper driving licence in his real name. He had shown them papers for the car and said that the licensing office had been told he had bought it, but perhaps the relevant certificate had not yet been processed. He was asked if he had hired a Sierra in the name of Frank Brown, giving a non-existent address in Liverpool; the number of the missing car was quoted. He denied all knowledge of the matter and, without the car and evidence, nothing could be proved, though someone from the hire firm might identify him.

They went at last, having gained nothing from the interview apart from establishing that the former convict lived at this address; patrol cars could keep an eye on it; any sex crime within the area would provide an excuse to bring him in. They'd made him sweat.

He strolled into the kitchen after they had gone.

'What did they want?' asked June.

'Just to check on the car,' he said truthfully.

He had shown them the insurance certificate; everything was in order, which was fortunate for him, but he had resolved not to run that obvious sort of risk; there was no reason why an ex-con with a valid driving licence should not buy a car. 'They thought it might have been stolen,' he said, and he laughed as if it was most amusing. 'What an idea!'

'How silly,' June agreed. 'That's harassment.'

'Yes,' said Adams, but he knew it was no chance that brought them there. It had to be the result of a tip-off, and they had checked the other car. The judge and Mrs Kent had set him up.

Well, two could play at that game.

6

The police reports noted that William Adams had been traced to 30 Endor Street, Titchford, where he had taken a room as a lodger. His papers regarding the Fiat 127 were in order. He had denied all knowledge of the hired and missing Sierra and had never been known as Frank Brown, nor had he been to Witherstone in his life; he did not know where it was.

Adams was calm about the enquiries. The Sierra would not be found. He had worn gloves when he signed the form at the time he hired it, with a tweed hat and spectacles: such simple precautions but now they were paying off. He had always intended to steal and sell the car.

An officer visited the hire firm, taking with him a photograph of Adams which was a prison mug shot and showed him clean-shaven. The clerk who had hired the Sierra to him shook her head; it could have been him, perhaps; the man she saw had had a moustache but wore glasses and a hat. She could not swear to it either way. She hadn't taken a lot of notice, just gone on with the job.

They were insured for the loss of the car. It was not a matter of life and death.

Meanwhile Superintendent Manners, having put in train the locating of the Fiat, had let the matter pass from his mind.

'Some policemen came to see Brian,' Sebastian told his father.

Donald Phillips was greasing a tin in which he was about to bake a large pizza. He paused and looked at his son.

'When was this?'

'Last night,' said Sebastian.

'Why did they want to see him?' asked Donald.

'I don't know,' said Sebastian. 'They didn't have a siren on the car.' He made a mimicking wailing noise.

'Do you know about this, Rose?' Donald turned to his elder daughter.

She shrugged.

'I was in my room,' she said. 'I don't know anything about it.'

'It was about his car,' said Amy. 'They weren't real police. They didn't have uniforms on.'

'Detectives don't,' said Sebastian scornfully.

'Was your mother upset?'

'Not that I noticed,' said Amy.

But Donald was. He didn't want his children mixing with criminals – nor their mother, for that matter. Of course it might have been simply a speeding offence: that was probably the size of it: but wouldn't a uniformed officer have come if that was all it was?

He meant to discover the truth, and when he took the children back that evening, he followed them up the short path to the front door.

'Tell your mother I'd like a word,' he instructed Rose, giving her a hug. Her embraces were always reserved, whereas Amy would cling to him, and even Sebastian would twine his arms round his father's waist and clamp his thin body against Donald's thighs. Each time they parted, Donald felt an ache in his heart. Parents didn't realise it would be like this when they split; maybe, if they did, they would give it another go before it was too late.

Rose went to fetch June, who always unlatched the door when the car arrived but only came out to speak to Donald if there were some special reason for them to communicate, which occasionally there was. She would tell him about parents' evenings at the schools, to which he never went. He telephoned about the children's arrangements, which varied from time to time to accommodate parties, his cricket in summer, and visits to the two sets of grandparents. There was still tension in their meetings, although it was easier now than in the first years of their separation, before the divorce. He wished she would find someone else, a decent man whose arrival in her life would make him feel less guilty. What he had heard about the lodger was not reassuring, were he to assume a different role.

June came to the door.

'Do you want to come in?' she asked, without enthusiasm.

'Well – yes, please. It won't take long,' he said, and she stood back to let him enter. He stepped awkwardly over what had been his own threshold and they went into the sitting-room. The man was not there.

'Is he here? Your – er – lodger?' asked Donald.

'No.'

'Ah.' Donald relaxed, although in a way he was disappointed. He would have liked to meet the man who had painted the kitchen and mended Sebastian's tractor.

The two younger children were clustering round; Rose had gone upstairs.

'Off you go, you two. Daddy and I have to talk,' June said. 'I'll call you when he's leaving.'

'Promise?'

'Promise.'

The children left, and June said, somewhat truculently, 'Would you like a drink? There's some sherry.'

'No, thanks.' Donald felt very uncomfortable standing there, an intruder in his own former home. 'I'll come straight to the point,' he said. 'I believe you've had the police here, talking to this man you've got living with you.'

'He's not living with me,' said June. 'He's lodging here. What about it?'

'Why did they want to see him.'

'It was something about his car,' she said. 'It's his business, not mine. I didn't enquire.'

'How much do you know about him?' asked Donald.

'What's that got to do with you?' she countered.

'Rose doesn't like him.'

'No – well, she's at a difficult age,' said June. 'He's done a lot to help me, mending things about the place, and the other two do like him. He's very good with them.'

Donald resented the idea of another man being good with his children, but he should have been pleased to hear it; if all three had been hostile to the man, he might have had more excuse to seek information about him.

'I just wanted to make certain it was nothing serious,' he said, lamely. He felt foolish now.

'Of course it wasn't,' said June angrily. 'Really Donald, don't you trust my judgement?'

'Your judgement let you marry me,' he said.

'Well, we may have our differences, but as far as I know you're not a criminal, and nor is Brian,' said June tartly.

'Well, I'm sorry,' said Donald. 'I suppose I feel anxious about him being here with the kids, when I'm not.'

'Jealous, you mean,' said June. 'And whose fault is that, anyway? Besides, they have to put up with whoever you've got at your place.'

He didn't reply. He had no defence.

'Is that all?' June moved to the door.

'Yes.' They had conducted their interview standing; an eyeball to eyeball encounter, he thought ruefully. He hesitated, wanting to tell her that he was around if she needed him, but why should she turn to him? And why should she suddenly need him in any particular sense?

Now that they knew where he was, the police would begin to harass him. Adams felt sure about that. It had been lucky that June hadn't heard them speaking to him, had not discovered that Cotton was not his name. Why couldn't a man, having served his sentence, be left in peace? Here he was, not hiding away, living openly with a woman and helping her with her kids, yet they had to come nosing round, looking for trouble, and they'd make it, if they were really determined. He knew that. It would be simple for them to fit him up, plant drugs in the car, anything to get him behind bars again.

He had already made one trip to Northampton to collect answers to his advertisement, first checking on the telephone that some had come for him. There were dozens of letters, each containing cheques or postal orders, even banknotes, from hopeful would-be slimmers. He'd paid the shopkeeper well to retain the next batch and had put the money in his bank account, writing a cheque to cash a few days later. While he was on this mission, June had supposed him to be pursuing a job.

After the visit from the police, he telephoned again and found there was another batch of mail. He had better collect it promptly, lest disappointed punters started to complain and someone came enquiring for him. As soon as June had left for work, he telephoned the store which was employing him to say that he was ill but hoped to be well enough to come tomorrow. Then he set off to collect his loot.

That night a young girl, Ann Green, who had been to spend the evening with a friend to discuss a planned birthday party, did not return to her home only four hundred yards away in the outskirts of a small town in Northamptonshire. Long before she was reported missing, Adams was back in Titchford.

She had fought hard when he bundled her into the car but he had soon subdued her, his knife no mere threat.

He had killed another one, once, years ago, but her body was never discovered and he put this one in the same place.

*

118

Christmas approached and the weather was grey, but in Titchford fairy lights twinkled from lamp-posts and in windows and the streets were crowded with shoppers. Adams continued at work, but once all the cheques he had just paid in had been cleared, he returned to Northampton to empty and close the account.

The hunt was now on for Ann Green, missing for almost a week. Adams felt that it had nothing to do with him; most of the time he forgot about it, unless it was mentioned on the news. There were shots of her anxious parents and pictures of her on holiday. They bore no relation, in his mind, to the real girl whose life had been snuffed out so fast. He felt no pity.

He thought about the judge again, ironically sitting so close, in Titchford Crown Court. It was only when he had seen a report in the local paper about a case where two youths had been tried for breaking and entering that he realised the judge did not travel to London every day. What could he do now that would worry that smug, arrogant man?

He tried telephoning but could not get through, and realised after a time that the number must have been changed. That, in itself, gave satisfaction. He'd caused enough trouble to force the judge to do something about it.

He could still write letters, and meanwhile there was Rose to annoy. He disliked the way she looked at him, which, just occasionally, she managed to do, an expression of contempt in her clear blue eyes. Snotty little bitch: she'd get what was coming to her one of these days.

He began leaving the house early, before she did, and would loiter nearby, then drive down the road behind her. Sometimes he followed her bus, aware that she knew of his car trailing along in the rear. It was a pity he couldn't leave the store in time to collect her from school and drive her home. That would give her something to think about, wipe that smirk from her face. He enjoyed indulging these fantasies.

When he had cleared his bank account, he turned in the Fiat and bought an old Allegro, just in case the police took it into their heads to look at his car, which might retain traces of its recent cargo. He sold the Fiat well away from Northampton, with its links with Ann Green, driving across the country to Shropshire to find a used car dealer to take it and sell him the Allegro. He bought it in Brian Cotton's name, and insured it for three months, but he gave an address in Cardiff, a false one.

It was time to move on. The police knew where he was, and that was bad; he would have to abandon June and the comforts of home, but he could soon find someone else to take her place; singles clubs existed in many areas and women picked up there were likely to be more lonely and easily gulled than those found in pubs. He would find one with no children, or very young ones; he did not want to live at close quarters with another sharp-nosed little cat like Rose.

He would wait until after Christmas. June would be alone for part of the holiday as the children were going to spend Friday and Saturday nights with their paternal grandparents and would return to her in the evening in time for Christmas Day itself, which fell on a Monday this year

He could take her away for a peaceful weekend. They could go to a quiet, luxurious hotel. He'd been promising himself a treat like that ever since his release, and he had plenty of money stashed in his bags. June would enjoy the break and it would make him feel good to treat her.

After that, he'd see.

June thought it was a wonderful idea.

When he proposed it, she hesitated at first, but then thought, why not? Why shouldn't she enjoy herself? The children would be having fun, indulged by their father and grandparents, so why shouldn't she let herself be pampered a little? She'd been feeling so tired lately; indeed, it seemed to her that she had been tired for years, ever since the children arrived. Small wonder, she thought now, in moments of honesty, that Donald had found her poor company and had not been eager to come home in the evenings. It wasn't easy to live together, especially when two became three, then four, then five, all clamouring with their needs.

At first she planned to tell Donald where she would be staying, in case some emergency arose; then she changed her mind. Donald and his parents could handle anything unexpected and she was going to be away only two nights. In the end she told no one, but she left a note with the address by the telephone. Just in case, she thought, slipping it there while Brian was loading their cases into the car. He had had difficulty finding a room: so many hotels were fully booked for the Christmas break. In the end, after telephoning a consortium, he was able to get a cancellation, but it was not in a beautiful country town or by the coast, but on the edge of a developing industrial town.

June masked her disappointment; they were lucky to get in at all at such short notice, she said.

The Allegro was bigger and more comfortable than the Fiat, but it was old and shabby; he said he had had the chance to buy it from someone at work, and that because of its size it would be better for the children.

June gazed out of the bedroom window at the surrounding factories and warehouses and wished that she had never agreed to come away. Then she scolded herself for being so ungrateful. Brian was spending a lot of money on their two-night stay, and it was not his fault that hotels in more attractive surroundings were all full. The room was large and adequately furnished; there was a bathroom; there was television. No doubt dinner would be good, and she would not have had to cook it herself.

Perhaps if Brian were livelier she would feel more cheerful. Their relationship seemed to have made no progress either way during the weeks he had been in the house, but this holiday would change it, bring them closer to each other. They had made love, if it could be called that, only five times since they had met: not a lot, when you thought about it; not enough to be discouraged about because it had been so unexciting. Perhaps tonight, with no risk of being interrupted by the children, it would be different. Anyway, the interlude would give her an opportunity to sort out how she felt about him, whether there might be any future for them as a couple.

Mrs Downes never came at holiday weekends, so there had been no need for her to learn about their plans, for June was certain she would not approve. She had already gone to stay in Reading with her daughter, whose husband was a prison officer. They had four children, so Maisie would have a lively time. June had given her a bottle of sherry and some bath oil for Christmas and had received in return a parcel which was probably a box of chocolate liqueurs, as last year.

Brian did not kiss her passionately as soon as the door of their hotel room was closed behind them. He set his own bag down on the bed nearest the door, asking if the other was all right for her, then turned on the television for the news.

Among heartening reports from Eastern Europe, now freeing itself from yokes of tyranny, there was mention that Anne Green was still missing though the police were following several lines of enquiry.

Adams knew what that meant: door to door in the area where she lived and where she was last seen – the friend's house. Had someone noticed anything suspicious? There would be dozens of useless calls to the police, wasting their time and keeping them busy. He was sure no one had seen him bundle her into the car; not a vehicle, nor a living soul, had passed in those few seconds – surely not a minute. The road had been deserted and was poorly lit; she was stupid to walk down it on her own, at night. You never knew who might be about.

He turned off the set. June was looking at him in a moony way which meant only one thing. He spoke abruptly.

'Let's get changed and go down to the bar. I could do with a drink.'

He'd need a few, if he was to go through with what was clearly in June's mind.

June lay wakeful in bed. What had passed between them, all over very swiftly, had been as mechanical as their other couplings. She felt hollow, dissatisfied; it would never do to build a life together with only this uncaring, almost casual connection linking them.

He was asleep. She heard his quiet breathing – he did not snore – and wondered at the manner in which you could be so closely joined and yet entirely separate. The comfort she had hoped for from his physical presence, free from other demands, was absent; they were like two strangers brought together by some outside agency, not drawn by mutual attraction. Perhaps only loneliness was what they had in common, she reflected sadly.

In the darkness, staring at the ceiling, she accepted that she had admitted him to her house and to her body too precipitately after their first meeting. She had needed someone; that was why she had gone to the club in the first place, though she and her friend had pretended to each other that it was simply for an evening's entertainment. She had been vulnerable enough to respond to anyone who showed interest in her, as long as he was not totally repulsive. Perhaps it had been the same for him, so lately back from New Zealand, knowing no one.

It wouldn't do. It would have to end. She saw that clearly, and a tear rolled down her cheek. She would tell him when they went home, but before then there was the rest of the weekend to get through, all tomorrow and Sunday, and further episodes unlikely to be any more fulfilling than what had just taken place. Her only other sexual experience had been with Donald and it had been different: warm, exciting, obliterating self, until the joy they shared had ceased; staleness had crept in.

She drifted off to sleep at last, and towards dawn lapsed into a deep slumber from which she found it difficult to rouse herself. Eventually, she woke up properly, and knew that something was wrong.

At first she could not remember where she was, but then she recollected. She pushed herself on to an elbow and listened for sounds from the other bed, but there was silence. It weighed on her, and she whispered his name softly.

'Brian? Are you awake?'

There was no answer.

June spoke again, more loudly, then switched on the bedside light, which took a bit of doing as she groped about for the unfamiliar switch, set into a plate on the wall beside the bedhead.

His bed was empty, the sheets rumpled.

She looked at the time. Nearly half-past nine! What an hour to be still sleeping! He must have got bored waiting for her to wake up and gone down to breakfast. He'd been very quiet. She'd better follow.

She swung herself out of bed, crossed to the window and drew the curtains back on a grey, unpromising day. Factory roofs glistened in the streets around the huge mass of the hotel which, most of the time, accommodated businessmen and conferences. She felt heavy and depressed; there was no light happiness, such as she had felt after early holidays with Donald. Still, she must put a good face on things until the weekend was over, and on Boxing Day she would tell him he must leave as soon as he could find somewhere else to live.

With that decision came overwhelming relief. She went into the bathroom and ran a deep bath, putting in the bubble lotion supplied by the management and soaking herself luxuriously. She felt better after that, refreshed and cleansed. She had washed her hair and dried it with the dryer provided. Then she did her teeth and make-up.

It was while she was doing this that she realised all Brian's things had gone. His shaving kit, his toothbrush and his green synthetic sponge had disappeared.

Even so, she took some minutes to acknowledge what had happened, checking the cupboard for his suit and jacket, and his extra pair of shoes. Everything had vanished. His two soft bags had gone.

She finished dressing; there would be a message at reception, she assured herself.

Hair in order, face assumed, she went to meet what had to be an awkward interview, and at the desk she learned that he had, indeed, departed, but had left no message for her.

'The bill?' she asked dully. He would have left that for her to pay.

But here she was wrong; he had settled the account. The hotel did not find out till later that the cheque that he had used, backed up by a bank card, would prove invalid.

'Do have your breakfast, Mrs Evans,' she was told. 'And do stay on yourself. Your weekend's paid for, after all.'

Mrs Evans? Why had he chosen to call himself by a false name?

She had her breakfast – a good one, eggs and bacon and a sausage, so she would need no lunch. Then she went to pack. How on earth would she get home?

As it was a Saturday, there were trains, and the hotel helped her catch one, looking them up and ordering a taxi. Had it been Sunday, Christmas Eve, she could have been stranded.

Her journey took a long time as there was no through train; she had to wait over an hour for a connection. When at last she reached Titchford, she was so exhausted that she took another taxi from the station. She had had to pay by cheque for her train ticket so that she would have enough cash to get the rest of the way. Going home had cost her nearly thirty pounds.

Sitting in the train, she wondered if he would be at the house when she arrived, as though nothing odd had happened, and if so, would he explain his flight? While she packed, she had blamed herself, imagining that her poor performance last night had exasperated him, made him regret the entire enterprise; but by the time she was in the second train, anger had replaced her self-condemnatory mood. Even if he had felt like that, he should have taken her home at least, and surely their failure had been mutual? And why Evans?

She reached home just before six o'clock and let herself in gingerly. He might be sitting there, waiting for her. But there were no lights on; why should he wait for her in darkness? She were being stupid. Perhaps he had meant to dump her all along and the weekend had been some awful joke; an expensive one, though, she reminded herself. He would not spend all that money on a hoax.

Although she had been away little more than twenty-four hours, the house felt alien, unlived-in. The heating had been left on, set low, and she turned it up, then went round checking everything. The Christmas tree still stood in the sitting-room window, and she put its lights on; they cheered her up. Cards were strung on ribbon on one wall; the children had hung paper chains about the hall.

She went upstairs.

Everything of his had gone. There was not a trace left, except his bed linen and his towel. She wrenched the cover off the duvet, took the towel and pillow cases and put them all in the washing machine, turning it up to a higher setting than normal to purge him from the fabric. She even flung a cupful of Dettol into the tub before switching on the programme. Then she opened the windows in the bedroom, letting in the pure, though damp, night air. After that she had a bath herself, and put her own clothes ready to be washed when the first load was finished.

She felt better then.

There was plenty of food in the house. She had done all the shopping before the children left and laid in stores as though for a siege, as was customary now at Christmas and bank holidays. She had eaten nothing since her large breakfast; there had been no buffet open when she changed trains, and she had had to stand in the second one. She had another fry-up, with fried bread and tomatoes added to her eggs and bacon. Then she drank some sherry.

Now she wished she had taken Maisie's advice given months ago, and fitted a chain to the door. He'd got his key; he hadn't left it in his room. Maybe he would post it to her. If not, she'd have the locks changed, but it was too late to get that done now until after the holiday, three days at least, if not more.

It did not matter. He would not be coming back.

PART FIVE

1

The prospect of spending another entire day with June, followed by a second night together, then Sunday, had proved too much for Adams. What had started as little more than a whim had become a sort of bondage. June was quite attractive if you liked her type; she had kept her figure and had worn a smart dress for dinner the previous evening; he had not minded being seen with her. It was the closeness he could not tolerate, having to speak, make small talk – what about, for God's sake? And her female smell – bewitching and at the same time a threat; to think he had been tempted to marry her! What a narrow escape! He did not want to be confined in the prison of permanent pairing. It did not cross his mind that, had he proposed, she might have turned him down.

He had soon fallen asleep, back in his own bed after their cold encounter. She had pretended pleasure; he knew it was faked and he despised her for the deception, unwilling to construe it as a sort of courtesy. If they were married, this meaningless ritual would have to be repeated or she would feel aggrieved; there would be rows and arguments, tears and recriminations. Women always let you down; not one could be relied on. The only way to deal with them was by force. He did not admit to himself that he was not confident of succeeding, were he to attempt to dominate June.

The police knew where he was, and that was bad. Because he was a known sex offender, they might decide, for no other reason, to question him about Ann Green, for all he was not living in her area. They could soon find evidence to link him with her disappearance if they chose; it would be simple to plant threads from clothes she owned, even hairs from her hairbrush, among his things to frame him. They wanted convictions; it didn't matter to them if they pinned evidence on the wrong man as long as they put someone away, and there were plenty of judges to help them do it by directing the jury to a wrong conclusion. When he woke on Saturday morning, with June only a few feet from him in the other bed, he knew that he had to leave.

He got out of bed and dressed quietly, not bothering to wash or shave, quickly packed up his things and hurried downstairs. It was only because the receptionist looked up and greeted him that he decided to pay. It would cost him nothing. It would serve June right to be left picking up the tab, but if she hadn't brought her cheque-book, it might lead to trouble. As it was, they would both be long gone before his fraud was discovered.

He had packed all his belongings before they left Endor Street; there wasn't a lot; he had few possessions, apart from his cash. There was no need to go back to June's place; perhaps he had meant to dump her all along.

Where should he go?

He stopped for petrol, and bought sandwiches in the shop attached to the service station, then parked in a lay-by to eat them. The day was grey, with showers of torrential rain at intervals. A container lorry parked ahead of him, and cars rushed past, their passengers on their way to friends or family for the Christmas break. Adams had a sort of brunch with the sandwiches while he wondered where to go. He had driven westwards after leaving the hotel but for no good reason. Now he thought of Witherstone. What about calling on Mrs Kent again, trying to upset her, seeing how she would react if he told her who Mr Baxter really was?

It would be something to do.

While he thought about it, he went into a pub and had a pint of beer; he bought two cans to take away and drove up the road to park again, and drink them. On the radio, he heard about the continuing search for Ann Green and the distress of her parents. Stuff them, he thought, opening the beer.

He was unused to drinking. Last night he had had wine, quite a lot of it, and two brandies. Now, the beer and the warmth generated by the heater in the car combined with stress and lack of sleep, made him drowsy and he napped off. When he woke, the rain was cascading down, and cars passing had their lights on. It was dusk when he reached Willow House, and the gates were closed. He left the Allegro outside and walked up the drive to ring the bell.

A man opened the front door. He was tall, aged about thirty, clean-shaven, tanned. He had switched on the porch light and in its rays he saw an untidy person, dark-haired, with a large, soft mous-tache and a day's growth of stubble. He wore no raincoat, and though it had stopped raining, was damp and dishevelled.

'Yes?' asked Tim Kent, home on leave for Christmas.

'I want a room for the night,' growled Adams.

Tim's fears for his mother's safety in her role as landlady magnified enormously as he looked with distaste at the caller.

'The guest-house is closed,' he said firmly, and shut the door in Adams' face.

His mother had a bad hour with him while she explained that she, too, would have turned away anyone who looked as unprepossessing as the man her son had described.

It never occurred to her that it was someone who had already spent a night in her house.

Thwarted, angry, Adams drove away from the town, blinding along the road at a reckless speed until he came to a junction where he turned north. There was very little traffic; one other car, going the opposite way, passed him before he met a main road, where he slowed down, his first anger fading. A police car went by and he realised that he might be stopped on no excuse at all; the papers had been full of warnings about drinking and driving over the holiday, and random breath tests. It would be just his luck to get caught for some stupid thing like that.

He turned to the right, now on a major road but with no idea of whereabouts it was; he had not read the signpost at the crossroads. After travelling some distance he came to a Little Chef with a Travel Lodge attached. Perhaps he should stop and have some food.

He parked the car and went into the washroom, where after looking at his reflection in the glass, he was forced to recognise that no one would want to let him have a room while he looked so unkempt. He washed thoroughly, smoothed down his collar and tie – he had worn his grey suit for the weekend break with June – and combed his hair, deciding that his stubble was, in some quarters, quite the fashion. To shave here would make him conspicuous.

After steak and chips with peas and tomatoes, he felt stronger, and went round to the Travel Lodge to see if they had a room. He was lucky. Most people had finished their holiday journeys and were installed at their destinations. Funny how the whole world dossed down at night, he thought. There were just a few folk awake, keeping things going: train drivers, and screws in prison, and the fuzz. He'd be much safer himself tucked up than driving around in the dark, and he hadn't decided where to go next. In the morning, he'd have another plan.

*

He slept fitfully, beset by dreams. He relived the night when he had killed Ann Green, though he did not think of her by any name. He had pulled her into the car, holding his knife at her throat to silence her, then shaking her. She'd lost consciousness and he thought that she had died like the other one, but she stirred when he stopped the car. He'd dragged her from it on to the grass, and he wasn't even sure that she was dead when, afterwards, he pitched her into the gravel pit beyond the bushes where he had parked. A lot had changed while he was inside: roads had been built, others closed; but this place seemed unaltered. He'd put stones in her pockets and tied her up with some jump leads from the Fiat, and he had watched her body sinking in the darkness. She might float to the surface one day, but the other one never had, and if she did, all traces of him would be washed away and she would be as rotten to look at as all women were inside.

It was better to kill them. Then they couldn't talk.

He cleaned himself up thoroughly in the morning, showering again, and shaving, and he took off his soft moustache – not an easy job, with nail scissors to trim the hair and then several scraping sessions with the razor. His revealed skin was white, and though he looked more like the mug shots of him taken when he was arrested, his appearance was much changed from how it had been since his release. Even June might not know him now, though the judge would.

The judge: the cause of all his present problems. If he had not been sent to prison all those years ago, he might be leading a normal life now, married to some ordinary girl, perhaps with children. The girl on whose account he was sentenced then had not died; she hadn't been badly hurt and it had been over in seconds, just like that business with June, only she had cooperated, if you could call it that, instead of resisting the inevitable. Help, not punishment, was what he had needed.

Ironically enough, had they been able to discuss it, the judge would have had some sympathy with this opinion, though he would have specified both help and punishment.

He'd go and trail the judge, find some means of vexing him, but covertly.

Adams drove to Rambleton, parking the Allegro in the market

132

square outside the judge's house. Sooner or later, he decided, some-one would arrive or leave.

This was false reasoning. In such bad weather – for it was overcast and windy – and on a Sunday morning, any family might choose to stay indoors. However, in this instance he was rewarded. The streets had been deserted, but now a few people began to appear, all from the same direction. It was twelve o'clock, and they were the congregation returning from matins in the church. Most people drove, but today the judge and Emily had walked together down the road, past the shops and the war memorial, to St Mary's with its Norman tower. Felicity had elected to go to the carol service that afternoon and Stephen said that he would go with her. Emily, however, had decided that the judge must have a companion, and wrapped up well in her camel coat, a red woollen hat on her head as protection against the wind, leaving Ferdy in the house, she had set off beside the stocky figure of her father-in-law.

Seeing them return and enter Waite House, Adams thought that she must be the judge's wife.

He sat there for hours. The Primrose Café was closed, and he did not go in search of food. That could come later. He felt himself boiling up inside to a familiar crescendo. Sometimes the seething feeling ebbed away if circumstances foiled him; it had been absent most of the time in prison because there was no scope there for relief and sometimes he had thought that it had gone away for ever, but past weeks had shown him that this was not so.

Activity helped: keeping on the move, being busy. He had enjoyed setting up his money-making schemes and until he was frustrated at Willow House, when he was denied a room, he had been able to control his restlessness. He still had money. He could go abroad, run a bar, perhaps, in Spain. Sitting in his car on that grey, blustery day, fantasising about the sunshine, he began to blame the British climate for his problems.

But that wasn't the real cause. It was what had happened to him as a boy, the hurts and the rejections. You couldn't be ordinary after that sort of start in life. He had learned then that no one helped you but yourself, and in the end the whole world turned against you, so it was best to attack before you got injured yourself.

He had kept within the law for a long time, working well at his first few jobs, but he had never been able to settle. Something would happen – some rebuff, criticism or imagined slight – very real to him though not intended – and he would know it was time for a change.

Then he began to blame the women. Girls in the office mocked him, he concluded. Sometimes he was teased because he was so quiet, or because he was excessively tidy; it was meant in a friendly way, but he interpreted it as malice. No woman could be trusted.

One dark night, after he had started tracking girls down and attacking them as he drove home after spending the evening at a cinema, he saw a girl turn down a side road ahead, and followed her. That was the one he strangled. He had offered her a lift, and, all those years ago, girls were less wary than today; she had accepted. She lay in the gravel pit, like Ann Green, beneath forty feet of water.

He carried on calmly at work as if nothing had upset the normal pattern of his life, staying in his current job a further month. Then he moved away. The case was deemed a mystery.

The girl had died so easily, when he had only meant to stop her struggling. After that, he changed his style, using a knife to frighten them and sometimes wearing a stocking mask.

He liked having a knife in his pocket. He had one there now, a flick knife, with a long sharp blade.

2

On the morning of that grey Christmas Eve, a woman who lived in an isolated cottage deep in the countryside some forty miles from Northampton took her dogs for a walk. She did this every day, going along field paths and bridleways, off the road, through woods and thickets. She often went past the gravel pit which was reached by a long rutted track at the end of the lane half a mile from her house, and here she could let them off their leads. The dogs – two black Labradors and a Jack Russell – snuffled about in the bushes and loped along, stretching their legs in the damp air.

She would be alone for Christmas. She was a widow, and had become almost a recluse, spending her time painting wild flowers which she found on her rambles. Others had already made fortunes from such illustrations and she had no plan to emulate them; her work was done for pure pleasure, and sheets and sheets of fine studies had accumulated in folders in the room where she worked.

She had bought a chicken to roast for her Christmas meal, a free-range one which promised flavour; she would listen to the carols from King's College, Cambridge, and when it was dark she would pile logs on her open fire and settle down with Jane Austen or Trollope. She was re-reading her favourite novels: nothing written today held her interest. She had a television set on which she watched nature programmes and occasionally the news; latterly, she had been transfixed by the revolution sweeping across Eastern Europe, and now it seemed that the Romanian despot had been captured. These were stirring times in which to be living, but she had been through other dramatic periods. She was in the WAAF during the war and had married a bomber pilot who was killed in a raid over Germany. They had had one child, a boy who had died in the poliomyelitis epidemic in 1947. After that, she had trained as a teacher and had worked in various schools in different parts of the country until she retired. By this time she had bought her cottage as a holiday retreat; it was well placed for the theatre, which she loved, at Stratford-upon-Avon, and by train she could soon reach London, but as time went on she did less and less of these things which took her away from home, concentrating on her painting and growing vegetables and flowers, which occasionally she sold in the village two miles down the road.

There were plans now to develop the land round the gravel pit: to turn it into a marina for sailing and water-skiing, make a golf course and attendant club-house in the fields on its further side, and add a hotel and conference centre. When that happened, the area would be ruined from her point of view, and from that of those who lived in the neighbourhood. A man from the city had bought one of the big houses in the district; a farm and nearly a thousand acres went with it, so there lay the potential. Letters had been written, protest meetings staged, but Lavinia Wootton feared that this was a battle which would be lost. She was thinking about it as she strode along, a small, sturdy figure in corduroy trousers, Wellington boots and a shabby Barbour jacket, a waterproof hat on her head and a big, stout stick in her hand.

The terrier had run on ahead of the Labradors, one of which was the son of the other, who had been mated with a bitch owned by a farmer in the village. Lavinia had wanted a younger dog as insurance for when the old one was no longer around, but at twelve he was still fit, portly now and with a greying muzzle. He nosed his way along the track behind his two more youthful companions; his son forged onwards, and now the terrier, who had scuffled down the side of the pit where bushes clung to the scree, began to yap.

Lavinia called to him, but he took no notice. She supposed he had flushed a rabbit, or found some other enticing scent which had lured him into happy deafness. Soon, though, the deeper voice of Dan, the younger Labrador, could be heard: gruff barks which made Rory, his father, put on speed and lumber into the scrub fringing the high sides of the pit, with its spread of deep, dark water.

None of the dogs paid the least attention to Lavinia's cries and whistles. The Labradors were usually obedient, though the terrier was less dependable, and she went towards them, irritated. Occasionally she met other walkers here, and now and then a tramp or a man who looked as though he did not belong in such scenery, so that she was always glad of the dogs, and her stout stick too, for these were violent times and peaceful spots like this one could be sites for horrible acts.

When she reached the edge of the pit, she looked down towards the water, which must be very cold. It was a dangerous spot; children playing there could fall in and local families had put it out of bounds, but you could not protect youngsters from every peril; they must learn to look after themselves. She knew that a scout pack had carried out a canoeing exercise here a few years ago without mishap.

The grass was beaten down at the end of the track, as though a car had turned there, but there were no fresh tyre marks to be seen; there had been a lot of rain lately, much needed after the long dry summer. In good weather, cars came this way and people picnicked; she had even seen a few optimists fishing but without success, though there was plenty of wild life around. She had seen wild geese, and a heron, and swans nested here; there were butterflies and water rats.

The dogs were making a deafening noise. They had slithered down the sloping side of the pit and were standing in a row at the point where it ended in a steep drop. Rory's bark was almost a baying sound, and now she could see what was causing all the excitement. Even from where she stood, high above them, she knew what it was.

She could not, with safety, go any lower herself, and it took her some time to get the dogs under control and back at her side. After that, it was more than half an hour before she reached home again and could telephone the police.

She had heard that a girl was missing from the Northampton area, but that was some distance away and she did not immediately connect what she had seen in the black water of the pit with her. The police, however, did, soon after they reached the scene. The sodden clothing exactly matched the description of what Ann Green had on when she disappeared.

Mrs Turner stepped down the road with a carrier bag.

Betty and Zoe had gone to Vienna for Christmas – quite a treat for them, it was, and well deserved. They had shut the salon until Wednesday, so they would have a nice break, and it should be lovely; they would eat rich cake and perhaps see those wonderful horses. They earnestly hoped the riding school would not be closed during the holiday; both of them liked horses and they often went riding on Sundays.

Mrs Turner would not admit that she would be lonely without them. Her friend Mrs Jones would be spending the day with her son; he lived ten miles away and would fetch her straight after breakfast. She preferred that to going to stay, for there wasn't much room to spare in their house and she did not like her granddaughter moving out of her room so that Mrs Jones could use it.

Mrs Turner had decided to keep busy, and there would be plenty of films to watch on television besides making sure that she saw the Queen's broadcast. She would tape it to add to her store of Royal occasions. Mrs Turner could imagine the fun the Queen would be having with all her family — Andrew playing jokes, no doubt, and the small ones over-excited, like children the world over — then church, of course. Like the monarch, Mrs Turner would attend matins where she would see people she knew, to exchange greetings, and would come home to a glass of sherry. The judge always gave her a bottle of Harvey's Amontillado for Christmas, and now she was on the way to collect it, for he liked to present it in person. In her bag were some cheerily wrapped parcels in red paper with snowmen on them: a fine lacy stole in a deep petunia shade which she had crocheted herself for the judge's wife; she could use it on summer evenings when she went on holiday with the judge, or to Glyndebourne — they had been two years ago and Felicity kept hoping that the judge would arrange to take her again. For Stephen there was a jar of Gentleman's Relish, which seemed apt, and for Emily six muslin bags filled with lavender from the garden at Waite House. It was a pity there were no children; Mrs Turner would have liked to make them some soft toys; as it was, she produced ducks and bears and elephants for various fêtes. Did the Queen sew? she wondered. You never heard about that, though everyone knew that Charles and his father painted quite nicely.

Mrs Turner never gave the judge a personal gift; for her to do so would have embarrassed them both.

With her bottle of sherry, there was always a cheque; twenty pounds, it had been last year. It might be as much as twenty-five this time, taking inflation into account, Mrs Turner thought, and told herself not to be greedy. Crossing the market square she noticed, among the few cars parked there, one with a man sitting behind the wheel. She supposed idly that he must be waiting for someone to come out of one of the houses. She glanced across at him, but his face was turned away and all she could see was brown hair. Who could he be waiting for? She knew who lived in all the houses facing the square: there was a solicitor and his family; several tradesmen who still lived over or near their businesses; a man who was a radio producer and his wife, who was a teacher; a pilot. The buildings were all pleasant, old, some timbered; newer places were hidden behind these fronts in roads radiating out round the town.

Mrs Turner rang the bell at Waite House. Naturally she would not use her key today.

Adams, who had looked away as she passed near his car, saw the broad figure in wine-coloured raincoat with false fur collar and wearing high boots, a black umbrella raised over her head, standing on the step in the drizzle. Then he saw the door opened by the same woman who had walked down the road with the judge that morning. She admitted the visitor to the house.

Twenty minutes later, Mrs Turner emerged.

Agog to hear the latest news from Romania, Colin had listened to the radio at one o'clock before they sat down to luncheon. He found that someone had tuned the set to the local station, and after listening to the headlines was about to retune when the announcer's voice informed his audience that police were investigating the discovery of a body in a gravel pit in the Midlands. At the moment they were not able to say whether it was that of Ann Green, seventeen, who had been missing for nearly a fortnight and for whom a search had been in progress ever since. It was hoped to establish the girl's identity later that day.

Colin stared through the window at the garden, where the high walls protected most of the plants from the blustery weather. The parents of the missing Ann Green would be confronted with the distorted features of the dead girl and might find her difficult to recognise after immersion. Dental checks would confirm identification if there was doubt. The body would be examined to detect the cause of death; the motive for the killing was almost certainly sexual, and her wretched mother and father would have to accept this confirmation of all their worst fears.

His mind flitted to Adams. This could be his work, though as far as was known he was not a killer. Had Superintendent Manners traced the Fiat he had been driving, found out where he was living? It might be pertinent now. Colin was not clear about the gravel pit's precise location, but it must be within fifty miles or so of Witherstone. The man should be checked, but the local police were probably already interviewing known sex offenders in the region and one of them might be responsible for this terrible crime. Would there be evidence enough to convict, when they found their man? The water would have washed away clues that could have yielded vital information.

He felt depressed by the weight of misery such a crime engendered. In court, facing petty criminals who fiddled money from their employers, stole items from stores, were guilty of drunk and disorderly conduct, he saw many examples of human weakness and was aware that those he was about to sentence were likely to do the same thing again when released; but when he was hearing a case of wife battering or assault, of child abuse or other violent behaviour, even now, after a lifetime spent dealing with such things, he felt real revulsion. He would sit on his dais above the court, making sure that the defendants had every chance to state their cases, never allowing a prosecuting barrister to get away with an improper question even though, beyond all doubt, the accused was guilty. He would weigh up extenuating circumstances, if any, and in some cases there was, if not excuse, at least explanation; but in others he was convinced that real evil was at work.

And a legal system which released wicked men to offend again without attempting to set them straight, merely content to keep them out of circulation for a period of punishment, surely had its own share of guilt to bear.

During lunch – Felicity had cooked a piece of gammon which they could eat cold for the rest of the week – they talked about the events in Europe. Colin, too young to serve during the war, had done his National Service in the Army. While stationed in Germany he had acted as prisoner's friend in a court martial and when he succeeded in getting a Not Guilty verdict, he had felt the allure of the law, which was what made him pursue his subsequent career. He had seen at first hand the post-war conditions in Berlin and other parts of Germany; he remembered all that followed in a much more personal way than Felicity, so much younger, and to Stephen and Emily it was simply history. Whilst he felt a surge of excitement – an emotion rare in one so controlled – he knew also a sense of foreboding; there were aftermaths to euphoria; peaks of triumph could be followed by anticlimaxes. No swift miracles should be expected.

He said something of this to the others, and they listened respectfully to his opinions, but they all agreed that this was a much happier Christmas than last year when a terrible plane crash had overshadowed everything else.

'No snow, either,' said Colin. 'It's unseasonable.'

'Was there always snow in your youth, father?' asked Stephen, who since his marriage had begun gently teasing both his parents.

'Not every year,' said Colin, with what passed, for him, as a smile.

Felicity related how she had once spent a Christmas holiday with a school friend and had skated on a lake near their house; she remembered digging snowdrifts away from their garage. Even here, since they came to Rambleton, there had been a New Year's Day when the world was white.

'Ferdy doesn't like it,' said Emily. 'It freezes his chassis.'

When Mrs Turner arrived with her gifts, they were all in a cheerful, relaxed mood. Colin had managed to lay his pessimism aside, and one cause for rejoicing was that thus far he had not been called on by the police to grant bail in some serious case or take out an injunction against a wife batterer.

Mrs Turner sat in the drawing room exchanging small talk with them all. Betty was enquired after and her jaunt to Vienna described – Felicity already knew as much about it as Mrs Turner. Emily had been to Vienna, and had seen the various palaces and had visited Mayerling. They discussed the romantic crime there: Mrs Turner had seen a film about it.

After Mrs Turner left, Colin went into his study to look over some papers for a complex case about which his opinion had been asked, and Stephen remarked that Mrs Turner seemed to enjoy life. Felicity was worried that, without Betty, she might be lonely in the next few days. Such a business was made in the press and on television about people being on their own while most of the world rejoiced.

'They don't always rejoice,' said Emily. 'Some people have awful quarrels instead of peace and goodwill.'

'True,' Felicity agreed.

'Mrs T's so nice, she's sure to have had lots of invitations,' said Stephen.

Felicity knew Mrs Turner had plenty of friends, but did they know that Betty was not coming home this year?

The weather was not too bad at the moment; Emily said she would take Ferdy out for a run. She slipped on her coat, her warm gloves and her woollen hat, clipped his lead to his collar, and set off, turning left towards the park. When she had gone, Stephen and Felicity went to get ready for the carol service. They had decided to walk because it was not very far and they thought it was blowing too hard to rain. While they were gathering up coats and boots, Adams, still sitting in the Allegro in the square, saw the front door of Waite House open again.

This time, the woman he thought was the judge's wife emerged, with a small brown and white dog on a lead.

3

She was much younger than her old man. She must have married him from greed, because he was rich, thought Adams.

He allowed a gap to open up between them before he started the car and began following Emily. She was tiny, her little booted legs moving briskly along, the dog at her side.

He didn't like dogs. They patrolled prison walls and they sniffed out fugitives, biting at their limbs, holding them down, snarling. Still, this particular dog was not much of a menace, no bigger than a large cat. The two figures went tittupping down the road and he stopped by the kerb, keeping them in sight, only moving when they disappeared round a bend. There was very little traffic, and most of it was going the other way, taking people to the carol service; the church lay at the other end of the main street.

He saw another woman, a much stouter one than his quarry, with a black spaniel on a lead, but she was coming towards him. Emily turned down a short side road which led to the park gates. She went through, and Adams stopped the car outside.

Emily decided that once round the perimeter path of the park would do for today. The place was almost deserted, for the wind was too strong for children to play on the swings or seesaw. Two boys were kicking a football in the distance, and as she walked on she saw three other people with dogs but they were on their way out of the park, moving towards the gates. They had been wise, she thought, starting out sooner than she; she pulled her cap down more securely over her ears to protect them from the wind.

When an Alsatian had gone safely by, she let Ferdy off his lead and he ran ahead with a couple of happy yaps. Emily folded her arms across her chest and marched on, hugging the bushes which grew alongside the boundary fence in an effort to keep out of the worst of the gale.

Adams had soon seen the scope of the park and guessed that there was only one entrance. Near it, there was a public lavatory, a brick building half hidden behind some shrubs, and that was where he waited for her to return as, inevitably, she must.

*

Lavinia Wootton had waited in her cottage for the police to arrive. Two constables in a car were there within seven minutes, which impressed her. She was ready for them, her coat on and the dogs locked in the kitchen. They began barking as she left with the officers to show them where she had been standing when she saw the body in the water.

They drove almost up to the gravel pit's edge but stopped short of the trampled grass, which she pointed out to the men. The figure still floated in the water; it was no dream.

The policemen radioed in their confirmation of the discovery, asking for help, and one of them remained on foot at the scene while the other took Lavinia home.

'No sense in you getting frozen through, Mrs Wootton,' he said. 'Keep warm, and we'll come in later to take your statement.'

'Do you think it's that missing girl?' she asked. They had all been able to see the spread skirt in the water, and the older police officer said that the body was that of a person who was not very tall.

'Could be,' said one of the officers. 'We'll know soon enough.'

Other cars passed the cottage: a second patrol car and then a large Rover with its blue light flashing, but there were no noisy sirens. Speed was not going to help the sad corpse. It was quite a long time before a black van drove by, and Lavinia knew that this meant the body had been lifted from the water and would be removed.

How infinitely sad to end like that, tossed into the deep dark water as if one were of no account, thought Lavinia. She supposed it must be the missing girl, unless some hapless suicide had leaped into the cold depths in a fit of despair. Whoever it was, there would be family and friends brought to the nadir of grief by the discovery and the ending of hope, for any missing person's safety must be hoped for until the last moment.

The two constables who had answered her call had swiftly assessed her as being one of that doughty breed of old women who were resolute and kept their heads, and knew she could be safely left to look after herself until someone had time to interview her. It was important to get on with retrieving the body while the light held, and frogmen went down to search for anything else that might have been dumped at the same time. There could be a weapon, though at first glance no outward injury was visible.

It was not until the next day, when the men went down again, that they found something of interest. One of them, casting around nearer the centre of the lake, found another body, one that had been there much longer, and was reduced to mere bones.

Detective Inspector Buchan and Detective Sergeant Drummond eventually came to the cottage. Lavinia described her walk, and the terrier's excitement.

'I go up to the pit almost daily,' she said. 'And he often goes off after rabbits – real or imaginary. It's not unusual. Sometimes he develops a convenient deafness when I call him back. But the Labradors are more obedient. I suppose they saw that poor woman – they couldn't have scented her from that distance.'

'They might have,' said Buchan, but decided not to go into details. Bodies immersed for a week or more often surfaced in this way.

Lavinia did not need to have spelled out for her the effects of putrefaction.

'The wind was blowing our way,' she observed.

'You'll be here over Christmas?' Buchan asked her, when Drummond had finished noting her words.

'Yes.'

'Alone?'

'From choice, Mr Buchan,' she said. 'I'm not lonely with my dogs.'

'Even after this experience? It must have shocked you,' he said. 'Isn't there someone we can get hold of to stay with you? Or some friends you could go to?'

'No,' she told him. 'I'm too old to go to pieces with shock. I'll have a good stiff whisky when you've gone.'

'We may need to talk to you again,' he warned. 'And there will be the inquest.'

'You'll want me there. Very well,' she said. 'When is it likely to be?'

'It depends when we get an identification,' said Buchan. 'Not for some days, at best. The coroner will want to enjoy his Christmas dinner, I don't doubt. It will be just a formality – adjourned to allow enquiries to proceed.'

'It's so sad,' said Lavinia. 'Why do people destroy one another?'

'If I could answer that, I could solve the riddle of humanity,' said the inspector grandly, and she smiled.

'Quite true,' she said.

As she showed them to the door, she remarked that they were both probably family men and this meant no Christmas for them.

'It's part of the job,' said Buchan.

'My wife's in the force too,' said Drummond. 'We've two boys, ten and eight. She'll do her best and I daresay I'll get some time at home. After all, that poor kid wasn't dumped last night. Any trail there might have been is pretty stale by now.'

'It is Ann Green?'

'We can't be certain yet, but I think so,' said Buchan.

'I hope you get him,' Lavinia said. 'And I hope he stays locked up for good, whoever he is.'

'You're not for topping them, then, Mrs Wootton?' asked Buchan.

'No,' she said. 'Not at all. But I'm not for letting them out, back into society.'

Colin was still in his study when Felicity and Stephen returned from church.

They had enjoyed the service, singing lustily, and had walked briskly home in the damp, windy dusk, looking forward to tea which they felt confident Emily would have made. When they let themselves into the house, it was quiet. No Ferdy came bustling to greet them, and though the drawing-room door was ajar, the room was deserted, the fire had burned low, and the lamps had not been turned on. Felicity started to make up the fire before she even took off her coat and boots, while Stephen, calling Emily by name, began looking for her, soon hurrying up to their room since she was not in the kitchen. Perhaps she was resting, he told his mother, and had taken Ferdy upstairs with her.

Felicity drew the curtains, then went to put her boots and coat in the cloakroom. She knew that Colin would have heard their return but would wait for them to tell him that tea was ready and ask if he would like his in the study. Sometimes he joined them, sometimes not; he seldom joined her when the young people were not there.

Today he was prepared to be sociable, and looked up with a pleased expression when Felicity entered the room.

'Where's Emily?' she asked. 'Is she lying down?'

'I've no idea,' said Colin. 'Isn't she in the drawing-room? I imagined she would be reading or watching television, as she wasn't going with you.'

'She took Ferdy out,' said Felicity. 'She left before we did.'

'And she's not back?'

'Stephen's gone to see if she's upstairs,' said Felicity, and at that moment he came hurrying down.

'She's not in the house,' he said. 'She can't have come back from her walk.'

'But that means she's been gone for over an hour,' Felicity exclaimed.

'She'd never stay out so long in this wind,' said Stephen. 'Twenty minutes, maybe half an hour, but no more.' His eyes had grown large in his face. 'Something must have happened to her,' he cried. 'She must have had some sort of accident.'

'Why didn't one of you tell me she had gone out?' Colin asked.

'Because we never disturb you if we can help it, when you've gone to your study,' said Felicity shortly.

'Am I such an ogre?' Colin demanded.

'No, Father, but your work is important, and we know we mustn't interrupt you unless it's urgent,' said Stephen.

'What difference would it have made?' asked Felicity. 'You wouldn't have noticed that she hadn't come back.'

'Well, we all know now, and I think we'd better go and look for her,' said Colin. 'It's getting dark. She may have turned her ankle and be unable to walk home.'

'She'd telephone,' said Felicity. 'If she'd done something like that, I mean. She'd go to someone's house. You'd have answered the phone.'

That was true.

Stephen said that it hadn't seemed so dark as he and his mother walked home from church, but that once you were indoors, the sky against the windows seemed quite black. It was true. Felicity had thought how pretty the town had looked as they came home, past windows showing Christmas trees decked with coloured lights, and with the streetlamps shining.

At that stage, none of them was seriously alarmed, merely puzzled and slightly anxious, and Colin was irritated with Emily for being thoughtless.

'She may have met someone she knows and gone in for tea with them,' he said, reasonably enough, though Emily's acquaintance in Rambleton was not large. He did not care to dwell on the implication that his privacy should be almost as inviolate as Fort Knox.

4

When a woman in her thirties, out exercising her dog, is not home when night falls, at what point do you call in the police?

This was Rambleton, not Liverpool or Glasgow, a town scarcely larger than a big village, with a population of some six thousand, three churches covering differing denominations, one two-star hotel and five public houses. Crime was not unknown in the town, even serious crime, but there had been no murder there within living memory. There must be some simple explanation for Emily's absence, but none that was swiftly proved correct.

Stephen went out to look for her, walking round the streets in the central area. He had been to the park, which was deserted. When at last he returned, without success, and having asked people he met if they had seen her, describing her and the dog, the possibility that she had met with an accident had to be considered. Colin could visualise a scenario in which that wretched little dog, as he thought of Ferdy, had somehow slipped his lead and run across the road in front of a car, with Emily in pursuit.

He telephoned the nearest hospital, then two more further afield, but none had admitted a woman answering to Emily's description.

Hearing Colin describe her, mentioning that she might carry no means of identification, made Felicity feel a sudden dreadful chill.

'There'd be Ferdy. His collar tag,' she said.

But it seemed no little dog was whining in a casualty department.

It was quite dark now. Any search made by the police would be very difficult, but it was time to notify them, and Colin did so.

Felicity and Stephen went together to the kitchen while he made the call. Stephen paced about, his face white, and he was shaking; his mother could see the effort he made to stop his teeth from chattering. She put the kettle on; tea could do no harm and might help.

'She'll turn up,' she said. 'Maybe she's met someone in trouble and is helping them.'

'She'd let us know. She'd realise we'd be worried by now,' Stephen said.

Felicity agreed, but said that Emily might have been prevented by circumstances outside her control.

'Like what?' asked Stephen roughly.

'Oh – I don't know. She took some distressed child home and there's no phone,' said Felicity. 'Or she's gone with a child to hospital.'

'I'm going out again,' Stephen said. 'I'll take the car.'

'You'd better wait till the police have been,' said Felicity. 'They'll need to know things – about her clothes and so on.'

'You know what she was wearing,' said Stephen. 'That tartan skirt and her camelhair coat and her woollen hat.'

'Do hold on, Stephen,' Felicity begged him. 'They'll be here very soon, I'm sure.'

She was right. Stephen was impatiently refusing to have some tea – he said he couldn't swallow – when a patrol car drew up outside. Ten minutes later a second car arrived and Stephen left to comb the countryside in his Peugeot.

'He'll feel better if he's doing something,' Felicity said, and, grudgingly, Colin agreed. He and Felicity added what information they could to the details he had supplied, and Felicity produced snapshots and a wedding photograph of Emily which the police took away. They set off to mount what sort of search could be carried out in darkness, leaving Colin and Felicity alone.

They looked at one another bleakly, and Felicity began to shake, just as Stephen had done earlier.

Colin made up the fire. Then he fetched her a tot of brandy and sat down beside her on the sofa. Tentatively, he put his arm round her, offering her the glass.

'Drink it, my dear,' he said. 'It's shock that's making you shaky. It does that sometimes, and this will help.'

She took a sip, and immediately felt the comforting warmth of the brandy as she swallowed it down.

'No wonder people take to drink,' she said, with a giggle that was half a sob. 'Don't you want some, Colin?'

'Not now,' said Colin.

'You're so controlled,' said Felicity. She wondered how he really felt; surely his nerves were as raw and vulnerable as her own? But it was for Stephen that she was suffering: the greatest hurt was to him and she could do nothing to help.

Colin gave her arm a pat, rose, and went out to the kitchen, returning soon with some cheese biscuits on a plate. Then he poured more brandy into her glass.

'You'd better have some blotting paper with that,' he prescribed, looking at her sitting there, knees drawn up, arms clutched against her body, rocking to and fro. 'And perhaps I'll join you after all.'

He poured himself a measure and sat down beside her once again.

'Waiting is the hardest part,' he said.

'Yes,' she said. She had steadied somewhat. 'Stephen was shaking too. I hope going out and moving around will calm him down.'

'I expect it will,' said Colin.

'Have you ever had the shakes like that?' she asked, curious. 'I never have, before.'

'Oh yes,' he said. Twice at least. 'Once was when you were having Stephen.'

'Really?' she was amazed. He had not been with her at the time; it was not yet fashionable for fathers to be present and anyway he had to be in court.

'I had to have a tot before I could make out a case for the defence,' he said. 'I remember it most clearly. A woman up for shoplifting.'

'Did you get her off?'

'Oh yes, although I think she was guilty,' said Colin. 'But it was trivial, a waste of everyone's time. Two tins of Heinz tomato soup: that was what she took. It was a gesture of despair. Her husband was having an affair with someone else.'

'Did they get back together?'

'I'm afraid not.'

She'd stolen some more things a month later, this time gin and whisky, and all that he could plead then was mental breakdown, but she had gone to prison, which was dreadful, and a marker to him on his road towards the Bench where he would have some control over the fate of others like her.

'Oh dear,' said Felicity. 'When was the other time you shook?'

He hesitated.

'Go on. Tell me,' she urged. Her head felt rather swimmy but she was not beyond realising that she was having a most unusual conversation with her husband, and it was stopping her from dwelling on Stephen's anguish.

After a long pause, he spoke.

'It was when my mother died,' he said.

'But you were very young then.' She knew his mother had died when he was a schoolboy.

'Youth doesn't protect you,' he said. 'And besides, I found her.'

'But wasn't she killed in an air raid?'

'I didn't tell you that, did I?' he asked in a gentle voice.

'No. I suppose – I just assumed – because it was during the war – ' her voice trailed off.

'She took her own life,' said Colin. 'It was suicide.'

It was snug in Lavinia Wootton's cottage. A wood fire burned in the open grate; the logs, from an old apple tree that had blown down in a gale, gave out a sweet scent.

She had put on a recording of Bach's *Christmas Oratorio* and was drinking a glass of good sherry, one of her treats to herself, while she listened, the volume turned up to give full effect to the music.

A policewoman had called earlier, to make sure that she was not suffering from delayed shock after the day's events.

'How kind of you,' said Lavinia. She supposed all this concern was due to her age, though in fact she was only seventy-two; in her book, you were not really old until you were past eighty, or until you felt antique, which she did occasionally, when physically over-tired. Still, it was good of the police to find time for this enquiry. 'I'm fine,' she said. 'And I've got the dogs for company.'

'And television,' said the young woman.

'Oh, of course,' Lavinia agreed.

But when Adams arrived two hours later, the dogs gave no warning of his approach.

There was no radio in Adams's Allegro. It had been stolen before he bought it, and he had thought about replacing it but decided not to because he wouldn't be keeping the car long; besides, it was an invitation to thieves. Sitting outside the judge's house, he would have liked to break the silence, but at the same time he did not want his attention to lapse so that he missed some movement, some chance to see the judge's wife again, if she came out. So he had not heard a news bulletin during the day; he did not know that a body, perhaps that of Ann Green, had been found.

All his previous victims had been young, small girls. Emily was not young, but she was small and thin, childlike in appearance, representing no sort of opposition. Had Felicity herself left the house while he was watching, he might have held back, for she was taller and more broadly built. He would have hesitated to attack her.

He had no plan when he followed the little figure and her dog, but after she entered the park, when he had left his car outside and watched her walking on, his actions became instinctive, and by the time he tackled her, he had forgotten her associations with the judge and the chance meeting at Willow House which had led him here today.

As she walked towards the gateway, leaving the park after her walk around its edge, she was totally unaware of his presence lurking in the bushes by the lavatories. He dragged her into them in seconds, silencing Ferdy, who gave a single yap, and her, and hid there with them until he was sure the place was empty. Then he backed the car up and bundled Emily into the boot, forgetting, now, about the dog.

No one had seen him. The park was not locked at night, so no keeper came along. He drove away.

The gravel pit had been his refuge before; that would be the place to put this one, with the others. All three could lie there for ever, undiscovered, and he would soon be half across the country.

It was a long drive through the dark, windy night. He drove on steadily, not stopping for anything at all. He felt no hunger, no sense of shock, no emotion at all. The dull anger that had surged up within him when he came close to Emily and seized her from behind had disappeared and he was icy calm, clear-headed, cool.

He maintained a speed of about fifty miles an hour on the main roads, less when he turned into country lanes. Several times he took wrong turnings, for he had no map and no real knowledge of how to reach the gravel pit from this direction, but at last he saw a familiar name on a signpost and knew that he was near his goal. He travelled on, driving carefully, along the road where he had brought Ann Green so recently.

Now he was close. There was the big tree on the corner, where he had almost run off the road that first time, so many years ago. Soon he would come to the track leading to the man-made lake.

As he rounded the bend before the track, he saw that the entrance was cordoned off with tape. There were signs beside the road, cones, and a police car was parked across the track's junction with the lane. Its blue light gently turned. A uniformed officer sat behind the wheel.

Adams drove straight past and round the next bend. Almost at once, the Allegro began to jerk and splutter, and it petered to a halt just short of Lavinia Wootton's cottage. The police car faced the other way and there were trees beside the lane, masking the Allegro's lights so the driver did not see that it had stopped. Adams doused them at once as he tried in vain to restart the car. Then he realised that he had run out of petrol. He had forgotten all about it, so intent was he on reaching the place where he could safely dump the body.

He pushed the car into Lavinia Wootton's gateway, for to leave it in the road would attract attention if more police cars came along. He had not yet worked out the reason for that one being present; he did not dare.

All was quiet. At seven o'clock on a Sunday evening, Christmas Eve, most people were at home.

He saw the light behind the drawn curtains at Lavinia's window, but there was no gap through which he could peer. Dan, the younger Labrador, lifted his head and looked about him, then, sleepy, warm and well-fed, settled down again. Bach obscured any further sounds from outside.

A young policeman, searching in the park, found Ferdy. His body lay under dense bushes among rubbish that accumulated there between visits from the cleaning team whose job it was to clear the park of litter and debris abandoned by the citizens.

The dog was dead. He had been stabbed.

Having established that, the officer left him there while he reported his discovery, and Stephen, who had already walked all round the park in his first search for Emily, and had now returned after a fruitless drive round the district in his car, saw the police activity which ensued. Torches shone. Blue lights flashed on cars parked beside the gateway.

They'd found something.

Feeling sick and faint, Stephen left his car and walked forward.

'What's happened?' he asked, as a policeman approached him.

'That's quite all right, sir. Just go along, if you don't mind. Everything's under control,' said the policeman, unaware of his identity.

'Have you found her?' Stephen demanded. 'Where is she? What's happened?'

'Just go along, sir, please,' said the officer, more insistently, now barring Stephen's way.

'Damn you, it's my wife you're looking for,' said Stephen. 'Have you found her? Is she all right?'

But she couldn't be, or he would have found her earlier, himself. The policeman dropped his arm.

'I'm sorry, Mr Drew,' he said. 'I didn't recognise you.' How could he? They had never met. 'No, we haven't found your wife, but we've found the dog.'

Another officer came over, and Stephen was allowed to move nearer to the spot where poor Ferdy's small white and brown body lay on the ground beneath a laurustinus, illuminated now by a brilliant light. Stephen made to move towards the dog, but was prevented.

'The animal must lay there for the present,' said the officer gravely. 'Sorry, sir. I think you should go home. We'll let you know directly when there's any news.'

But Stephen would not leave, and in the end they let him help in their renewed search which, by torchlight, covered the area very thoroughly.

They found nothing else, not even Emily's red hat.

5

At first light on Christmas morning, teams of police officers renewed their search for Emily.

Stephen and his parents had not gone to bed. They had made up the drawing-room fire, and sat around it, saying little. Occasionally one would hazard a theory of a consoling nature in an attempt to comfort the others, but such efforts were ineffective. Felicity had heated some soup and made sandwiches, but no one felt like eating. They had discussed whether they should tell Emily's parents about her disappearance, but Colin decided that it should wait until the morning.

'Let them at least get some sleep,' he had ruled, knowing that this could be a wrong decision, but the parents could do nothing to help and might at least be spared some hours of anguish. They must be told early, however, before there was any risk of hearing about it in a news bulletin.

The dog had been stabbed but no knife had been found, and the inference had to be that whoever killed Ferdy had abducted Emily and may well have used his knife on her.

Felicity refused to imagine what might have happened to Emily before death released her. Exchanging glances in an accord so rare in the years of their marriage that neither of them could remember when it had happened before, Stephen's parents strove to prevent him from speculating about her possible fate. After a while, despite his misery, Stephen, who was sitting on the sofa, dozed off, and Colin gently turned him and lifted his legs up, so that he was lying down. He left Stephen's shoes, afraid of waking him if he removed them.

Felicity watched, amazed. He had done almost nothing for Stephen when he was a child.

'I'll get a blanket,' she said, and went upstairs to fetch one, which she tucked around him. In the end, all three of them drowsed. Colin and Felicity kept waking, and whichever one of them stirred tended to the fire so that the room stayed warm. Felicity woke to find herself covered with a duvet; Colin must have done that. She looked across at him: he had taken his shoes off and had a rug over his knees; with his glasses off and his head, the hair now almost white, leaning against the high back of the armchair, he looked old.

I don't know him at all, she thought. The revelation about his mother's death had stunned her.

'I thought it was my fault,' he had said. 'I thought she couldn't bear the struggle any longer and that it was my coming home that was the last straw. Her life with my stepfather was dreadful. He beat her up, but she stayed with him because the house was hers, and she never surrendered it to him. I suppose she thought she wouldn't get him out of it, if she took me and left, but under the Married Women's Property Act, I think she would have managed. When she died, the house became mine; the trustees sold it and the money paid for most of my education.'

'Why do you think she took her life?' asked Felicity. 'I mean, as you were wrong at the time, what do you think was the real reason?'

'To save me. My grandmother had left all she had in trust for my education, but it wasn't enough.' He had paused, looking down at his big, strong hands. 'Sending me off removed me from my stepfather. He didn't like me and sometimes he beat me, too. She had managed to send me away for some of each holiday – to holiday schools or camps, and once to a vicar in the country who took in boys and coached them. I liked it there. The vicar's wife was a wonderful cook. Next to staying with my grandmother, it was the nicest place I remember in my childhood.'

'Why did you never tell me all this before?' asked Felicity.

He shrugged.

'I didn't want pity,' he said. 'And perhaps I only came to terms with it myself while Stephen was growing up.'

She asked him no more then. There would be time to hear the rest of the story later.

Adams moved quietly round the cottage, an old stone place with a tiled roof. Beside the building there was a garage which was locked; it had a window, and, hand against the glass, he peered in and could see a car inside. With a bottle and some rubber tubing, he could milk petrol from it, but would there be a bottle or a tube in the garage? Could he break into it without being heard from the house?

He still had the knife, now wiped clean. He could ring the bell and overcome whoever came to the door. But there could be several men living here, farm labourers, perhaps, each one big enough on his own to kill him with a blow. He did not know that only one elderly woman, and her dogs, were resident within.

He crept round the house, listening, and heard the music Lavinia was enjoying. It was loud, clearly audible through the curtained windows. That gave him hope that it might drown any noise he might make. The back door was firmly locked, and a blind was drawn over the kitchen window. If he could not see in, those inside the house could not look out.

After surviving several minutes undiscovered, and with no traffic having passed down the lane, Adams grew more confident, though he felt very angry. The police must have found that girl, and he could not think how such a thing had happened. She had sunk out of sight in a most satisfactory manner, like the other one all those years ago. However, there was nothing to connect him with her death and if he could get clear of the area and dump the body of the judge's wife – for so he still thought of Emily – somewhere else, none would be found. He had kept calm before and had not been caught; he must keep calm now.

He turned away from the house, back to the garage. He would try there before tackling the house.

Carefully, skilfully, using his knife, he forced the window in the garage and climbed through. He had a torch; one was vital to nocturnal adventures and it made a useful subsidiary weapon if required. He shone it round the garage.

The car was a Volkswagen Polo. What if he took it?

He tried its door. It was not locked, but there was no key in it, and even if there had been, he would have had to move the Allegro, now in the drive, to get past it. He poked about. The garage, sturdily built of bricks when the cottage was modernised many years before, was tidy; at one end there were some garden tools, including a wheelbarrow, rake, spade and fork, and a motor mower, an old Suffolk Colt. That made him think. Such mowers ran on petrol. Though it was winter, there might be a can of fuel. He looked about, and soon he found one, made of yellow plastic, with a filler cap attached. It was half-full.

That would take him away from here, at least as far as a filling station and out of reach of the policemen guarding the path to the gravel pit.

No one came by while he poured the petrol into the Allegro. He even replaced the empty can, so that the owner might not discover his loss for some time. He could not close the garage window properly when he emerged for the second time, but only close inspection would reveal that it was not securely latched.

Turning the ignition key, he held his breath, but the engine, still warm, fired at once and he was in gear and out of the gate in seconds, only putting on the headlights when he was in the road.

Lavinia Wootton dimly heard the sound of a car's engine, but her music was still playing and she paid no attention. Few cars passed along the lane at night, but there might be police traffic now; she knew there was an officer at the track leading to the pit, and others at the pit itself. She felt herself quite safe.

The Jack Russell uttered a soft bark, his head raised, ears pricked, and she thought he must have had a dream about a rabbit.

The police were out early in Rambleton on Christmas morning.

There had been some traffic during the night. People attending Midnight Mass had seen the activity and the cordoned-off park entrance, and in the morning they heard on the local radio that a woman had disappeared from the town during the afternoon of the previous day.

At first she was not named, but as soon as the police began their door-to-door enquiries her identity was revealed.

No milkman – an obvious early messenger – came on Christmas morning, but one of Mrs Turner's friends who lived near the park and was questioned soon after eight o'clock telephoned her and told her that Emily had disappeared.

Mrs Turner had planned breakfast in bed as a treat, then a lazy morning, perhaps watching videos or past Royal broadcasts in preparation for the new one later in the day. This altered everything.

'How?' she gasped, and 'Why?' but her friend knew only that police were going round the town asking if anyone had seen Emily Drew who had gone for a walk with her dog and not returned.

'But you can't disappear in Rambleton,' said Mrs Turner.

'It can happen here as well as anywhere,' said her informant. 'Maybe she's lost her memory and wandered off.'

'Humph.' Mrs Turner did not think Emily the type to do that, though how could one tell who was such a type? 'Well, thanks for letting me know. I'll get over there right away. They'll be needing help.'

She bustled into her clothes, her good navy skirt, as planned for Christmas Day, but, in case bad news was to come, not her scarlet jacket over her cream polyester blouse; she found a navy cardigan instead. The morning was fine, but she wore her raincoat and took her umbrella as she set forth for Waite House. It was wise to be prepared.

As she hurried along the road, Mrs Turner was asking herself what could possibly have happened. Emily was an unusual person, sharp, and given to making quite curt remarks at times, but she was direct, which Mrs Turner liked: no sweet smiles and smirks to your face and then cutting you up behind your back, like some did. She had had a sister-in-law like that and it had been hard to endure. Mrs Turner did not meet Emily often as she went to Waite House at weekends only if there were people to dinner on a Saturday night. Once a year in the summer, a large garden party was held, out of doors if the weather allowed, which it had this year. Mrs Turner would hand round the canapés which she and Felicity had prepared, and Emily would help, saying that as she did not really know the guests, this was the best way for her to cope with the occasion. Mrs Turner found her attitude refreshing.

As she crossed the market square, something nudged at the back of Mrs Turner's mind, some memory, but at the moment that was all it was, a blur niggling at her vaguely. She half expected to find a policeman barring the entrance to Waite House but it looked normal, the gates closed, the front door solid. She let herself in with her key, having calculated that if she rang, the judge himself might answer and might turn her away. She knew Felicity would need her.

They were all downstairs. By the look of them, none of them had been to bed. Mrs Turner, pink with distress and looking very smart, stood in the drawing-room doorway and cleared her throat.

'I thought you'd be needing some breakfast, Madam,' she said. Very rarely, in the judge's presence, she used this form of address to Felicity. Today it had the effect of making her employer burst into tears.

She pulled herself together very quickly, blowing her nose on a tissue and dabbing her eyes, but not before Mrs Turner had noticed the judge touch her arm gently, almost in a caress. Mrs Turner had time to be astonished; togetherness was not something she had observed between them.

'Oh, bless you,' Felicity was saying. 'How did you hear? Oh, how good of you to come.'

Mrs Turner was bustling forward now, seeing the blankets and the duvet thrown down where they had been used, the plates and soup bowls and some glasses. She began clearing everything up.

'Why don't you all go upstairs and have a wash?' she suggested. 'I'll soon have coffee made, and what else would you like? Stephen, you must keep your strength up. I'll boil you an egg.'

She was as brisk as an old-style hospital sister.

'Mrs Turner's quite right. Stephen, dear, go up and have a bath and a shave. You'll feel better then,' said Felicity.

'I'll come, too,' said his father. 'There will be things to see to, today, and we must be ready to face up to them.' He was thinking of newspaper reporters, even enquiries from neighbours. He had already spoken to Emily's parents, stealing out of the room while Stephen still dozed, calling them from his study, telling them what little was known, trying not to destroy their hope.

Now, he put his hand on his son's shoulder in a brief gesture, then propelled the younger man out of the room before him. The judge had aged ten years, thought Mrs Turner, really shocked at seeing him with stubble on his chin and his tie loosened, his shirt undone. He was always so dapper.

'There's no news.' Felicity interpreted Mrs Turner's questioning look. 'The police are carrying on searching today.'

While she and Mrs Turner cleared up the remains of their nocturnal snacks and dealt with the fire – as it burned logs, the ash merely piled up in the hearth and did not need clearing every day – Felicity told Mrs Turner about Ferdy.

'That's bad,' said Mrs Turner. 'Oh dear! It means – ' and she could not go on.

'Yes,' said Felicity. 'They met someone, and he had a knife.'

It was while Mrs Turner was spooning coffee into the glass jug with the plunger which Emily had given Felicity last year that she remembered the man she had seen sitting in his car outside Waite House the day before, when she came with the parcels. He was still there when she left and crossed the square to go home. She told Felicity, who thought it important enough to go up at once to tell Colin, even interrupting him in his bath. She came running downstairs again to report that the judge was at that very moment telephoning the police from upstairs.

Within ten minutes Mrs Turner was sitting at the kitchen table trying to describe to a detective sergeant what she had seen of the man, and the type of car, but she was not much good at that. It was not very large and not very small, she remembered, and a sort of dingy beige, rather old, she thought. She hadn't seen the man clearly; well, she thought it was a man; you couldn't be sure these days. She'd noticed only brown hair and a dark sort of coat; she'd not taken much notice, really, except to think it odd for someone to be sitting in a car in the square on a Sunday, and Christmas Eve at that.

'I suppose he was waiting for someone,' she said.

'Other people will have seen him,' said the detective sergeant. 'Now you've given us this lead, somebody else may have noticed what make of car it was and a bit more about it, or the man.'

He wasted no time in passing the information on to the investigating team. The officer looked alert now, with definite information upon which to act. At least this car and its driver could be traced and, if not connected with Emily's disappearance, be eliminated from the enquiry.

He had already gone by the time Stephen and Colin appeared, both looking refreshed, if haggard, and in clean clothes and shaved. They all had breakfast together, Mrs Turner too, democratically at the kitchen table, for she had stopped only for a cup of tea before leaving home. She was briefly the heroine of the hour as she described her sighting to the judge and Stephen.

'A beige car,' said Colin.

'Yes,' agreed Mrs Turner.

Colin was turning something over in his mind. Had the choice of Emily been random, or had the man in the beige car been waiting specifically for her? How could he have been aware of her existence? He could not have known she would certainly leave the house that afternoon, and alone except for the dog, for that had not been a long-planned excursion. Felicity and Stephen had set out, too, though some time later. Had the man been watching Waite House, or merely seeking some woman alone?

But he might be innocent, not involved at all.

Would the police succeed in tracing him? If so, how soon would he be found and questioned?

6

Adams knew that the half-gallon of petrol he had put into the Allegro's tank would not take him far. Driving up the road, away from the cottage and the gravel pit with its sentinel police car, he wished he had kept the empty can; then, if he ran out again, he could have walked or got a lift to a pump. But how many were open on a Sunday night? He realised he might have to drive miles before finding one when he passed through a sleeping village, its garage and pump in darkness. By then he had clocked up eight miles; he would be lucky to get another eight out of what was in the tank.

Long ago, he had known the area well, which was why he had dumped the first girl in the pit; he had camped nearby with the scouts, and had returned once with the girl he later married. They had had a serious quarrel by the edge of the pit and he had put his hands round her throat and started to shake her, but had not persisted when she struggled and kicked out at him; she had been a strong young woman, not small and thin like his victims, and when he had begged forgiveness, she had soothed and comforted him as if he were a child; at the time, this had appealed to him, and her mothering technique was what had bonded them at first. Later, it had palled for them both.

His own mother had abandoned him when he was eight, going off with a lover. His bitter father eventually found a new wife who had picked on the boy and been viciously jealous of him. His father had two more children by her, and after that his life became still more wretched, though he had tried to appease both his father and stepmother. The stepmother had gone to chapel twice every Sunday, taking him and her own two children with her, until he became old enough to rebel. He found her a poor advocate for what she professed, if all that praying and hymn singing permitted her to whip him round the legs with a cane and shut him in the coal cellar when he transgressed. He began wetting his bed, and that earned him more punishment. At last he left home to live with an aunt, his father's sister; she was strict, too, but just, and he had some better years there, doing well at school. Then she died and he was on his own.

The car began to falter again. He was not going to reach a pump. The road ran slightly downhill, and, coasting, he saw a turning ahead to the left; he pulled into it, and the car continued by its own momentum down the sloping road. When he saw a gateway, just before it levelled out, he stopped and got out of the car. The gate was a strong iron one, but not wired up, opening with an ordinary latch when you lifted it. The ground was damp, and he was afraid the car would stick as he tried to push it forward. He attempted to start the engine again, and it coughed into life just long enough to edge off the road and into the field, though he could not move it far from the entrance where it would be less noticeable to anyone passing.

Then he lifted the body out of the boot. Rigor had set in, and Emily was rigid, like a curled up puppet. He dragged her over the wet ground to a ditch and left her there, half buried under soaking grass and hedgerow growth. The car would soon be found, but she might not be noticed for some time. No one would start searching for her here.

He took his two bags from the car and trudged back to the main road, where he started to walk. After a mile he gave up and sat on a case by the roadside. The strong wind had dropped and the air was damp, but it was not raining. Half an hour later a lorry driver stopped and picked him up, and two miles further down the road they passed an all-night filling station.

Colin needed to talk to Superintendent Manners. He had heard no more from him about the Fiat which Adams had been driving; he wanted to hear that it had been traced, and Adams, not that he could in any way be connected with Emily's disappearance.

Manners was not on duty but at home, hoping to have a peaceful Christmas Day with his family, which included his first grandchild. He received a message that Judge Drew was anxious to speak to him and would Manners please ring him at home. By the way, went on the duty inspector who had called Manners, did the superintendent know that the judge's daughter-in-law had gone missing?

Manners didn't.

It wasn't a local matter, but the inspector filled him in with such details as were known, and after their call, Manners dialled the judge's number.

What did the old boy want? The young woman's disappearance was not something for Manners to take on board; it would become his business only if she turned up on his patch. Still, it might be very serious, unless the woman had simply run off, as could be the case. Judges' families were no exception to troubles of this nature.

There was the dog, however, allegedly stabbed to death. That was nasty: sick, if no worse, and a crime in itself.

As he dialled, Manners remembered the judge's interest in William Adams, but there could be no connection there. Adams had attacked a very young girl in a dark lane. This woman was no girl, and had, it seemed, disappeared in broad daylight in the middle of town.

When the judge answered, he asked Manners if the whereabouts of Adams and his Fiat had been traced. Manners protected himself by saying that he was uncertain; he would check and get back to the judge as soon as he could give an answer. Then he commiserated with the judge about his missing daughter-in-law and asked if there was news.

'A man was seen sitting in a car outside my house yesterday,' the judge told him. 'He could have been watching the house, or there may be an innocent explanation.'

'Is the make of the car known?' asked Manners.

'No. It was beige – rather shabby,' said the judge.

'Your local force will soon trace it,' said Manners encouragingly.

'I hope so,' said the judge. 'And I shall expect you to tell me about the Fiat very soon.'

Manners replied that he would do so, and hung up.

It could wait. The old boy seemed almost paranoiac about Adams, but the Fiat was black and so could not be the shabby beige car seen outside the judge's house the day before.

Manners returned to his family and the happy scene of parcel unwrapping. Then he got an urgent call about a break-in at a warehouse where guns had been used and a man was wounded; for this, he had to return to duty.

On the way to his headquarters he remembered the Fiat, and after making immediate plans concerning the break-in, he put in motion steps to discover what had been done about tracing the car. Eventually a young policewoman began chasing the information.

*

The lorry driver who had picked Adams up was self-employed and hurrying home to his family. His ultimate destination was near Watford in a village from which he ran his haulage business, and he dropped Adams, who said he was going to Newbury, at a service station before he turned off to the east.

'You'll probably pick up another ride here,' said the driver cheerfully.

In fact Adams had no plans. All in a few hours, his confidence had ebbed away. But he was free, and had with him all his cash and his few possessions. He simply lacked transport.

The lorry driver had told him, when he mentioned a railway station, that there were no trains running over Christmas and seemed surprised that Adams did not know that. He had trotted out his old excuse about recently returning from New Zealand, which did not deceive the driver. He reckoned he had picked up an old lag, but did not report this to his wife when he reached home. She did not approve of his practice of giving lifts, but he liked the company and sometimes met interesting people.

Adams went into the shop and bought himself coffee from the dispenser and some sandwiches, which he ate in the building.

The till assistant had a radio on, and he heard a news bulletin. There was something about a search for a missing woman which was called off because of darkness but would be resumed at dawn.

'Terrible, isn't it?' said the assistant, a big, strong girl with unnaturally orange hair and a lot of make-up. There was a man on duty with her, but he was in the rear office at the moment, having a rest. Such places were vulnerable to attack, but the customer drinking his coffee looked meek enough, and respectable in his rainproof jacket worn over a grey suit. The assistant did not notice the mud on his shoes and trouser ends, but he had a somewhat rough-dried air and later she described him as needing a good ironing.

'I didn't hear that properly,' Adams said, advancing. 'What did it say?'

'Some woman gone missing,' said the girl. 'A judge's daughter-in-law, it said. If she can be done, no one's safe, are they?' She smiled at him warmly. He looked very tired, she noticed now.

'Daughter-in-law?' asked Adams. 'Not wife?'

'That's what the man said,' the girl answered cheerfully.

*

His head was pounding.

He had walked out of the shop and across the forecourt to the point where vehicles turned in and out, and he stood there staring at the brightly illuminated signs, the grey sweep of the road, the streetlights beyond the service station. He had begun harassing the judge by writing to his wife and telephoning her, but ultimately his wish to hit at the woman herself and through her at all women had become dominant: he had been sidetracked by his discovery of the judge's hypocrisy, but when the woman appeared, he had recognised his true target. Only it seemed he had got the wrong woman.

He watched, without really taking it in, as an old Mini drew up at the pumps. A young man in jeans and combat jacket got out and filled it with petrol; then he went off to pay. Adams had not made a conscious decision to steal the car; after all, unless the keys were still in it, he would not be able to drive it away: perhaps he was thinking of asking the youth for a lift.

But the key was there, and in seconds Adams had thrown his bags into the back and had driven off. The driver, buying sweets and sandwiches, never noticed until he came out again quite two minutes later and saw that his precious car had gone.

'You should never leave the key, dear,' said the orange-haired girl, lifting the telephone to call the police. She, busy chatting to the customer and with her radio on, had not noticed, either. It never crossed her mind to connect the theft of the car with the well-spoken man who had been asking about the missing woman some ten minutes earlier.

June was asleep.

She had filled the children's stockings – Sebastian had remained awake until nearly midnight – and had collapsed exhausted into bed, worn out by the emotions of the past twenty-four hours. She had had two glasses of sherry which had helped her to relax and finally dropped off about two. She did not hear Adams open the front door with the key which he still possessed.

He stood in the hall, swaying to and fro. He had left the stolen Mini in a car park in the town centre. It was so quiet; there was hardly a soul to be seen, nor a vehicle moving. It was still only five o'clock in the morning, and dark. He dumped his bags on the floor and thought about going upstairs to claim his bed and fall into it to sleep, for he was reeling with fatigue, but first he went into the sitting-room. There might be some liquor there, in the sideboard; she'd be sure to have got something in for Christmas. Now was the time for one of his rare moments of indulgence; it could give you a boost when you were low, as he was now, with the world against him.

This was the only place he could think of to go to; he'd be safe here: June was wild about him, and the kids, too, apart from that stuck-up Rose, too conceited to make her friend. They'd be glad he was there for Christmas; kids needed a man about.

He found the bottle of sherry, which was nearly empty, and drained it straight down, without using a glass. The room, with the small, brightly decorated tree in the window, was tidy; June had swept round and polished while she waited for the children's return. A pile of parcels was heaped under the tree. Those spoiled brats: nothing was too much trouble for them; she'd have spent a fortune on toys and rubbish to keep them amused for an hour or two. He flopped down on the sofa with a big square parcel wrapped in red paper covered with Santa Claus figures, with Sebastian's name on the label, and thought about opening it.

Before he could do so, he fell back against the cushions, asleep.

Rose saw him there when, coming down early to make her mother a cup of tea as a treat before they all undid their stockings in bed with her – the two younger ones had already unpacked theirs together, but would refill them to let their mother witness their delight at the contents – and she almost screamed. Her mother had said he had gone, but here he was, and to her fastidious eye he looked unkempt and dirty, unshaven, his tie askew and his shirt undone, and his shoes, which were covered in dried mud, still on his feet.

She rushed upstairs to her mother.

'He's back,' she cried tensely. 'He's back, downstairs in the lounge.'

'Oh God!' said June. 'Oh, no!' Then she pulled herself together. 'Perhaps he had nowhere else to go,' she said, more truly than she knew.

7

A boy who had roller-skated along the pavement in front of Waite House to the end of the street and back by way of the market square had seen the shabby beige car parked outside the judge's house and was certain that it was an Allegro. He was convinced of this, and when challenged by the police officer who had called at his parent's house in the course of routine enquiries, took the man up to his room and showed him, pinned to the wall, row upon row of pictures of cars, among them an Austin Allegro. He had cut them from advertisements over the years to decorate his walls. He had not noticed the registration number of the car, but he had seen the man inside as he did a swooping manoeuvre past the car.

Other witnesses were found who endorsed this statement. Some were less positive about the make of car but confirmed it was beige; they had noticed it because it seemed odd that someone should be sitting in a car parked in the market square for such a long time. Several people had seen him in the morning when they returned from church, and there were two who had noticed him again in the afternoon, when they went down early to the carol service; they were in the choir, hence their two visits in the day. Neither had imagined that he sat there all day but beyond noticing his presence, they had not thought about him at all. No one had seen the car there when the carol service was over.

Find the Allegro was the message. But by this time it was marooned in a Midland field, and as Christmas Day progressed, torrential rain was falling all over the countryside.

Cars passed along the sloping lane down which Adams had rolled the Allegro during the night. There were people going to church, or visiting friends. A doctor called out to a man with a heart attack went past the quiet field where Emily lay among grass and brambles in a shallow ditch. No one noticed the car as they drove by. There were no cows in the field, for at this time of year they were all in byres, with no journeys to and fro for milking, but there were sheep in a neighbouring meadow, ewes heavy with lambs which would soon be born. The farmer, with his dog, strode out during the morning to look at his flock, so that he could, with a quiet mind, enjoy his midday meal. Where animals were concerned, accidents could easily happen and beasts stray to wander in the road.

He caught sight of the car through the low, leafless hedge dividing the two fields, which were both his, and, muttering angrily, went over to investigate what seemed to be the dumping of some clapped-out old heap on his land. He walked all round the Allegro. The windows were closed and the key was in the ignition, but the doors were unlocked.

It was the dog who found Emily's soaked body in the ditch at the side of the field.

Waite House seemed to have shrunk: it was as though the walls had drawn closer together as the building filled with the tension and fear of those within.

The rain beat down outside, but it was warm in the house, with a good fire in the drawing-room, a room much admired by Mrs Turner who thought it must resemble some of the homelier apartments in the Queen's various residences. After consultation together, she and Felicity had decided to cook the turkey, which had been intended for dinner on Christmas night, so that it should be ready at lunch-time. For one thing, Mrs Turner said, it would give them something to do, and for another, people must be fed even in a crisis; there were policemen coming and going; a cooked turkey would be more use than one in its raw state. When it was ready, looking and smelling good, even Stephen might be persuaded to eat something. By now, unspoken between them, was the shared view that Emily would not be found alive.

Her parents' first impulse, when Colin telephoned early that morning, had been to come over to Rambleton to be on the spot if there were any news, but it was a long drive, and there was nothing they could do to aid the search. Emily's mother had recently had a bad attack of bronchitis, and was still not very well; besides, there was the other family there, and the grandchildren; it was decided that they should remain where they were and keep in touch by telephone.

Afterwards, Felicity wondered how she would have coped without Mrs Turner, so stalwart in the background. She produced coffee and biscuits at mid-morning, and when Stephen said he could not swallow, suggested a cup of Bovril, which he consumed, with some thin dry toast; he had been unable to eat any breakfast. Between ministrations, Mrs Turner was self-effacing, keeping out of everyone's way. Felicity saw her dab at her eyes once or twice with a fine lawn handkerchief; Felicity herself was now in the state of calm which sometimes follows shock, moving like an automaton round the house.

Stephen had been round the town again on foot, and was allowed by the police into the park, where the area in which Ferdy was found, and the lavatories, had been cordoned off. Men were examining the ground; soil was being sifted; polythene bags were being filled with various specimens. He did not learn if anything of significance had been found; it would depend on the results of tests, he was told.

But there were footmarks in the toilets; a thread of red wool had been retrieved from a shrub. If Emily were found, the wool might prove to have come from her hat; the footmark might match that of a suspect. Stephen was not told about these examples of possible evidence.

Emily's body was discovered around midday. By two o'clock, when Colin had just finished his turkey, followed by cheese and biscuits, Detective Superintendent Winslow, in charge of the local search, came to the house to break the news. The dead woman must be identified. She had not yet been moved from the ditch because forensic scientists and the pathologist would want to examine the scene itself, but by the time someone could travel from Rambleton to identify her, she should have been transferred to a more appropriate place. For more appropriate, thought Colin, read mortuary. He and Stephen went off together in the police car, and Mrs Turner remained at Waite House to be with Felicity. They settled in the drawing-room to watch the Royal broadcast, which, by a miracle, came into Felicity's mind as she saw her companion glancing somewhat wistfully at the television set, kept, when not in use, in a corner and wheeled forward when required.

While the men were away, a call came through from the Metropolitan police. The message was to tell the judge that William Adams had been traced to a house in Titchford, 30 Endor Road, the home of one Mrs June Phillips where he was, apparently, a lodger.

Felicity wrote down the address and said she would tell the judge as soon as he returned. She had no idea who William Adams was, or why this message should be important enough to transmit today.

*

When they had watched the Queen – very informal this year, speaking to children in the Albert Hall – Mrs Turner suggested that Felicity might care to have a rest, upstairs in bed.

'You can't have had much sleep last night,' she said. 'If you have a nap now, you'll be all the more able to deal with things when the judge and Stephen get back.'

Felicity looked at her kind, concerned face, the neatly waved hair framing the anxious brown eyes and soft lined cheeks. She felt a wave of affection for this woman who, she suddenly perceived, recognised and understood loneliness.

'I'll fill you up a nice hot water bottle,' Mrs Turner said.

'Perhaps it would be a good idea,' Felicity admitted. 'They'll be away at least four hours, I'd guess, even if they come straight home afterwards.'

'You think it must be Emily?'

'I'm sure,' said Felicity. 'And there was the car, too, the beige Allegro. And the clothes they described were what Emily had on. Even her red woolly hat.'

The police had not mentioned how Emily had died, merely saying that the doctor had not yet given his opinion.

'But don't you wait, Mrs Turner,' Felicity went on. 'You must go home. This has wrecked your day.'

'I'd only be on my own, if I did go,' Mrs Turner told her. 'I wasn't going anywhere. The girls are away, and so is Doris Jones. I didn't let on to my friends. I don't want anyone's pity and I'm happy enough with the telly. I'll bring you a cup of tea in plenty of time for you to get yourself together before they come back. You go on now, and I'll be up in a few minutes with the bottle.'

Mrs Tuner had been amazed to discover that neither the judge nor his wife had electric blankets.

Like a child, Felicity obediently went upstairs. Mrs Turner, arriving with the bottle, drew the curtains and waited while Felicity, in her petticoat, slid beneath the duvet, and almost tucked her in, if you can be said to tuck in people with duvets.

Felicity's eyes were closed and she was already nearly asleep when the older woman left her. No one had shown Felicity such tender care since she was in hospital, giving birth to Stephen.

There was no doubt that it was Emily. Her body, now released from rigor, lay neatly beneath a sheet, not yet subjected to the forensic

171

pathologist's examination. Colin, inured though he was to knowledge of such matters, did not like to think about what this entailed, and hoped that Stephen, because more ignorant, would not give it consideration. She looked peaceful; apart from the pallor of death, there was no outward sign of distress, no wound on her face. Her hair had been neatly combed into approximately its normal style – easily done, with her short bob and straight fringe.

Colin nodded an affirmative, took Stephen by the arm and led him out.

'How did she die?' he asked the detective superintendent who had accompanied them to the mortuary.

'We don't know yet. There's no visible wound, nothing obvious, and she wasn't strangled. There would be signs in the eyes and her colour if that was the cause of death.'

'I see,' said Colin. 'Well, no doubt you'll tell us when you can, Mr Bowes. We'll go home now.'

Stephen, accepting a cup of strong tea before getting into the police car for the return journey, felt as if he were living in a nightmare. He had never seen a dead body before, and this one was the wife he loved, his little Emily who looked so fragile but was, in fact, so strong, wiped out in an afternoon, never again to be his dear companion and exciting lover. He could not take it in.

Bowes mentioned that the car's ownership was being checked, and the vehicle was already in the laboratory awaiting examination. When Stephen was out of earshot, he told Colin that it looked as if the body had been dragged along the grass from where the car had been left to the ditch. A dead weight, even so small a corpse would have seemed heavy. Hypostasis showed that she had lain, after death, in a different position from that in which she had been found.

Going home, Stephen began talking, almost babbling, declaring how he had tried to protect and look after Emily, but yesterday had failed by being absent from her side.

'You were with your mother, Stephen,' Colin answered. 'Good God, Emily should have been safe, walking her dog in Rambleton park on a Sunday afternoon. Who could imagine that a maniac would be passing by?'

It was an impassioned speech from this usually calm man, and Stephen fell silent; then, lulled by the heat of the car's interior and the rhythmic swishing of the screenwipers sweeping to and fro, he dozed, leaving his father free to attempt to bring order to his own confused mind.

He reviewed what facts there were. A man in a beige Allegro had been parked outside Waite House, and could have followed Emily along the road when she emerged. Alternatively, by then, he may have moved his car to the park entrance, looking for a victim. Either way, it had to be a chance attack. There could be no connection with William Adams, who had telephoned Waite House anonymously, leaving messages he knew the judge would understand. William Adams had a blue Sierra, then a black Fiat, and was last seen in Witherstone, sixty miles from Rambleton.

But there could be a link with the killing of Ann Green, whose body had been found the day before in a gravel pit less than twenty miles from the field where Emily was left lying in a ditch. The same man may very well have killed them both.

Detective Superintendent Bowes was already regarding the two deaths as possibly related, although both victims lived so far apart. The murderer may have planned to leave the second body where he had left the first one, and been foiled by the police presence. It was already known that the Allegro had run out of petrol, but there had been no reason to suspect that its driver had stopped earlier, at the cottage in the lane.

There was the second body in the lake to be considered. It had been there a long time. Lists of missing people must be checked, and dental records looked at; the skull and teeth were intact.

After Stephen and Colin had gone, Bowes learned that a car, unidentified in the dark, had passed the police car stationed at the lane leading to the gravel pit during the night. It was one of only three vehicles which had come that way during the officer's shift, and he had attached no importance to it, only mentioning it when he came on duty again and learned about the body discovered in the field and the abandoned Allegro.

A different type of constable, in the spirit of wanting to miss nothing, might have taken down its number, might even have waved it to a halt and checked its driver's reason for passing down the lane. Bowes sighed. Most coppers were made, not born.

He decreed that someone must visit Mrs Wootton and enquire if she had heard or seen the car pass.

She had not, though she remembered that her little dog had yelped once during the evening. It need not mean anything, she assured her questioner: just a dream after his dinner. But the officer noticed a fresh tyre mark, filled with rainwater, at the side of her entrance drive. He covered it with polythene sheeting. If it wasn't made by

Mrs Wootton's own car, or the milkman's van, or the postman, or, indeed, a police vehicle, whose tyre mark was it? It was deeply indented, and though soft because of the rain, might just yield an impression.

8

Felicity had slept so soundly that when she woke, after more than an hour, she could barely haul herself into consciousness. She had submerged again when Mrs Turner appeared with the promised tea.

'There's a good fire going, and I've got the kettle on,' she told Felicity. 'But perhaps they'll feel like something stronger when they come in.'

'Very likely.' Felicity struggled to rouse herself. 'Bless you, you've been wonderful.'

'Oh well, we're here to help each other, aren't we?' Mrs Turner said. 'The Dunkirk spirit in a crisis.' She fidgeted with the curtain. 'I'll let you get dressed,' she added. 'There's more tea in the pot downstairs.' She left the room.

I've embarrassed her, thought Felicity, and reflected that people grew accustomed to living without expressing their emotions.

She splashed her face with cold water to wake herself up properly before dressing again and going downstairs. Another long night lay ahead.

Colin and Stephen arrived ten minutes after she was ready. Mrs T had judged it to a nicety, she thought. Both looked pale and tense, and Stephen said he was going to Essex to see Emily's parents and break the news to them himself before they heard it in any other way. Because it was Christmas Day, the police would be able to sit on it for a while, he said, something Colin confirmed.

He didn't look fit to drive to the end of the road, much less some hundred miles or more across country in darkness and in pouring rain.

'Don't try to stop me,' he warned his parents. 'I've had a sleep in the car, and I'll be careful. I want to be around to see whoever did this put away for the rest of his life.'

White and haggard though he was, Stephen acquired dignity as he said these words, and Felicity and Colin both saw that they must let him go, and go alone.

'Of course you must go, if that's how you feel, Stephen,' said

Colin. 'You'll want to be with them for a while now, I'm sure.' A few trite clichés came into his mind, comforting platitudes handed down through generations, but he left them unsaid. 'Are you all right for ready cash?'

Stephen had twenty pounds in his wallet; he used plastic most of the time. His father produced fifty in ten-pound notes and handed them over.

'I don't want you at some wayside pump unable to buy petrol, or needing a meal and penniless,' he said. 'Come back when you're ready, and I – or your mother and I – will join you if Emily's parents want us, or you invite them here – whatever seems indicated.' He paused. 'Things – they'll want to know. There can't be a funeral yet, but there will be an inquest fairly soon. It will be adjourned, but then you will be able to make some arrangements. You'll want to work it out with them – her parents. Decide what you'll all prefer.'

'Yes. Thanks.' Stephen hesitated.

'Get your things together while your mother sees to some sandwiches for you, and a flask of coffee,' Colin went on. 'You'll need to stop.' It was an instruction.

'Yes,' said Stephen. 'I suppose so.'

'You will,' his father insisted.

Stephen began to climb the stairs. He moved slowly, like an old man. Felicity made as if to follow him but Colin stopped her.

'Let him go,' he said. 'He can manage, and he'll be better keeping active.'

He remembered being shepherded away while his mother's body was removed from their small house, the kind neighbour who had tried to distract him from what was happening, the sense of helplessness that filled him and turned his grief inwards. 'They'll talk about her,' he said. 'It will help them all.'

'I'll make the sandwiches,' said Felicity, turning, away, and went into the kitchen where Mrs Turner, who had heard most of this since the conversation took place in the hall and the kitchen door was ajar, had already begun assembling buttered bread and slices of cold turkey and ham.

'Does he like mustard?' she asked Felicity.

When Stephen returned, with his bag, Colin suggested telephoning Emily's parents to warn them that he was on his way.

'Better than if you just turn up, quite late at night,' he pointed out. 'Less of a shock.'

'I suppose you're right,' said Stephen. 'I can't get there much before ten, I suppose, in this weather.' He moved towards the door, then turned. 'If they ask, I suppose you'll have to tell them she's dead,' he said.

'Yes,' agreed Colin, grateful for this dispensation. 'But you can give them details. They'll want to know, Stephen, however distressing it is for all of you.'

Stephen nodded.

'Yes,' he said.

When his white Peugeot had gone, swallowed up in the wet night, Colin turned to Felicity.

'Victims and their families suffer so much,' he said. 'And they rarely receive official help. This will get Stephen through the next few hours, and he may be able to comfort that poor couple, her parents. Trying to do so will make him feel better.'

Felicity agreed.

'It's awful, being powerless to help,' she said.

'It is.'

They went into the drawing-room and Colin said he thought they both needed a drink. He poured them each a brandy and added soda.

'Very medicinal in times of crisis,' he declared. 'I'll take Mrs Turner some sherry.'

'She'll have to go home,' said Felicity.

'I'll drive her back after we've all had some supper,' he said.

But that did not happen, because Felicity remembered the telephone call from London and gave Colin the message about William Adams' address.

'What? He's been living in Titchford?' Colin gasped. He lost all his colour and had to sit down abruptly.

'Whatever is the matter? Who is this man?' Felicity exclaimed.

Colin was breathing heavily. He chose his words with care.

'He's a man I prosecuted in a rape case, and he came out of prison recently. I think he telephoned asking for Mr Baxter. You mentioned it.'

'Yes,' said Felicity. 'I remember.' He had mentioned Mrs Kent, Willow House, and Witherstone, as well, and all of them existed, as she knew. 'Who is this Mr Baxter? Why should the man Adams ring up about him?' He must be real, too.

'I'm not sure,' said Colin. What should he tell her?

'Could it be connected with these?' She rose and crossed the room to her desk, then took from it the two letters she had received and showed them to him. He could see that one had been crumpled up and then unfolded.

'I threw the first one away, and then for some reason retrieved it,' she said lamely, standing before him twisting her hands together, rather frightened, now, of what she might be unleashing.

Colin was studying them, his expression blank.

'Why didn't you show them to me?' he asked at last.

'I thought the first one came from some crank and decided not to bother you,' she said. 'The second one arrived a few days later. Pretty sick, I thought.'

'Yes,' said Colin.

'There were some other phone calls – I mean, odd ones, like the Mr Baxter one, but it was Mrs Turner who answered that time. I suppose it was the same person.'

'It was a man each time?' asked Colin.

'Yes.'

'What did he say?'

'One call said, "Ask him who Mrs Kent is", and the next said, "Ask him about Witherstone", and the third was, "Ask the judge about Willow House". I wrote them down, after the first one.' But the words were etched into her memory. 'You understand these messages, don't you?' she said. 'You know what they mean. Who are these people? Where is Willow House?'

She knew the answer. Would he give it to her?

'Mrs Kent is a doctor's widow who lives in Willow House, in Witherstone,' said Colin. 'It's in Warwickshire. I stayed there when it was foggy one night about three years ago. You were in London. There was no need for you to know about it, and I never told you. I'd just missed running into a traffic pile-up and I turned off the main road to avoid it and look for somewhere to stay. For some reason I don't understand, I gave my name as Mr Baxter. Perhaps I thought I was too high and mighty to stay in a mere boarding house.' But it had not been as simple as that. 'Stupid, wasn't it?' he went on. 'After all, if I'd given her my own name, she wouldn't have known that I was a judge, not that it made any difference.'

'Why Baxter?' asked Felicity, who could not believe what she was hearing.

'It was my mother's maiden name,' he answered.

'I don't see much wrong with that,' said Felicity, though she thought it an extraordinary thing for him to do. 'How does Adams come into all this? Didn't you say he'd only just come out of prison?'

'He has. But I've been going back to Willow House ever since that first visit,' Colin told her. 'I stay there whenever I go to trust meetings, and I've let you think I was staying with Peter.'

'And you've been Mr Baxter every time?'

'Yes.'

'This Mrs Kent,' Felicity began, then did not know how to finish. The notion that Colin might be the lover of a woman in Warwickshire, or anywhere else, was still so incredible that she could not give it even a tiny space in her comprehension.

'She's a pleasant woman, much my age, with three adult children all well settled in life. We're friends, I suppose,' he said. 'We don't talk a great deal. There isn't time. I have dinner in Witherstone – she doesn't do dinner, only breakfast – and then go along, and once or twice we've had coffee together, or a drink, when I arrive.' He sighed. 'I lose myself there, somehow,' he said. 'I'm not the judge, I'm not a husband, I'm not a father. I'm no one.'

And he was not the poor boy who felt his mother had abandoned him by dying. Did he see in Mrs Kent his mother, or the woman he should have married?

'Adams,' she prompted. 'He found out about this, somehow?'

'The last time I stayed there, so did he,' said Colin. 'I saw him at breakfast. We recognised each other at once and we each heard the other's false name. Mrs Kent called me Mr Baxter – we're always formal,' he added. 'No Christian names.' But he knew that hers was Judith.

So they couldn't be lovers, Felicity decided, though she had a feeling that people could be lovers in spirit without committing the act.

'He was blackmailing you?'

'No. Harassing me, as they say, but through you,' said the judge. 'If I had used my own name, there would have been nothing for him to pick up, but because I was using another name, he thought I had something to hide. In a way, I did.'

'It sounds fairly innocent to me,' said Felicity. She needed time to think about his revelation. She had had so many shocks and surprises in the last twenty-four hours that her powers of absorption had run out. For years Colin had been carrying on this mild deception; it could just as easily have been a full-blown love affair.

'Mrs Kent thinks I'm some sort of policeman,' he said. 'I didn't tell her that – she assumed it, and I let her go on believing it was true.'

'I suppose you paid cash,' Felicity remarked, and he nodded. 'But these letters and telephone calls – they're only nuisance actions, aren't they?'

'Not when carried out by such a man,' said Colin. 'He brutally raped and assaulted a girl. The police thought he might have been responsible for other attacks but they could prove nothing and he never confessed to more. He's violent, possibly unstable, and seeing me like that may have given him the idea of getting at me in some way for having him convicted. Men like him should not be at large. It's no use locking them up for a number of years and then freeing them into the population again unless they've been successfully treated, which in most cases I believe is impossible. Certainly they should be supervised, when released.'

'And be tattooed with "I am rapist" on their foreheads,' she said.

'Something like that.' He almost smiled. 'You're being very good about this, Felicity,' he said.

Felicity was so astonished and curious that she had no room for any other emotion.

'What do you expect me to do?' she asked. 'I don't exactly understand, but then I've learned more about you since Emily disappeared than in all the years of our marriage, and that must say something about me too – about my inadequacies as a wife.'

'You're not inadequate, my dear,' he said. 'But I took your youth from you, when you should have been enjoying yourself at parties and falling properly in love.'

She did not insult him by declaring that she had fallen in love with him. She had fallen in love with the idea of love, and of being married.

'Adams,' she said, returning to the point.

'He knows where we live – he telephoned and wrote letters. It would have been easy for him to look me up after he'd seen me in Witherstone.'

'But you don't think he – that it was him who took Emily away and –?' She could not finish.

'I don't know,' said Colin. 'The car's wrong, but it seems he's been living in Titchford.'

'One of the letters was postmarked Northampton and the other was too blurred to read,' Felicity said.

'That means nothing. He could have arranged that easily.' But Ann Green had lived near Northampton.

'You don't seriously think he was sitting outside waiting for Emily? It was sheer chance she went out alone with Ferdy.'

'I don't know.' Colin told her how Adams was driving a Sierra when they met, and that he had returned to Willow House in a Fiat but Mrs Kent had turned him away.

'Thank goodness she did,' said Felicity. The idea that men like Adams could be at large, unrecognised, in banks, in supermarkets, next to you in a train or on a bus, was horrifying. A petty thief was one thing; a violent criminal quite another. 'But this girl they've found – Ann Green – they think it's her, don't they? Could he have done that?' She echoed his thought. 'Didn't she live near Northampton?'

'There is no evidence to prove it yet,' said Colin carefully. 'But the man in charge up there thinks there may be a connection with Emily's death. Immersion will have destroyed evidence which might have trapped Ann Green's killer – that is, if she was raped. Genetic fingerprinting, I mean.'

She nodded.

'I understand.' Poor Colin, he was embarrassed at the possibility of having to explain.

'They'll have to hunt for witnesses who may have seen Ann Green with Adams,' he said. He paused, then added, 'If Emily was raped, they will be able to prove who did it, providing they catch him.'

'Adams, or another?'

'Yes.'

'He'd get put away properly this time.'

'This time, it's murder,' Colin said.

He stood up. His colour had returned and he looked more himself, ready to give a full summing up and address a jury. He knew that the doctors had seen no obvious sign of sexual assault; if there had been recent intercourse, Stephen would have to undergo a blood test to establish if he had been her partner.

There was no need to mention any of this at present.

'Please put the letters away safely,' he said. 'I'm going out. I may be some time, and I would prefer you not to be alone. Ask Mrs Turner if she will stay overnight.' He took two ten-pound notes from his wallet and gave them to her. 'Get her to take a taxi home to fetch her things. That should cover it adequately, Christmas notwithstanding.'

Felicity was amazed at the flow of banknotes which had come from him in recent hours.

'Where are you going?' she asked, but she thought she knew before he gave his evasive answer.

'To attend to some unfinished business,' he said.

Someone else, somewhere, had famously said that he was going out and might be gone some time, and he had not returned. Who was it?

Oates, she thought: that man with Scott at the Antarctic, who walked to certain death.

9

He'd shaved off his moustache. It made him look so different, thought June, entering the sitting-room in her dressing gown.

'Merry Christmas,' Adams greeted her, sprawling on the sofa. 'Sorry I haven't got you any presents, kids,' he added, to the two smaller children who stood behind her, using her body as a shield as they peered at him around her. Their chief emotion was curiosity, but they had learned to accept that adult behaviour was often inexplicable. Rose had gone back to her own room.

'We've got some for you,' Sebastian said. He came forward and ran to the Christmas tree, where he rummaged among the pile of parcels on the floor, surfacing with two packages which he handed to Adams.

It broke the spell. June, who had temporarily lost all power of movement, regained control of her limbs.

'I'm making coffee,' she said, going out to the kitchen. She put the kettle on, then went upstairs to dress; you were at a disadvantage if not properly clothed. As she did her face, she made a resolution: she would not allow him to remain. If necessary, since it was Christmas Day, he could stay and share their turkey, but afterwards he must be made to leave.

Downstairs, Adams was undoing his parcels, helped by Sebastian, who knew that one contained a sweater from June and the second three pairs of socks from the children. He had so few clothes, she had told them, coming from overseas and not wanting to bring much luggage with him. The children had thought that odd: surely, when you moved, you took everything? Amy regarded him thoughtfully as he undid the paper, tearing it, not removing it carefully so that it could be used again as their mother always did. Her worry now was that she would have to surrender her room again.

Adams seemed pleased at the contents of the parcels.

'You could put them on,' Amy suggested. 'The sweater I mean, and a pair of socks. You look rather dirty.' He smelled, but she was too polite to say so.

'I got in late last night,' he told her.

'Mum says you can change the things at Marks and Spencer's,' said Sebastian. 'She's got the receipts.'

'I shan't do that. They're fine,' said Adams.

'Why have you cut off your moustache?' asked Amy.

'I felt like a change,' he answered. 'Don't you like it?'

'I don't care,' said Amy bluntly, and she went away to find her mother, who reassured her about her bedroom but said they wouldn't talk about it now; she'd speak to Brian later.

The turkey had to go into the oven, the pudding must be put on to boil, and the table laid. The sprouts were already cleaned and the potatoes peeled. Then there were presents. While June and the children were dealing with all these important matters, Adams went upstairs to have a bath, and while he was in it, Rose came down. She had twisted her hair into a knot and looked two years older than her schoolday self.

'I hope that creep's not staying,' she said.

June repeated what she had told Amy about talking to him later, and Rose muttered something under her breath. June let it pass, just as she had made no comment on the epithet Rose had used.

'Come on — let's enjoy our presents,' she suggested, and the children had a happy, noisy time doing exactly that while June went in and out of the kitchen at intervals to inspect the bird and finished laying the table. Rose helped her set out crackers and scarlet table napkins with holly motifs. Adams did not reappear, and eventually June went to look for him.

He was in her bed, asleep.

She closed her bedroom door with a snap, which did not wake him up. What had he been doing since he left the hotel, and her? Where had he been? She looked out of the landing window and could not see the Allegro in the road, though there was ample space for parking just outside the house.

The bathroom was full of steam; the bathmat and her towel were sodden. She had not put a clean one out for him. She picked them up and put them in the linen basket; some of his clothes were already in it.

How dare he? She had done his washing while he stayed there; it was obviously the simplest arrangement and because they had sometimes slept together, it had seemed the natural thing to do. But all that was over.

The children relaxed with their presents, and the younger ones, who had been given various games, wanted to play them. They settled down with Monopoly, which an aunt had given to all three of them. Rose knew how to play; the others soon caught on, and June took a place with them, saying they could take her turn for her if she had to attend to the meal.

The game was still in progress when the turkey was ready, and just as June was wondering whether to call him, Adams appeared.

He was in a good mood. There was no sherry left because he had finished it, but there was a bottle of wine which had been among June's presents, a gift from Mrs Downes.

He offered to carve the bird, and she let him, for she was not very good at carving. He took the knife and ran his thumb along the blade, his gaze on Rose, who looked away. Suddenly, he frightened her. Until now she had merely thought him boring, a wimp, but today there was something about him that was more than that: perhaps it was only that the moustache had gone and his lips were visible. They were long and thin.

He made some remark about liking nice young birds and then addressed himself to the turkey, which he sliced up after expertly sharpening the knife with rasping strokes on the steel. For a time he had worked in the prison kitchen and had acquired some expertise.

Outside, it had begun to rain and now the heavens spilled down water as though from an upturned bucket, as Amy colourfully remarked. She said she had been discussing similes and metaphors with her grandfather, who was now retired but who had been a journalist. She tried to explain what they were, and they all began to think of examples. Sebastian inspected his fork before loading it with food, and said the prongs were like prison bars.

Adams said nothing, but June felt his *frisson*. He had eaten stolidly, staring at his plate; he seemed extremely hungry. June talked brightly, almost hectically, and Rose could sense that her animation was not normal. Somehow it was connected with Brian and after a while, when Rose began to understand that her mother was deeply uneasy, almost frightened, she entered the conversation, trying to help it along, thinking of comparisons for the other two, getting beyond feet like lead to wearing snowflakes on your head like lace caps. They prolonged the exercise, but Brian made no attempt to join in; however, he pulled crackers and they all read the jokes, blew whistles, and put on paper hats.

Washing-up filled in some time, but he did not help. June left the children to finish it while she went to tackle him about leaving.

He was in the sitting-room before the fire, with a cup of coffee and a full glass of wine. June had drunk very little; he was now finishing the bottle. He looked sleepy.

'You seem very tired,' she said. 'Where have you been? Why did you leave like that?' By asking such an obvious question, she postponed tackling the real issue.

'Something came up about a job opportunity,' he mumbled.

'You could have left a message.' She did not mention that it was odd for something so urgent to arise on the weekend before Christmas.

'Sorry. I could have, I suppose,' he said.

How had the job people known where to find him? She didn't believe a word of it. And there was the Evans business.

'I didn't expect to see you again,' she said. 'I'm afraid you can't stay. Would you like to telephone some hotels and see if you can find a room?'

'You can't turn me out,' he said. 'Not on Christmas Day.'

'I can,' she replied. 'I'm doing it.'

'I won't go,' he said, and he left the room, pulling a knife out of his pocket as he went. It was a flick knife, opening at a touch, and, in the hall, he cut the telephone line close to the box, then returned to where June stood staring at him. She began to tremble. 'I'm staying until I want to go,' he said. 'And that includes tonight, and as long as I choose.'

He put the knife back in his pocket and sat down.

'If you're sensible, you won't alarm the children,' he said. 'If you're not sensible, I shall go and take Rose with me.'

June bit her lip to steady herself. She could not believe what she had just seen him do.

'Who are you?' she whispered. 'You haven't come from New Zealand. You've been telling me a whole lot of lies.'

'I've given you a good time,' he sneered. 'You've been glad of me, you sex-starved, dried-up bitch.'

She had not found an answer to this when Sebastian, followed by the others, came breezing back into the room wanting to continue the game of Monopoly. All the children still wore their paper hats, and Adams seized another that lay on a chair and rammed it on to June's head.

'There's your crown,' he said. 'Keep it on. Finish the game.'

She could think of nothing else to do. Perhaps, while playing, something would occur to her or he would change his mind and go, but he watched intently while they finished that game, then joined in the next quite naturally, as if he enjoyed it. June kept making silly mistakes, but Sebastian kindly helped her. Rose, alarmed because her mother was so much on edge, did her best to be cheerful and keep things going. Brian made no attempt to stop her when she left the room to prepare tea, setting out the Christmas cake with its robins and miniature fir trees, but when June said she must go the bathroom, he followed her and stood outside the door.

What could she do? She couldn't climb out of its small window, and even if she were able to do so, she could not leave the children with him. How could she get help? What sort of a man was he? Had he done something terrible with that knife? He had never been rough with her, only cold and unfeeling, but he had threatened Rose; perhaps he liked young girls. Rose had never taken to him, as the others had done; perhaps instinctively she had known there was something to fear.

Now, because she felt it happening to her, June understood that blood can run cold with terror.

Could she somehow get hold of Rose and send her to call the police and persuade them to turn him out of the house?

What she did do was to return downstairs, pour out the tea and cut the cake.

Rose took charge of the clearing away, gathering her brother and sister up to help her, shutting the three of them into the kitchen, where she spoke to them quietly.

'Something weird's going on with Mum and Brian,' she said. 'I don't like it. Mum's all tense.' She did not want to say that their mother was frightened.

'He's drunk,' suggested Sebastian.

'Maybe.'

'She said he'd go today,' said Amy.

'Well, he hasn't and it's raining cats and dogs,' said Rose.

'A simile,' said Amy with a feeble grin.

'Could we ring Dad?' This was Sebastian's idea.

'Good thinking,' said Rose. 'But he's miles away, with Gran and Granddad.'

'He'll know what to do,' said Amy.

He would.

'You two go back into the sitting-room and keep them talking,' said Rose. 'I'll telephone.'

But she soon discovered what had happened. When she heard no sound after lifting the receiver, first she pressed the rest up and down, trying to get the dialling tone. Then, almost by chance, she saw the severed flex. The fact that it had been deliberately cut did not sink in at first, until, viewer of television thrillers that she was, she understood. The next step was to deduce who had cut it. There was only one candidate.

She was terrified, but she did not panic, going at once to the back door. She would slip out and phone from up the road – dial 999 – that was what she must do. But the back door was locked, bolted top and bottom and the key turned and missing, so that even after she had undone the bolts, she could not unlock the door. When she ran through to try the front door, the man she knew as Brian was standing across it, blocking the way.

'Going somewhere, are we?' he asked her, with that look on his face which was not a smile; she did not know how you would describe it, unless it was a leer.

In his hand he held a knife with a long thin blade. He pointed it at her.

June was instantly by her daughter's side. She thrust Rose behind her.

'Go into the sitting-room with the others,' she said.

'I'm not leaving you with him,' said Rose. The words were valiant, but the tone was shaky. Her hand slid into her mother's.

'You don't need that knife, Brian. Give it to me,' said June. She tried to speak calmly.

For answer, he brandished it.

'Why the melodrama?' asked June. 'You're being very stupid.'

'I was going to ring up Dad,' said Rose. 'The line's been cut.'

'Of course. To stop silly little girls like you doing silly things,' said Adams. 'And bigger girls, too, like your cow of a mother.'

'She's not – ' Rose spluttered.

'Shut up, you,' said Adams.

'If you go now, just go, I won't ring the police. I won't say anything about all this,' said June.

'There's nothing you can say,' he told her. 'I've hurt none of you, have I?' He waved the knife again.

'You've threatened us,' said June. 'You've refused to leave the house when I asked you to.'

'Why should I? I'm your common-law husband,' Adams said.

June heard Rose's intake of breath.

188

'You are no such thing,' said June. 'You were my lodger. That was all. And now you're leaving.'

He'd blown it. Standing there, facing the woman and the girl, Adams knew it. As soon as he'd pulled the knife, he'd lost control of the action. He didn't want June – never had – that was just for manners – but Rose was different; she'd be sweet and juicy. He saw her looking at him now with contempt on her face, and he recognised that expression which was stronger than fear; he'd seen it on the other face, too, in Rambleton Park yesterday, when he stabbed the dog. Contempt had turned to fury; then he'd grabbed her. But there'd been no satisfaction; she was dead too soon.

He moved uncomfortably, and June felt the atmosphere alter.

'Come on, Brian. Keep your knife, if you daren't move without it, but turn round, open the door, and go,' she said.

He looked at her, and the girl beside her.

'I'm taking Rose,' he said.

'You're not,' said June. 'If you go alone, I won't tell the police about any of this, but if you take Rose, I'm running screaming down the street behind you and you'll be caught.'

'I'll kill you all,' said Adams.

'No, you won't,' said June. 'It isn't worth it to you. Why go to gaol for us?'

Rose's grip on June's hand was now so tight that a ring dug into her finger, but the grasp gave both of them courage as they stood firm, facing him.

Adams advanced towards them.

10

When Colin left, Felicity looked for the piece of paper on which she had written the message from London, with the address in Titchford, but he had torn it from the pad beside the telephone. She could not remember the name of the road, or the number.

Colin believed that the man Adams was responsible for the telephone calls and the anonymous letters, and she understood that in spite of the fact of an Allegro being involved, not a Fiat, Emily's death might be linked to Adams in some way.

She felt sure that Colin had set off to confront Adams.

What a thing for him to do! He was a cerebral person, not a man of action. She must ring the police at once and tell them to get to the house ahead of him, but how, when she did not know the address?

Mrs Turner appeared behind her.

'Would you like me to stay with you, Mrs Drew?' she asked. 'Overnight, I mean. With all this trouble, perhaps I can be useful.'

'Oh, Mrs Turner, thank you. Yes – my husband did suggest I should ask you if you would. He said to take a taxi home to collect your things, if you could really stay without all your own arrangements being upset.'

Should she bother? Mrs Turner thought about it. If she could borrow a nightie from Mrs Drew, and if there were a spare new toothbrush in the house – as she knew there was, in the store-cupboard – she could manage. Her smalls, washed overnight, would soon dry on a radiator. But perhaps she would be more comfy with her own belongings. She accepted.

Felicity rang the taxi first, and it arrived to bear Mrs Turner back to *Balmoral* while she was dialling the police. There was no need to mention the letters or the telephone calls; she merely told them that the judge had been anxious about William Adams, whom years before he had prosecuted successfully, and who had recently been released. The judge had reason to believe he was driving a Fiat car, and this vehicle had been traced to Titchford. Now she feared that her husband had gone to see Adams, suspecting that he might know something about Emily's death. She could give no address in Titchford, nor the number of the Fiat, but she did know the registration number of the judge's Volvo.

The police said that they would go and look for him.

Mrs Turner was not absent long, and when she returned, with a small valise, Felicity told her where the judge had gone. Mrs Turner immediately inspected the telephone pad, holding it to the light. Then she took a pencil and lightly shadowed the top page. Sure enough, faint indentations revealed the address, 30 Endor Road, Titchford, which Felicity had written on the page above.

'Well, Miss Marple, you're a wonder,' said Felicity, reaching to the telephone again.

Colin drove fast to Titchford. He was sure Felicity would tell the police he had gone after Adams, but he did not know if she would remember the address. If not, he had a head start. He wanted a chance to settle the score himself, find out if Adams had waited for Emily. He'd have traces of her on him, if he were guilty.

He had never acted so impetuously in his life, nor, in adult years, without a plan, and what he was doing was contrary to any advice he would have given someone else in his position. 'Leave it to the police,' he would have said. But this was personal. Adams, even if innocent of Emily's death – and how to account for the Allegro, except that he had changed the Sierra for the Fiat and could soon have changed to another car – should be challenged over the nuisance he had committed with the calls and letters.

He had to concentrate on driving; the rain was still pouring down in torrents, and he did not know where Endor Road was. As he always tried to anticipate problems, he kept a street map of Titchford in the car, and he stopped in the outskirts of the town to consult it. Endor Road lay to the north west, a little distance from the centre of town, but he knew the area, and today, with very little traffic on the road, he had no difficulty in finding it.

There was no black Fiat outside number thirty. There was no car there at all, just a large space where he could easily park the Volvo, which he did. He turned off the lights and removed the keys, but for once in his life, he did not lock the car.

Everything in the road seemed peaceful. No cars passed. Many of the houses had vehicles parked outside them, but there were spaces, too, for people were away from home for Christmas.

He looked at the house. The upper floor was in darkness, but a lighted Christmas tree stood in the bay window on the ground floor, beside the front door. The practice of leaving curtains undrawn so that coloured lights shone out was a charming one, he thought, but hazardous, since it could attract prowlers.

He wondered how to proceed. There was no precedent to follow here, no famous case to offer guidance. Was Adams really living in this ordinary house in this ordinary street? Had he a wife here?

He would ring the doorbell and ask for him by name, then see what followed. If he had had anything at all to do with Emily's death, surely Colin, a judge, a man of intellect, could trap him into an admission?

As he was about to get out of the car, he saw a movement at the window where the tree was: the lights were obscured as a figure came between the tree and the glass; then he saw the window open and someone emerge.

A prowler?

Many thieves entered by a window but left by the door, letting themselves out with their booty, but there were always exceptions. Colin advanced towards the figure he had seen, regretting that he had no weapon with him, not even a simple walking stick.

Then he saw that the figure was extremely small.

Larger boys often used smaller ones to gain entrance for them, pushing them through fanlights too small to admit the real thieves.

He caught the little boy by the gate.

Sebastian struggled, kicking hard against his captor's shins, but he had no chance of escaping. Colin thought it shameful that such little boys were being introduced to crime.

By now Sebastian was shouting, demanding to be released.

'Calm down. I won't hurt you,' Colin said, holding the boy in the air by his upper arms, his legs flailing. 'What have you been up to?'

'There's a man in there with a knife,' wept Sebastian, his tears those of frustration, not pain. 'He's got my sister and my mother.'

Colin was perhaps the only man in existence who would instantly believe those words, thus uttered.

'A dark man with a moustache?' Even he needed confirmation.

'He had one. He's cut it off,' cried Sebastian. 'Oh, please put me down. He's holding them to ransom.'

Colin glanced at the house and now saw another figure at the lighted window.

'That's my other sister,' said Sebastian. 'I've got to go and dial 999. Please let me go.'

Colin set him on his feet, but still held him.

'Where is the man? Upstairs?'

'No. In the hall. We wedged the door with a cupboard so that he couldn't get in at us,' Sebastian said. 'Then me and Amy thought about getting help.'

'Well, luckily I'm here.' Colin said. 'I'm a judge. Do you know what that is?'

'Yes. You send people to prison,' said Sebastian.

'I do, and we'll send that man there too, shall we?'

'Yes,' agreed Sebastian, with fervour.

'What are they doing? Your mother and your sister and the man?'

'I don't know. They were talking, but we looked out and saw the knife. He didn't see us peeping. So we made the plan.'

'And it's a good one,' Colin commended him. 'Let's get Amy out of the house. Do you think I could climb in through the window? Then I might be able to take him by surprise.'

'I don't know.' For the first time, Sebastian studied his new friend. 'You look a bit old for climbing.'

'I am rather old,' Colin agreed.

'What if me and Amy pushed you?'

'Perhaps Amy could pass out a stool or something, for me to stand on,' said Colin, who knew his ability to step up to any height was limited. 'Is there one in there?'

'There's a little chair I had when I was young,' said Sebastian. 'It's quite small,' he added doubtfully, surveying Colin's portly figure as revealed by the streetlights.

Would it bear his weight? Time would soon provide the answer.

In moments, Amy was apprised of the plan. She caught on at once, passed out the small chair and then climbed out herself. Neither child wore a coat and the rain was bucketing down. Colin took off his raincoat and wrapped it round them both. He would climb more easily without it. Then he prepared to enter.

'When I'm in, count to two hundred, not too fast,' he said. 'Then you, boy – what is your name?'

'Sebastian.'

'An excellent name. Well, Sebastian, you ring the doorbell very hard, and run. Meanwhile, you Amy, will have opened the door of my car – that's it, there by the gate – and got in yourself. Sebastian, you run and get into the car too, and lock yourselves in. Do you think you can do that?'

'Yes,' they said.

The Volvo's locks were not complicated. They should manage it.

'If the man comes out, blow the car horn and keep on blowing it hard until somebody comes, then tell them what's been happening.' said Colin. 'If nothing happens, and you think about five minutes have gone by, blow the horn anyway. Someone will soon come along and you must tell them to get the police. Off you go, now.'

They stood watching him climb in, which he did with difficulty. He wrenched his knee, sliding over the window ledge. Then he turned. They had vanished.

Ringing the bell would distract Adams. Either he would open the door, or he would get the mother or her child to do so, and Colin would, he hoped, be able to come up behind him, unawares.

Of course, Adams might simply freeze, let whoever was there think the house was empty, wait till they went away. Perhaps it hadn't been such a good idea after all. But it might work and anyway the children would sound the Volvo's horn.

In the room, he looked about for a weapon. There were no fire irons because the realistic fire was gas. Then he saw the empty wine bottle standing on the floor beside the sofa, where Adams had left it after finishing the contents. There was no time to search for something better. He pulled the small chest away from the door – it would not have held back a grown man for more than seconds – and took hold of the doorknob with his left hand, the bottle in his right. As he did so, the doorbell rang very loudly with a shrill, sustained intensity that startled even Colin, though he expected it.

He opened the door a crack and could see the woman and the girl, their backs towards him. He pulled the door wide and thrust past them, pushing them aside, the bottle raised as Adams turned towards the front door, undecided, in those moments, about what to do. From the corner of his eye he saw Colin coming for him, whipped round and lashed out at him with his knife, but Colin was bigger, and very, very angry; he hit Adams' head extremely hard with the bottle.

Reasonable force, he thought to himself: force could be used that was commensurate with that threatened, in such a situation.

Adams stumbled and fell, and Colin stood on his wrist as the man dropped the knife. Then, with very great pleasure, he stamped hard on Adams' hand.

The man writhed and moaned on the floor, only stunned by the blow on the head, not really hurt. Colin made to pick up the knife, then drew back: it would bear the man's prints. Instead, he sat on

Adams' chest, thumping down on him and winding him. His weight would keep the fellow down and with luck might break a rib or two in the process.

Then he looked up at the woman and girl, who were clinging together, too startled to do more.

'Your little boy and girl are outside in my car,' he told June. 'They're perfectly safe, and very brave, but if, as I suspect, your phone isn't working, go outside, madam, to a neighbour, and ring the police. I think I can keep this person under control until they come.'

As he spoke, he thought that the woman's face looked familiar. Had he ever sent her to gaol, or heard her plea for maintenance?

At that moment, they heard a car horn outside start up, loud and strident, and almost simultaneously the siren of a police car as it arrived at the scene.

Sebastian was very impressed at this response to his tocsin. He never really understood that the police were already on their way.

Meanwhile, his mother had been staring at their saviour.

'Why, Judge Drew,' she said, half laughing, half about to cry. 'How very lucky that you were passing by.'

11

It is often difficult to place people seen out of context, and Colin did not recognise June as his dentist's nurse until they were all sitting round her kitchen table having cups of tea under the aegis of a young policewoman. Something about a gesture she made, putting tea bags in the pot, reminded him of her movements as she refilled the glass of mouthwash.

How had she come to be involved with such a man as Adams?

There were several police officers in the house. One was going through the contents of the linen basket, removing Adams' discarded clothing and putting it in polythene bags to take away for testing. Another, in the sitting-room, was dusting for prints. Although the judge had positively identified the man whom June knew as Brian Cotton as William Adams, it would have to be established in court that it was he who had threatened June and Rose with a knife. So far, that was all he could be charged with, but it was enough for his arrest. There was nothing to connect him with Emily's death; no results had yet come through from examination of the Allegro.

The police had told Felicity that Colin was safe and the man Adams in custody; at the judge's request, she was told nothing of his deed of derring-do. She, in turn, asked them to pass on information about the post-mortem report on Emily, which Bowes had telephoned through. She had not been sexually assaulted, nor stabbed to death, but had died of a massive heart attack probably brought on by shock. It seemed she had a congenital heart defect, something which had never shown up before but could have led to death in any circumstances of sudden strain. She had probably died instantly, in the park, at the time of Ferdy's killing. Adams might face a manslaughter charge on her account, but not murder; and an allegation of abduction might not hold; he might face a lesser charge of concealing a death. Colin mulled these possibilities over when he heard the details. However, the police might establish that he had killed Ann Green and put her body in the gravel pit; Detective Superintendent Bowes had a theory about a tyre mark possibly made by the Allegro near the scene, and more enquiries would be made of a local resident, the woman who had seen Ann Green's body in the water.

There was also the second body taken from the water. It had not yet been identified, but could be that of Sharon Wood who had vanished ten years ago. Dental records would be studied, and there was a gold chain and locket round the victim's neck, which offered possible clues to her identity.

Colin knew that the police would sift all the evidence carefully. They might seek to make it fit Adams, but there would be facts. He numbered them off in his mind: the Allegro, so near the scene; perhaps traces from Ann Green which would link her with Adams. If the Fiat were found and examined, it might yield more information, since that was the car he was driving when Ann Green disappeared, and if she had been transported in it, even with a new owner, something might be detected.

Sebastian was a hero, and Amy a heroine, but all four members of the Phillips family had been extremely brave. A policewoman would be spending the night in the house with them, since June refused to leave – and where could she go, in the late evening on Christmas Day? Before Colin went home, he promised to come and see her in a day or two, to make sure that none of them was any the worse for their ordeal. He thought the children would soon recover, especially the younger ones, but Rose might be affected more seriously, and June, if she had been involved with Adams, as seemed all too probable, could be badly scarred.

Later, she told Colin how they had met, and how she had been gulled. She was afraid it would come out in evidence when Adams went to trial but Colin said it might be possible to retain his definition as her lodger.

The police had found a large sum of money in one of Adams' cases, and documentation which led, much later, to the exposure of his confidence tricks.

Eventually, his prints were found in the Allegro, so that there was no doubt of his responsibility for what had happened to Emily.

Some days after Christmas, the Fiat was traced. Adams had sold it to the dealer where he bought the Allegro; the new owner was located, and after very careful examination in the police laboratory, bloodstains were found under the carpet in the rear. The amount was very small, but it was sufficient to get a match: DNA fingerprinting established that it had come from Ann Green. There were also threadlike fibres from her clothing. It was enough to make a case.

The newspapers took it all up quickly, but were unable, before Adams was charged and it became *sub judice*, to expose the fact that he had only recently been released from prison.

Lavinia Wootton, questioned again, took a look round her property, but it was a constable who noticed that her garage window had been forced. They found the empty petrol tin; there were no prints, but Adams had snagged his trousers on the window getting through. There was a scrap of thread which could be tested for comparison.

Felicity was astounded at Colin's courage, even though she thought that he had been reckless; he should, she said, have waited for the police.

'I know,' said Colin. 'But this had become personal. And there was no time for fear. That child – that little boy – was so brave. It had to be done.' He paused, then said, 'I wanted to stab Adams. I wanted to seize his knife and stick it into him. There was murder in my heart.'

'But you didn't do it. That's the difference between you and him,' said Felicity.

'If I hadn't met him at Willow House, Emily would still be alive,' said Colin heavily. He would have to live with that knowledge for the rest of his life.

They knew that death might have come at any time for Emily, but it would have been a different ending, one without the terror which she must have known, even if only for an instant.

'I was just beginning to appreciate her,' said Felicity. 'She was very perceptive. Quite a girl, in fact.'

'Yes,' said Colin.

'It wasn't such a dreadful thing to do,' Felicity declared. 'Stay at Willow House as Mr Baxter, I mean.' How could she console him?

'It was a sort of betrayal,' Colin said. 'I could have used my real name. Perhaps I was repeating what had happened to me in childhood – betraying you, by denial, because I felt that I had been betrayed myself. Sometimes we hurt those we love the most,' he added.

Felicity heard this statement with astonishment. Was he telling her he loved her? She could not remember every hearing him say so, even when he asked her to marry him; he had made some flowery speech about holding her in high regard and would she honour him by agreeing to become his wife? She had thought his high-flown language wonderfully adult, part and parcel of his calling; she had not, at the time, found it pompous, as she would today.

'And we are hurt most by those we love.' She turned his statement round. 'Only those we love have that power.'

He thought about her words. How did she know this? Whom did she really love, apart from Stephen, and, perhaps, Emily? Her parents, who had gone to live in Australia, near her sister? How had they treated her, in childhood? Would she, one day, tell him?

'I used to visit my grandmother,' he told her now. 'I loved her and was happy in her cottage. Then, one year, she was cool to me when I arrived – aloof – and sent me home after only a few days. I thought I had offended her – lost her affection. Later, she died. I think now that in her own weird way she was preparing me to lose her – cutting the bond between us. Of course it was cruel, wrong of her, but now I think that was her motive.'

'Then you thought your mother did it too?'

'Yes. But I see now that in releasing me, she also released herself and gave me the only chance that lay in her power.'

'So they were both acts of love, if misdirected,' said Felicity.

'Perhaps.' He sighed, then added, 'I shall resign, of course.

She didn't argue, but he went on as if she had.

'A judge must be above suspicion. I acted most unwisely, and when he comes up for trial, Adams may expose my folly even though it won't bring him any benefit.' What had Mrs Kent thought, he wondered, when she read about it in the papers? His photograph had been in all the tabloids and several of the quality newspapers. 'We must hope that the police will be able to make the murder of Ann Green the main charge, because if he can be convicted of that, he will go down for a very long time. What he did to Emily would not carry such a sentence.'

Felicity thought that some people would take more seriously his attack on Ferdy than his other offences, but perhaps this was not the time to say so.

'What would you think of backing me in an antique shop?' she said lightly. 'Quite a small one. Porcelain, Victorian jewellery – that sort of thing. I would like to do it, but I would need some capital.'

He hid his astonishment at this suggestion. It seemed he had a lot to learn about his wife.

'I'd consider it,' he said carefully. 'I thought I would direct my attentions towards the Victim Support Scheme and other connected efforts.' Work would come his way, he knew; work he could accept, chairing committees, acting as consultant, and some of it might be paid.

'That sounds excellent,' she said. 'I would offer you moral support but might not be able to spare much time from my business. First I have to learn to drive.'

She would not waste the driving lessons Emily and Stephen had given her for Christmas, and if Colin backed her with the shop, she could buy a car with her hidden savings.

They sat in silence, staring at the fire. Soon they would have to talk about their son, who at the moment was spending all his spare time with Emily's anguished parents.

One day, though maybe not for years, Stephen would marry again, and when he did, there might, after all, be grandchildren.

Felicity smiled with quiet pleasure at the prospect, and, watching her, Colin thought she smiled because they had resolved the future to their mutual satisfaction.

As, of course, they had.